THE DISPOSABLES

ALSO BY DAVID PUTNAM

The Replacements
The Squandered
The Vanquished
The Innocents
The Reckless
The Heartless

THE DISPOSABLES

A Novel

David Putnam

OCEANVIEW  PUBLISHING

SARASOTA, FLORIDA

ISBN: 978-1-60809-164-5

Published in the United States of America by Oceanview Publishing, Sarasota, Florida

www.oceanviewpub.com

10 9 8 7 6 5 4 3

PRINTED IN THE UNITED STATES OF AMERICA

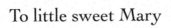

To little sweet Mary

Acknowledgments

I would like to thank some of those who helped make this book possible: Jerry Hannah, Judy Bernstein, Asilomar Writers' Group, Mike Sirota and his writers' group, The Writers of Solimar, the De Luz Writers, Fictionaires, Squaw Valley Writers' Conference, Mary Maggie Mason, Doug Corleone, Sue Readon, my agents Mike and Susan Farris, and the wonderful folks at Oceanview. And a special thanks to all those in law enforcement and social services who are out there doing their best to help at-risk children.

THE DISPOSABLES

Chapter One

The bell above the door jangled. I looked up from the open *Wall Street Journal* on the scarred, grimy counter. A kid came in with a brisk blast of Southern California winter, his ball cap skewed on his head, pulled down over the top of his hoodie. He was black with dark skin that made him difficult to recognize under the navy-blue sweatshirt hood. Both hands were in his pockets.

The kid was about to die.

I was helpless. Knew I couldn't save him. I looked out the window in between the discount posters advertising cigarettes and cheap twelve packs of generic beer. The street appeared normal for a late Saturday night, pedestrians, cars all going about their business on Long Beach Boulevard, nothing out of the ordinary. Yet I knew they were out there, sensed it.

The only customer who'd come in before the kid was a small Asian gal, her hair cut in a pageboy and streaked with dark maroon. She'd put a Big Hunk candy bar on the counter and tried to catch my attention as I watched the kid saunter to the back by the walk-in refrigerator and disappear behind the Doritos rack. I'd told the overtly greed-driven Mr. Cho too many times to move the rack just for this particular problem.

"Gimme a bottle of that Hpnotiq vodka and some Virginia Slims one hundreds."

I pulled my eyes away from the kid to look at her. She was

barely sixteen, hidden behind makeup, piercings, and some hard years on the street. She had potential to be a real beauty. I rang her up quickly, justifying the minor law violation — selling alcohol to a minor — in order to get her out of the store. It hurt to do it, went against everything I had worked for since I got out. I tried to put the guilt aside and concentrate on saving the boy's life. When the door closed, the bell had not finished its little jangle before he came at the counter in a rush. The gun out, turned sideways like in the gangsta videos.

I put my hands up. I searched for his eyes. When I found them, they were wild, out of control. As calm as I could, I said, "Listen. Just listen to me, okay?" There wasn't time to make him understand.

He jabbed the air with the gun. "Put the money in the bag. Now, Pops, before I blow a big hole in that ugly face."

The gun came up close enough to smell the oil and burnt cordite from within the huge round hole of the barrel. I moved slowly, opened the cash register, and carefully put the folding money in a small, brown paper bag usually reserved for pint bottles of liquor. "You can have it all. But you have to listen to me. They're out there waiting for you. You step out that door, and they won't give you any warning, none at all. They won't give you one chance in hell. They'll blast you right out of those designer kicks. You understand what I'm sayin'? I'm on your side."

"Shut up, old man. Just shut up. You think I'm some kinda fool or somethin'?"

"You need to listen to what I'm telling you. This is for real. Two steps out that door, and there won't be any second chances."

His jitters went to full vibration. His eyes flitted from the window several times then back to me as he wrapped his fried brain around it. His tongue whipped out and wet his lips again and again. The dope made him that way. He was a dope fiend, a sketcher jonesing for some crystal meth, desperate, ready to do anything it took.

"That's all you got? You got more under the counter, don't ya? Give it to me." He again jabbed the gun at the air. It went off accidentally, blasting a shelf of Old Granddad whiskey to the right, less than a foot away. The concussion from the muzzle blast bounced off my flesh. I dropped and crawled. Glass shrapnel punctured my palms and knees. The alcohol burned hot.

Two more explosions.

Bottles shattered and fell on my head, raining down glass and wet liquor.

There came a long pause in the noise, the calm in the center of the violence. I froze to listen. Sticky sweet liquor dribbled off the shelves as I held my breath, waiting for his footfalls to track me down, to fire one last shot, to silence the only witness. I thought of my girl, how much I loved her, how much I'd miss her, how I had been remiss in telling her so. I thought of all the kids stashed over at Dad's place and who would take care of them if I were gone.

Clump, clump. Two long foot strides. The bell jangled. I closed my eyes still holding my breath, knew the next sequence of events. Outside came the muffled yells, "Freeze. Police." The words punctuated by shotgun blasts. Lead pellets shattered the front window of Mr. Cho's cherished money-making store.

I got up, brushed my hands on my apron, streaking it with blood, and walked like an automaton to the door. The bell jangled as I went out.

Chapter Two

"You," they yelled at me. "Police, get on the ground. Get on the ground right now."

I stared down at the dead kid, the meth freak rolled up against the store wall like so much dirty laundry, the gun still in his hand, the paper bag of money soaking up the thick, red blood that ran from a massive chest wound. I'd done this. This was my fault. They'd been out there waiting, these hunters of men, waiting, watching me. The dead kid, in their vernacular was "collateral damage," icing on their cake.

The yelling grew louder.

People rushed in.

"I said get down, asshole." The butt-stroke from the shotgun turned the night a bright flash of white and the air too thin to breathe. I went to my knees. The second blow hit my kidneys. Face first, I fell onto the sidewalk pocked with smashed-flat gum and cigarette butts. Someone jumped on my back, wrenched my hands behind me, and cuffed them.

Police radios squawked. Sirens rolled up the street.

I turned my head and saw the kid's vacant eyes, empty, wasted. The eyes of Derek Sams even though I was smarter than that and knew it wasn't Derek. No way it could be. Derek had been dead a long time. My voice hoarse, "You could have given him a chance. He would've surrendered."

"Shut your pie hole."

"You didn't even give him a chance. He would've put his gun down."

The boot came from off to the side, a fleeting shadow in a long, wide arc, aimed to broadside my face. I flinched defensively, only not far enough. My head exploded for a second time.

"What'd I tell you, asshole?" The words came as an echo in water that warbled and vibrated in the unkicked ear.

Gradually, the world came back into sharp focus. I realized what I had in my pocket and went absolutely still. I didn't want to provoke them further. I couldn't afford to. But it was already too late, they had me cold. There was no reason to believe, that under the circumstances, they wouldn't search me.

Two men moved in, stood close, their shoes a foot away, men evaluating the scene. "You capped two of them?"

"No, he ran out into our crime scene and refused to follow orders."

"So you capped him?"

"No, he resisted. We had to put the boot to him. No big deal. This is all good. It was a clean shoot. The puke had a gun in his hand. Look."

"Clean, right? So you got it all on video?"

The other man remained silent.

"Ah, man, tell me you got it on tape."

"The video broke."

"Sure it did. Here's the lieutenant. Shut your face and let me handle it."

A third man walked up. "I heard the call and was in the area."

A voice, one I recognized, one that made me want to shrivel down into the crack in the sidewalk.

"Whatta ya got?"

"Two-eleven, armed, came out of the store like Butch Cassidy and the Sundance Kid. He was ordered to stop. He didn't comply and we had to put him down."

"You got video?"

"No, the machine malfunctioned."

"Ya, right, how many times you think they're going to buy that one." The lieutenant paused. His shoes took a couple of steps back. "Hey, this is Sammy's Market Number II. Who's this dude?" The lieutenant nudged me with his toe.

The thug cop spoke up, "Sir, he came out of the store into our crime scene and —"

"Knock off the party line. I'm not some paper-pushing bean counter from downtown. I know what time it is. Get him up."

Two sets of strong hands helped me to my feet. The thug cop, who'd put the boot to me, had a flat, white face, blue, deep-set eyes, and buzz-cut white-blond hair. His shoulders were humped with muscle. He was nervous and flexed them again and again as if at any moment he would reenter the ring for round two. He was still pumped with adrenaline and had not yet registered the cold evening. He wore a t-shirt and jeans and a shoulder holster with his Los Angeles County Sheriff's badge clipped to it.

I kept my head bowed. Robby Wicks, the lieutenant, leaned down to try and see my face, my one good eye, not swollen shut from the kick. "Ya, I thought it was you. Hey, Bruno, what's goin' down?"

The thug cop was stunned. "You know this asshole, Lieutenant?"

"That's right, and you call him an asshole again, I'll bust you back to working the cell blocks at Men's Central Jail. Take those cuffs off. You okay, Bruno? You want to file a complaint against this guy?"

I didn't know how to take his congeniality after what had

happened the last time we met. He acted as if nothing had come between us.

My right eye was swollen shut and the other watered, blurring everything. I didn't say anything and rubbed my wrists, then daubed the eye with a sleeve.

The thug cop was angry. "Man, that ain't right. We didn't do anything we didn't have to, that we weren't forced to do. It was his fault. This was all by the book."

Robby Wicks said, "We'll never know for sure, now will we? Not since your video recorder just happened to malfunction."

"Bruno, say the word, and I'll start the paper on this one, do it myself."

I looked down at the dead kid pushed up against the wall of a shitty little market on a dirty sidewalk in South Central Los Angeles. Then I looked the thug cop in the eye until he looked away and he asked, "Who is this guy?"

Robby Wicks reached over and pulled up the t-shirt sleeve stretched tight around the thug deputy's large bicep. He revealed a recent tattoo, still red and enflamed against his too-white skin, "BMF," in bold black letters. "Looks like you recently made your bones and joined up, got initiated, huh? Good thing this doesn't smell of a blood kill. God forbid."

BMF, the insignia of the Los Angeles County Sheriff's elite Violent Crimes Team.

The thug pulled away from Robby, anger in his eyes.

Robby stepped over to me and pulled my sleeve up. My skin was black and made it difficult to see, but it was there, "BMF," only more crudely etched.

"This guy you called asshole is none other than Bruno the Bad Boy Johnson. The man who started the BMFs."

BMF, that's right. Robby had to rub my face in it. People do stupid things when they're young, things they regret for all time, things they wish with their very soul to take back. Only it was too late, like the kid on the ground, it was too late.

The thug deputy's mouth dropped open. "You're *the* Bruno Johnson?"

My left fist snapped out and connected with his right cheek—the diversion—as I came out with a right roundhouse—the heat—and laid it right on his nose. Cartilage crunched. Blood burst out as his knees gave way and his eyes rolled up. He melted to the sidewalk. His sergeant caught him. Uniform deputies moved in fast, batons out, ready to beat me until I was dead.

Robby held up his hand to stop them. "Hold it. Hold it, it's all over." He looked at the sergeant who was easing his unconscious man down to the same dirty sidewalk as the dead kid. "We done here, Sergeant? We going to call it even or do I call in IA and take this incident apart piece by piece?"

His eyes angry, "No, we're done here, Lieutenant."

"Good."

Robby put his arm over my shoulder, turned us around, and guided us back into the shitty little market. I felt sick at his touch and would have shrugged him off had I not needed the insulation, the cover to protect what I had in my pocket, a small piece of what I needed to fight the underground war.

"Christ, Bruno, your hands are bleeding. You want me to call med aid?" He reached for the handie-talkie on his belt.

"No, I think you've done quite enough. That big white boy out there's not going to forget what happened. Especially, the way it went down right in front of all his homeboys. There's no way he can leave it alone."

"He can't lay a hand on you. Everyone would know about the bad blood. Besides, I'll whisper in his ear, make sure he knows exactly who he'd be pissing off."

The lieutenant of the elite violent crimes unit carried more clout than a deputy chief.

Robby looked around the store. "This the best you can do, Bruno?"

I got a broom from the back and started to sweep up. The handle instantly turned slick.

Robby took it away. "Man, you of all people know the routine. The forensics gotta have a go at this mess first. Come on, I'll give you a ride to the hospital. You need stitches on those hands and maybe even an X-ray of that rock-hard head of yours."

Doom-and-gloom depression descended and gave the night's darkness a hard edge. I should've done more to stop the kid's assassination. He was someone's child, someone's grandchild. A mother, an auntie would be waiting up for him tonight and, instead, they'd get a coroner's house call.

Chapter Three

Outside, everyone had been moved away from the front of Mr. Cho's store and stood behind yellow crime-scene tape. An instant crowd had gathered. Both ends of Long Beach Boulevard—a major drag through town—remained blocked off. Robby had me by the arm, escorting, letting all concerned know I now came under his protective veil.

"I'm working a serial killing, down south of here on Cookacre," he said, "heard the call and stopped by. Good thing or your black ass'd be on its way to county about now."

The lump in my pocket grew warmer, even though it was physically impossible. When I didn't answer, he kept up the rhetoric to cover the uncomfortable silence.

"This case is a bad one. You've seen it in the news. I know you have. All the good citizens are staying indoors because of this guy. After dark, they're afraid to come out from under their beds."

Robby didn't wait for me to answer. He knew I had heard of this suspect. Like he said, everyone had.

"The dude tosses a coffee can of gas on the victim, holds up a lit lighter, and says, 'gimme all your money.' The victim complies, and the suspect lights his ass up anyway. Then he stands by and watches. Just stands there, cheering like it's Saturday night at the fights.

"There have been three so far, and we don't have a clue.

The victims are too random. Wish you were still on it with me. We'd tear this town apart until someone told us. Right now they're all too scared to give up the dude. Who could blame them? What a way to go, huh?"

In the twenty years working for the Sheriff's Department I'd seen my share of burnt people, charred people, an image sewn into all your senses, the reek, the stark fear forever frozen in the victim's eyes.

We made it over to the police line. The short, dumpy Mr. Cho elbowed his way through the crowd and pointed a stubby little finger at me. "You fired. You hear me, you fired."

Robby gripped my arm tighter, spoke to me out of the corner of his mouth, "Sorry about that, man."

"Don't be. I was looking for a job when I found this one." I had to make it look like I didn't care, even though I did. I had a parole agent who insisted the members on his caseload remained gainfully employed. Worse, I didn't know how Marie was going to take it. I needed the job for the kids.

We rode in silence in the undercover cop car. Neither of us wanted to talk about the stolen couple years that had slipped by. Largely unnoticed by him, I was sure. My hands and knees and eye throbbed with enough pain to keep the past embarrassment at bay. He took Roscrans west then Willowbrook up to 120th and over to Wilmington and up to Martin Luther King Hospital. The people in the area serviced by the hospital called it "Killer King."

I basked in some relief. I'd been wrong about the surveillance. They had been staked out looking for this torch. I hoped with all my heart that's what it was and that they weren't there for me, watching me in order to find the kids I had stashed. Now I could see Marie without the worry of pulling her into what I had going on.

Robby stopped. Blood had pooled in the lap of my apron.

I got out, flopped it out on the ground in a wet little splash, and closed the door. He rolled down the window. "Don't be a stranger, huh?"

I turned and waved over my shoulder, more interested in seeing my Marie than to dredge up hot, angry memories with the likes of him.

Inside the packed emergency room sat a sorry lot of humanity, the sort in every ghetto across the US. Folks on the lower socioeconomic scale, who drank on Saturday nights to forget their hunger, folks in a dead-end life with nothing to look forward to and who picked up a knife, a club, or brick and took it out on their neighbor.

I checked in with the overworked receptionist then wedged myself into the only seat available, an unwanted half-seat next to a big mama who had one child clinging to her breast and a second on her lap, cute well-fed children who looked like they might have a touch of the flu.

An hour later when a seat with a view of the ER room door vacated, I jumped over to it. Thirty minutes after that I got a glimpse inside of a harried Marie who did a double take when she saw me. The ER door closed on automatic hydraulics as she approached, blocking her from view. It opened again. She cautiously ventured out, looked around, afraid the cops were about to jump her.

All because of me.

I had come into her life and fed her an idea, sold her some fantastical plan. I used her love for me to seal the deal. She'd agreed for only one reason, to help save the children. Guilt in the pit of my stomach overrode pain in my lacerated hands. She asked with her eyes if it was all right to contact me. I nodded and stood. We hadn't seen each other in going on two weeks. A long, lonely two weeks that now made my heart ache just to see her.

A hot-blooded Puerto Rican fifteen years my junior, put her right about thirty-three. Five four and a little too lithe, she was feisty and not afraid to speak her mind, in rapid-fire English, heavily accented with Spanish.

She rushed out with a big smile. Until she saw the blood, the chewed-up hands, the eye all but welded shut with purple. Her face melted into sympathy that enlarged a lump, made it rise in my throat, and choke me. I didn't deserve a woman like her, not after all I'd done in my previous life, not with what I had in the works and was now too afraid to tell her. She knew some of it, but not all. And she had already warned me if I held anything back, we would be "kaput."

She hugged me and kissed the uninjured side of my face. "Come on." She tugged me toward the ER door, hesitated, looked around, said in a low tone. "You sure it's . . . it's okay?"

"Yeah, I was all wrong about who was watching. It wasn't me they wanted. The kids are safe. It was just the Boulevard, Long Beach Boulevard. A two-eleven team was staked out for a hood pullin' robberies. They gunned him tonight, right out in front of my store. Shot him dead. There was nothing I could do, Marie. Just a kid."

I tried hard but couldn't stop the tears as they welled in my eyes and burned in trails down my cheeks. I had degenerated to nothing more than a tired, shot-out, overemotional old man.

"Aw, babe, come on in here and let me get you cleaned up."

She guided me past the long queue in the hallway behind the ER doors, folks in chairs and on gurneys, who had waited hours in the waiting room and now waited their turn to see the overworked doctors in another line on the inside, their angry eyes blazing a path right through me for the unfair favoritism. We went on past all the curtained-off beds and into an empty trauma room with a hard door, that when closed gave us privacy. My Marie was a physician's assistant and went right to preparing the tray to suture my hands.

She looked behind us one more time, even though the door was closed. I'd done that, made her paranoid to the point of distraction. I wasn't any good for her. If I kept it up, before too long she'd need tranquilizers and a good shrink.

"You sure it's okay now?" Her eyes big and brown yearned for a positive answer.

"Relax, okay." Her paranoia turned contagious. And maybe I wasn't so sure. Maybe they had been set up outside the store watching me, and the kid they gunned was nothing more than collateral damage, words from the BMF—a bonus.

She sighed. All the tension left her shoulders, and the muscles in her face, tense for the last two weeks, finally relaxed. In the next instant, her Puerto Rican blood flared. She pulled back and socked me in the stomach.

Not too hard.

"Then what the hell you doin' gettin' hurt like this?"

I didn't have the nerve to tell her and make things worse. Tell her that I was going to court day after tomorrow, on Monday. In reality, it was already early Sunday morning. I'd be in court in a few short hours. I used to face down armed and dangerous suspects who would not hesitate to drop the hammer on me, and yet I didn't have the guts to tell her.

To top it off, if she knew what I had in my pocket, well, she'd be done with me for sure. No questions asked. I wouldn't blame her one bit. Not one damn bit.

Chapter Four

The cuts were jagged around the edges and time consuming to stitch up. I watched her closely, her every move, her hair, the way her hands moved, her delicate fingers inside the latex gloves, the gold ring on her finger. We'd been together six months, and she'd still not taken it off.

She didn't look me in the eye the entire time. I knew what she wanted to ask. But it was still too soon to see each other. Too dangerous. Too much at stake, other lives besides our own to consider. I had to be absolutely sure it had been a robbery surveillance for the kid, that the cops I'd seen for the last two weeks out in front of the liquor store weren't really out following me. Hunting me. I needed to make sure the kid robbing the store wasn't collateral damage who'd just wandered into the wrong place while the team was watching me.

"Cho fired me."

She stopped, looked up, "Ah, Bruno, now what are we going to do? You didn't make a lot of money but you needed the job to keep—" Again, she looked around at the closed door. "—to keep that punk Ben Drury off our backs. And the money. We need every penny."

"Ben's not that bad a guy."

I leaned forward and gently bumped her forehead with mine, "I told you I got the money thing handled."

The corner of her lip came up in a snarl. She pointed a latex-gloved finger brown with Betadine antiseptic. "You promised. No more stealing. We're hurting enough people with what we got going on."

"I can't come over tonight." We'd planned to meet, the first time in two weeks because of the surveillance.

She stepped back, mouth open.

I hated to hurt her even a little bit. She was everything that was right in my life. I wished every day I had met her years before. But back then she'd have taken one good look at what I was at the time and run away screaming.

"You said it was all right. You said not five minutes ago that they were looking for a robber. You said—"

I held my hand up. "There's too much at stake to be careless. One, maybe two more days, and I'll be absolutely sure."

"You think that's fair to me? You think that's fair to the children?"

"One more day's not going to matter."

"To them it will. You don't remember what it's like being their age."

She went back to work on my hand, shaking her head in disgust. After a couple of minutes of thinking about it she said, "I know it's not right but—" Her brown eyes were vulnerable and the most beautiful I had ever seen. With my other hand I gently pulled her into me and kissed her long and hard, a kiss I wanted to go on forever. She kissed back, the heat rising between us. I'd missed her so. In a way, I wished I had not set in motion the events that now threatened to overrun us both. Only, I realized a long time ago this had been what I was put here for, what I was made for. Fait accompli.

At 117th Street I stopped under a streetlight and looked around. Nothing moved. It was too early in the morning. I stepped out of the yellow halo into the shadows and waited twenty minutes. Nothing. I walked across the street on a diagonal over to an ancient pepper tree to check, the way I always did every time I came home. The way my night had gone, I knew it was going to be bad before I looked. Lately, things had been going too well.

The empty Gatorade bottle stuck up in the Y of the thick boughs, the red-labeled punch flavor signified an emergency. The last five days the tree cradled the green-labeled bottle, and meant, "Situation still okay." Yellow meant hurry. Red meant emergency. I'd half expected the yellow, but the red scared the hell out of me. It made me want to run full-out until I got there.

Shit.

What else could go wrong?

I suppressed the dangerous urge to throw caution to the wind, took a couple of deep breaths, and started the long tedious process of bob-and-weave to make sure my tail remained clean. In and out of side yards, into backyards, cutting across streets, stopping, waiting, and listening, a different path each and every time. There wasn't much time. It would be dawn soon. I cut it short, shorter than I should have risked.

In the last backyard, just north of 133rd, I moved quietly along the familiar path.

I saw the glow of his eyes moving fast right at me. I was downwind. He hadn't caught my scent. "Junior, wait, wait, it's me. Junior!" He skidded on all fours in the dirt.

"Keyrist, dog." He snuffled and jumped with his huge paws up to my chest. I'd almost been eaten by my own dog. I gave him as much love as the little time I had left allowed. I hadn't planned on coming, so I didn't have his treat. He didn't seem to mind. He was in it for the lovin'. He was a good friend with a big heart, as long as you were on the good-guys team. I shoved him off and moved to the back door. Just in the few months I'd been coming, I knew every inch of the place, and still the porch wouldn't let me by without a creak.

I turned the knob. It wasn't locked. My heart skipped a beat. Damn, he knew better than that.

The stuffy air inside the small lath-and-plaster house smelled of bacon grease, okra, and greens. It sparked a nostalgic moment that took me back many years and made me wish I was back there, away from all the pressure, these problems. The feeling hadn't happened in a long time. The shooting of the kid at the liquor store, the sudden realization of being old and helpless was what set me off.

The dim orange-yellow glow from the living room lamp filtered into the kitchen on the floor. I eased the door closed. The house was absolutely quiet, minus the snore. I stopped and opened the refrigerator. The bright light near blinded me. Just as I thought, they were out of milk and low on just about everything else. I was a fool. The old man had begun to panic. I couldn't blame him.

I peeked around the corner. He sat in his easy chair his head back, his mouth open, gums exposed. His teeth were on the end table next to him as he quietly snored. His short-cut afro was cotton white. I carefully put my hand on it and remembered a time when it was jet black and glistened, a time when he was built like a world-class boxer and wasn't afraid to keep the neighborhood safe from the thugs. Feeble now, and too old to care about anything but the two small children asleep on his lap and the others, two over on the couch in a makeshift bed and three more on the floor with pillows and blankets. Dad slept too soundly to be an effective night watchman. I felt bad that he was left with the job of caring for the children. I felt even worse about what I had to do to him in a couple of weeks. He knew the plan. He was unafraid to be alone looking into the backside of forever. My old man never complained, never.

Because of the situation, he wasn't allowed to leave the house and had to pay the neighbor kid to buy the groceries. Had to pay him extra so the neighbor kid wasn't inclined to talk and ruin the good thing we had going. The cover we wanted people to believe — crazy old man living by himself, a recluse who doesn't want to venture out into the real world — so far it had worked fine. It just cost double for the food and supplies.

The kids looked as if they'd grown in the two weeks I'd been away. The responsibility of their safety caught me up short. How could I keep them safe? Who was I to think I was better than the county system? Was I doing the right thing here?

Of course, I was. Each one of these kids had been returned, by a judge no less, to an abusive home. Returned to parents who only wanted custody to keep the welfare checks coming. Some people were just plain wired wrong, mentally and emotionally. They did not consider kids to be living, breathing human beings. Children were disposable, even their own. Of course, I reassured myself, the kids were better off with Marie and me.

The kids needed to be in their beds in the bedroom. Dad was a soft touch and had let them stay up late watching TV and he'd fallen asleep with the rest of them. One at a time, I picked up the Bixlers, Ricky and Toby, two black boys, six and seven respectively, and carried them to their bedroom. They'd been taken into custody after their mom's boyfriend's PCP lab caught fire in their apartment. They hadn't escaped unscathed. Their arms, legs, and backs rippled with scar tissue. They'd spent two months in the burn unit and were then dumped right back with the same mother who still lived with the same boyfriend, now out on bail.

I came back and lifted Sonny Taylor. He'd almost died overdosing on some meth his mom had left out on the living room coffee table. I'd found him in a closet where his mom had left him while she went out foraging for dope money.

Little Marvin Kelso was so light in my arms, so young to be a victim of abuse. Even though there was a court order keep-away, his mom, Julie Kelso, had snuck the molesting slime ball suspect back into her house.

Wally Kim, a Korean kid, lost his mother, a prostitute who died of an overdose, and left him without relatives to care for him. And half-Mex-half-white five-year-old Randy Lugo came to our attention after his fifth visit to Killer King hospital for a broken bone.

I carried them all into their bedrooms and tucked them in. Albert was conspicuous by his absence. I missed him dearly.

In the six months we'd had the kids, I treasured every minute I had with them. We wrestled on the floor, tossed a ball in the house, and played silly games. It didn't matter what we did so much, what mattered was the laughing, giggling, and cheering. And the hugs. It wasn't complicated. They hungered for attention and love. For me, maybe they partially filled Albert's empty place, but I'd come to love them as my own. I gave all I had and wished I'd had more time to give. I couldn't imagine letting anything bad ever happen to them again. I wouldn't allow it. These kids' lives and security were more important than any petty crime I might commit to keep them safe.

I lingered a little longer with Alonzo, my grandson, Albert's twin, and watched him sleep. The gentle rise and fall of his chest, the baby softness of his pudgy cheeks, his pure innocence, he was pure vulnerability.

I left Dad asleep in the chair and went into the kitchen. From my pocket, I took out the wad of bills, that if caught with, I couldn't explain and would violate my parole. I peeled off twenty hundreds from the roll of two hundred and fifty bills, 25K, and laid them on the table. Two grand would be more than enough to last him until I could make it back the following week. I started for the back door, stopped, went back, and added another ten one hundred dollar bills. The money was important but not more than my dad's peace of mind.

I had my hand on the doorknob when the old man's voice from around the corner reached out, "Chantal called, said it was real important."

Dad had been so proud when I joined the Sheriff's Department, even more proud when I was promoted to detective on the Violent Crimes Team, working the South Central Los Angeles area, making the ghetto safer by putting away the violent predators. He told all his friends over and over, told everyone on his mail route, as well.

I'd been out of the joint now six months, had seen him on many occasions in those six months, and still I felt overwhelming guilt for having let him down. He'd lived by a code of honor with a strong work ethic like I've never seen in anyone else. He never missed a day in forty years as a mail carrier for the post office. He never backed down from what was right.

The worst part of it, after it was all said and done, I was nothing more than a common street thug, now an ex-con on the dodge trying to keep from going back.

I let go of the doorknob and went back into the living room. He had his teeth back in and smiled broadly, his brown eyes clouded with cataracts. He was always happy to see me, even from behind the thick glass wall in visiting.

"I got your message at the tree and came over directly. I put some cash on the table out there and didn't want to wake you. Sorry it took so long to get over here. Thing . . . things have been a little out of control."

"You touch my kids, you're going to wake me. You should know that."

I got down on one knee, put my hand on his. "I know, Dad. I'm sorry, but we're almost through it."

I'd taken off the apron in the hospital and thrown it away, but some of the blood had soaked through to the dark work shirt and left unmistakable blotches. His eyes scanned my swollen eye, the bandaged hands. His palsied hand came up involuntarily to touch my face but stopped short. "I know you would've come sooner if you could've. I didn't want to give you the emergency signal but . . . but I was worried about Alonzo, his asthma medicine is running low, and Alonzo, he wants to see you something fierce. I know it's not fair to you with what you got going on, but it kills me to see him so sad."

"It's okay. You did right. I left you enough to last you through."

I fought a lump rising in my throat and tried not to think about Alonzo or I'd probably tear up again. "Did Chantal say what it was about?"

"Yeah, something about a guy named Ben something."

I sat back on my heels. "Ben Drury?"

"Yeah, I think that's it."

"I have to go." I got up and kissed him on his forehead. Ben Drury meant bad news, the worst. Chantal wouldn't have risked calling unless Ben meant to make a home call. I had to roll fast. Parole agents didn't make home calls on Sunday. Something was up.

"I talked to Marie tonight, she said she was going to have some meds dropped off tomorrow, okay?"

He nodded.

"She'll check over Alonzo. And, I think I forgot to take the

Gatorade bottle down. Can you have Toby do that for me, old man, right away so I'll know the next time?"

His hands were crippled up with arthritis. He patted my arm with a weathered claw, "You take care, son, you hear?"

"I always do, Dad. I wish I could stay longer. I have to go."

He closed his eyes and nodded. I started for the back door and then switched direction, went down the hall to the bedroom. I stroked Alonzo's soft hair and kissed his forehead one more time. In his sleep he mumbled the name, "Albert," his brother. Alonzo was small for a three-year-old, so vulnerable in such a violent world. The clock ticked in the back of my brain. I had to go. Soon it would be over. Then I'd make it up to him.

I grabbed a cookie from the cookie jar on the kitchen counter on the way out, stopped at the door, and looked back at Dad, Alonzo's great-grandfather, who stood at the entrance of the living room. "Tell Alonzo, no matter what, I'll come see him tonight. Okay?"

"I shouldn't tell him that if there's any chance at all you won't make it. It'll break his little heart."

For a second, I thought about Ben Drury, calculated the odds, then said, "You go ahead and tell him."

Chapter Five

On the porch I gave Junior the cookie and patted his head. There was nothing else to do but run for it. Taxis didn't come into the ghetto when it was dark, not this far south. I had to make it back to Killer King, the farthest place a cab would venture down from Imperial Highway, and only if the money was right. Short of carjacking, a taxi was the only way I was going to get to Chantal's in time.

Five blocks west and thirteen long blocks north. I couldn't run the whole thing and had to walk-run, my face and hands throbbed, my old body yelled that the brain had gone off line into the red zone and threatened a full meltdown.

At Killer King I used the pay phone out front, hoping Marie wouldn't come out for a smoke and see me. She didn't know about Chantal. She knew about the apartment, but not about Chantal. Marie wouldn't understand. I paced in the shadows waiting as the sun broke on the horizon. I wasn't going to make it.

According to my parole officer, I was supposed to be home in bed on Sunday mornings. I was labeled High Risk because of my commitment charge. Drury had my work schedule, my entire life schedule. He had the ability to drop in on me at anytime. Until now, Ben had been cool and always called first, a professional courtesy only extended from parole agent to ex-cop.

The situation now called for a serious two-step shuffle, lie to him about how my job was going, and hope Mr. Cho wasn't mad enough to call him to rat me out. Then hope Ben didn't find out for two more weeks. That's all I needed was two more weeks.

I paid the cabby twice the fare to take me up to Crenshaw and then gave him a twenty-dollar tip for busting some of the red signals at empty intersections. At the gate to the apartment my hand was almost too swollen to get in my pocket for the keys. Chantal lived in a three-story apartment building, one as upscale as they came for the Crenshaw district. I fumbled the keys, got the gate open, and looked back to the street for the light-blue, nondescript government car Ben always drove. Still too early for his visit. Though, this was an extraordinary situation that added variables. He never made a home visit on Sunday. Something was definitely up. And added fuel to the theory that the cops on Long Beach Boulevard may have been watching for more than the torch, the guy robbing his victims and afterward tossing the can of gasoline on them.

I had a key to the apartment door and had promised to always knock out of courtesy to Chantal, a kept woman, a high-dollar executive's, on-the-side squeeze. She allowed me to give her address as my residence of record as long as her sugar daddy never knew about it.

I'd met Chantal back before the big fall, back when I was running and gunning on the Violent Crimes Team. I'd helped her out with a problem her nephew had with the law, and she returned the favor. Ben Drury promised to always call and it worked out as long as I let Chantal know where I could be reached.

I stopped at the door, fist raised to knock. If her sugar daddy was in there, that would be it. The jig, as the saying goes, would be up. I'd have ruined her life, and she'd be mad enough to tell Ben some simple, basic details to get me a year's violation back in the joint. And worse case, an add-charge, a new case with ten to twenty years' exposure.

But she'd been the one to call. She had to know I'd be coming over. I knocked and waited. Knocked again. Out on the street I heard a car pull up. A door slam. I went to the open balcony in the hallway and looked out. The light-blue nondescript government car sat at the curb. I saw the top of Drury's brown hair bob as he walked toward the gate. Back at the door, I knocked again, this time with more urgency.

The door opened a crack. I shoved my way in. Chantal started to protest. I put my hand over her mouth and closed the door behind us. "It's okay, it's me. Paroles are coming up right behind me, right now." Her body hot, against mine, my hands slick on smooth silk.

I yanked my shirt off, the white t-shirt underneath was splotched with drying blood from my hands. I yanked my t-shirt off and tossed them both to her.

"What happened to you?" She asked, calm as if nothing of import ever happened, her eyelids pinned and her pupils constricted. Heroin. Shit. Perfect timing, girl.

"Ditch that stuff, he's going to be here any second."

"Relax, would you?" She sauntered back into the bedroom. She wore a silk eggshell-white nightgown that clung to her body and let every beautiful curve in the cleave of her lovely heart-shaped bottom show off with each rise and fall of her long, perfect legs. Her skin was cocoa smooth, without blemish. She kept her hair down around her shoulders, a different look. She always wore it up.

I sat on the living room couch and tried to control my breathing. The couch, made of cushy white leather, matched the white fur carpet. I sank in. Everything else in the room was hand picked, all chrome and black.

Ben knocked at the door. I looked to the hallway. Chantal was taking her sweet damn time.

"Chantal, someone's at the door."

"Can you get it for me, babe?"

"I guess, yeah, sure why not?"

I quickly untied my boots and kicked them off as I walked to the door. I was about to open it when I realized what I still had in my pocket, twenty-two thousand dollars, a red-hot parole violation. Again the knock, more urgent this time. "Open up, police."

Police? Ben Drury, State parole, right? Not the police, it can't be the police.

I tossed the wad of bills in a waist-high fake oriental vase with silk flowers, next to the entertainment center, and shoved it down its throat. I went to the door, took in a deep breath, and opened it.

A big hand shoved my chest. I stumbled backward and almost fell. The hand came in attached to the thug cop I'd only recently met out in front of Mr. Cho's store. The cop who'd kicked me in the face. The cop whose nose was red and swollen three times its normal size from the roundhouse I'd given him.

Chapter Six

The thug cop had run a check on me, found out about the parole, called Ben Drury at home, got him out of bed early on a Sunday to come out for a little get-even time. Back in the day, as a young and full-of-testosterone copper, it wouldn't have been out of the realm of something I would have done. The parole tail on me gave him the balls to overlook Robby Wicks's warning.

The thug said, "Morning, Mr. Bruno Johnson. We're here on a routine home check."

I looked over at Ben, who looked away. No doubt, the thug had something on Ben.

"Nice digs you got here, Mr. Johnson. How can a piece of shit like you, who works at a chickenshit little hole-in-the-wall grocery store, afford a place like this?" He kept walking, shoving me on my chest until I was back at the couch and sat down hard.

"What's going on?" Chantal came from the hall, her eyes a little more alert from the adrenaline, her nipples poking straight out of her nightgown like a couple of number two Black Warrior pencil erasers. The thug cop moved closer to her for a better view, lust apparent on his shovel face.

His sudden change in behavior, from aggressive to ogling, stopped her cold. "Mr. Drury, who is this? He has no right to come into my home."

"Just calm down, Ms. Sykes, he's a deputy with the Los Angeles County Sheriff's Department. His name's John Mack, and he does have a right to be here."

"Chantal," I said, "I'm sorry."

Mack made no effort to hide his ogle as he kept his stark, blue eyes locked onto her breasts.

Chantal crossed her arms on her chest. "If you say so, Mr. Drury, that's fine. I trust your discretion. I'm not happy about it, but I'll go along. For now."

"For now?" Mack said, "Who do you think you are? You uppity little nig—"

Drury stepped in between them and pointed a finger at Mack, looking him in the eye as he addressed Chantal, "We're sorry for the intrusion this morning. I promise this won't take long."

"How can we help you, Mr. Drury, to get you out of here sooner?"

He turned back to face her. "I heard some disturbing news about Bruno. I came over to make sure everything was okay."

"Is that right? Exactly what did you hear?"

"He had a run-in with the police last night. He slugged one."

Chantal looked at Mack, and brought her hand up to her mouth, stifling a smile. "Oh, really, who could that be?"

Mack's gaze snapped off her breasts, his expression instantly transformed to ugly. He took two quick steps toward her. I jumped up to stop him. He pivoted and shoved me back down on the couch. Chantal brought her fists up to defend herself as her eyes flared. She had grown up in Nickerson Gardens and knew how to defend herself.

"Hold it. Hold it," Ben yelled. "Let's everyone just calm down."

Mack looked at Chantal, his expression softening. "Hey

now, lookee here, the arrest gods have shined down on me this lovely Sunday morn. It looks as if our lovely lady is smacked back. She's under the influence." He reached to grab her wrist. She jerked away. Ben moved in between. "Stop it. We had a deal, no misdemeanor bullshit."

"Okay, but if she's under the influence, then she has to have her kit and dope somewhere in the pad. And dope is a solid felony. I'll just have a little looksee."

"You have no right to search my house without a search warrant."

Ben had her by the shoulders. "This is Bruno's residence of record. We don't need a search warrant."

Her head whipped around, her eyes ablaze, burning a hole right into me. "Is that right, Bruno?"

Too ashamed, I could only nod.

Mack stood at the stereo, tossing all the CDs to the floor. He pulled the pictures off from the wall, tossed them on the floor, and started to move systematically through the room conducting a professional search.

"Ben Drury, you stop this right now, or I swear I'm going to make a call."

Mack hesitated.

Drury said to Mack, "I warned you."

Mack smiled. "Grow some balls, Drury. All we have to do is find her stash and then nobody can touch us. Nobody. We'll be bulletproof. Trust me." He picked up the vase and turned it over. The silk flowers fell out. Green Benjamin Franklins cascaded to the carpet.

Mack threw his head back and laughed. "Lookee, here." He turned toward me, "Peekaboo, asshole."

This, a term I myself had coined years ago, and it had become a standard BMF catchphrase. He knew its origin and purposely used it on me. Threw it right in my face.

"What?" Chantal said, "That's my money. It's not against the law to be leery of banks and to keep cash in your home. Is it, Mr. Drury?"

"It is if it belongs to a parolee."

"I just told you that it's mine."

Mack came over to the couch, "Stand up, asshole, it's time to go to jail."

I knew I could take Mack, he was younger, stronger, but overconfident. The problem was whether or not Ben would stand by while I put Mack on the deck. I had no choice. No way could I go back for a year on a violation. Not right now, not with everything already in motion. I stood up, the decision made. I'd chance it, put him down. Go on the run until everything ran its course.

Drury's cell phone rang. He looked at the incoming number. "Hold it. Hold it, the both of you, give it a rest." He pushed the button, said, "Drury. Yes, sir. Yes, sir. I understand." He punched off. "We're through here."

Mack's head spun. "What're you talking about?"

"You heard me. We're done. We're leaving right now."

"You can't tell me what to do. I work for the Sheriff's Department."

"You're absolutely right. I'm leaving. You can do what you want. But be warned I told you the setup here, and if you stay, it's at your own risk. You're no longer sanctioned by state parole for this search. You will need your own probable cause." He turned to Chantal, "I'm sorry, Ms. Sykes, for bothering you on Sunday." He walked to the door, opened it, "You coming, Mack?"

Mack looked at me, gave me his best cocksucker eyes. "We're not through. You and me are going to tangle. Count on it."

"I look forward to it."

The words locked his jaw tight and screwed his muscles down. He hesitated, weighing his options, as if he could weather the shit storm he'd stir up if he jumped now instead of later.

It passed.

He stomped over to the door, turned, and said, "Lady, you know what kind of piece of shit you're living with? He's a murderer. He hunted down a twenty-five-year-old kid and shot him in cold blood right in front of witnesses." Mack pointed an unloaded finger at me. "The kid wasn't wanted by the law and he had nothing in his hands. This piece of shit gunned him in cold blood. Think about that the next time he's kissing on your neck, running his hands up to grope that sweet little ass of yours, and then ask yourself, when's he going to snap and kill again. Kill again for no reason. Think about it."

Chantal walked over to Mack, smiled, put her hand up, and stroked his face. "And you, honey, try and keep your big nose where it doesn't belong. Next time you might not be so lucky."

Mack's face bloated red. For a long second, I thought he would just say, screw it, pull his handcuffs, and take us both down. He finally gave it up, kicked the doorjamb like a spoiled little kid, and followed Ben out, slamming the door so hard the walls shook. I would now have to be careful and not give him my back. Without witnesses around, given the chance, he'd surely gun me.

Chapter Seven

Chantal's shoulders quaked as she walked unsteadily over to a chair, sat, and lit a cigarette from the box on the end table.

I didn't know what to say or do. I walked over, got down on my sore knees, righted the vase, picked up the silk flowers, and replaced them. My voice croaked, "I'm sorry. I didn't mean for that to happen."

She took a long drag on her cigarette, held it in, and then blew it out of her nose in one long exhale. "What a prick, that guy."

I started shuffling all the cash together. "Boy, we were lucky. If Drury hadn't gotten that phone call —" I stopped and looked at her.

She took in another long drag and spoke as the smoke came out her mouth. "The way you came in, I knew there was going to be trouble so I made a preemptive call."

"I don't know what to say. Thank you. I owe you big."

She held out her hand. "Yes, you do. You have no idea how much explaining I'm going to have to do. Calling him at home on Sunday morning, telling him that state parole was at the door, and could he do something about it? That's going to cost me dear."

I looked at her hand, then down at all the money in mine. It represented a good a chunk of what was needed. To give it up meant I'd have to venture back out on the edge to replace it, take the risk all over again. Another delay, another big risk, when I'd thought I was all but done with that part of the plan.

Had she not stopped the law machine from running me over, I'd have been on the run from parole with an armed-and-dangerous warrant out for me, or worse, in the can waiting for a parole hearing. How much was that worth? More than twenty thousand, that was for sure. I set the money in her hand and said, "Thank you. I mean it, you saved my ass."

She got up with a big smile, sauntered over to the stereo, and set the money on top in one tall pile. "You know what? That big ugly bastard made me feel dirty all over." She slipped the spaghetti strings to her nightgown off her shoulders and let it fall to the floor. "I think I'm going to take a shower."

She walked down the hall, her perfectly shaped naked bottom over spiked high heels rose and fell with each step.

She'd put the heels on when she'd gone in the bedroom, put them on purposely for the overall presentation. While at the same time making that phone call that saved my ass. She was one cool, conniving woman who knew what she wanted and how to get it. She hesitated, looked over her shoulder to see if I followed. Her eyes and smile beckoned.

I shuddered and closed my eyes and tried to think of something else, about Marie, her smile, the way her eyes flashed when I said something that made her happy, made her laugh with the little crinkle at the corner of her lips. When I opened my eyes, the hall had turned drab in Chantal's absence.

I went into the second bedroom, shut the door, quickly stripped out of my clothes, entered the bathroom, and locked the door. Locked Chantal out. Just in case. If she walked in the bathroom, opened the shower door, and stepped in while I lathered up, I didn't think I'd be able to—I shuddered again at the thought and turned the hot water off and the cold on high. "I'm with you, Marie. I'm still with you, babe."

Chapter Eight

Violence in its purest form will surge and ebb with a common rhythm, and if you're familiar with it, you can predict when it will next surface. I'd been out of the business too long. Those last two weeks out in front of Mr. Cho's, I missed the signs, the indicators.

Had I been on my game, I might've been able to stop the kid, been prepared for him the second he'd walked in. Maybe if I'd have thrown a forty-ounce bottle of Cobra beer, chunked him in the head with it. Instead of just watching, letting it all play out as if I were some kind of bumpkin sitting on a country fence.

Sleep in Chantal's spare bedroom didn't come easy. I tossed and turned and slept little in the four hours I allowed.

When I got up, Chantal was gone. On the kitchen table sat a note and a couple hundred dollars.

> *I'm not a total witch. I left you something. At least you can eat. You're a survivor, Bruno. I know you'll bounce back financially. I have to think of my own retirement. You understand. Please don't hate me. Be out no later than five o'clock.*
>
> *Love you, Babe.*
> *Chan*

She'd always talked about when her looks started to fade, how would she live in her old world after she'd become so accustomed to the "easy life," how a nest egg was so important. I should've been mad about the money, but I wasn't. I went over to the phone and dialed a number from memory.

The tin-hard voice of Crazy Ned Bressler said, "Yeah."

"Let me speak to Jumbo."

"You pissed in your Wheaties, pal. He doesn't want nothin' to do with yo sorry ass."

I said nothing.

Bressler hesitated, then set the phone down with a clunk. Harsh rap music along with low murmurings in the background mixed and danced in my ear, then another voice on the phone. "What the hell's this about? You said no more. Yesterday morning you said no more, that it was the last time. No if, ands, or buts, you said. Threw it right up in my face and laughed. You laughed at me. So, what am I hearing now, huh?"

"I know," I said. "I'm sorry, something's come up."

"You laughed at me, my man, when I asked you to do it one more time. Just one more."

"I said I was sorry. What more do you want? A formal apology? You want me to say I was a fool that I wasn't thinking clearly? Okay, I was a fool and I wasn't thinking clearly."

"Fool? More like an asshole. Say that you're an asshole, and I'll think about it."

I let the silence hang, then, "You know I don't hold with your obstreperous language."

He paused. I knew it would get to him. He gave it a little chuckle.

"Obstreperous? What kind of word is that? You some kind of sissy-pole smoking asshole?"

"You want me or not?"

"You know I do. I told you that yesterday."

"Man, yes or no?"

"Meet at the usual. No, make it at the Bun Boy in two hours. You know where that is?"

"Yes, but it's way to hell and gone out in the desert and that's too early. It's twice as far out. You said yesterday morning that the gig wasn't until—"

"Not on the phone, asshole. Just tell me now. You in or out?"

"I have to—"

"You going to punk me or you going to show some sack and—"

"I'll be there." I slammed down the phone.

Bun Boy was in Baker, the home of the world's largest thermometer. With a fast car and no cops it was the better part of three hours away. No chance could Jumbo make it there that fast. I called him at his home in Downey. He was leery about my sudden change of heart. He smelled cops and a setup. I couldn't blame him. But all I was going to do was get there before him and sit around and wait while he scoped the area, made sure everything was cool, and I wasn't bringing the cops down around his neck. He already had two strikes. One more and it was twenty-five to life.

"Shit." I was going to miss the visit I promised my grandson Alonzo.

I picked up the phone to dial Jumbo back to reset the deal in four hours, not two, so I could keep my promise with Alonzo. I slammed the phone down. Went to the closet, took out a pair of Chantal's sugar daddy's chinos and a blue chambray shirt, pure white-man-yuppie. The pants were too large and the shirt too tight through the shoulders and arms, the guy was a pear. I cinched the belt up tight and hung the shirt out over it. I searched the sock drawer for something other than the thin stretch nylon jobs he had tons of. My hand came

across something cold and hard. I knew the make by feel without looking. I took it out. An H&K .40 caliber. Too much gun
for a pear to hold up, let alone shoot. I'd held a gun my entire
career and it felt as natural as if part of my hand. For a brief
second I thought about taking it along to keep Jumbo honest.
Only a gun was a misdemeanor for Joe Citizen and a felony
for an ex-con. And if I took it, there might arise an occasion
where I'd have to use it. If I didn't have it, I'd have to run. I
wiped off any fingerprints and put it back.

   I still had to boost a car, a calculated risk that it wouldn't
be reported before I was done with it. I had to get on the road
now. The Sunday traffic, everyone would be coming back
from Vegas, opposite direction than I would be going. At least
that much fell squarely in my favor.

Chapter Nine

I sat in the parking lot across the street from Bun Boy and waited. Just the way I'd figured it, Jumbo was late, although I hadn't made him or any of his boys driving around the area. Baker was nothing more than a gas and food oasis in the middle of the desert, a "wide spot in the road" as Dad would call it, and easy to pick out a car that made more than one pass.

Finding the right car and the ride out took three and half hours. Another two put it at about four thirty. It wouldn't be absolutely dark until five fifteen. I'd give him another forty-five minutes, then call it a day. Dad's words about not telling Alonzo unless I was absolutely sure, echoed in my brain and hurt just a little bit more each time I thought about it. Anger started to rise up unbidden and soon I'd need an outlet. I tried to focus it on that shovel-faced Deputy Mack. He was the true reason why I was going to miss the meeting with my grandson. Mack was the reason why I'd lost the money, not Chantal. She just did what she needed to do to survive. Without her, I'd have been a lot worse off.

I had about fifteen hours to get the job done, make the drive back, and be in court.

Off, down the road by the ramp that dumped folks from the freeway onto the frontage road that led to the restaurant, came a sleek, 700 series BMW, black with tinted windows. Jumbo had arrived. He drove by and slowed, then accelerated on past. He wanted me to follow. I started up, pulled onto the frontage road and fell in behind. We drove five miles, then turned off onto a dirt road, that had Jumbo not turned on it, I would have missed for sure. This had to be something big. Jumbo wouldn't get his car dusty or bang his suspension like this for small potatoes. I was tired, but the thought of the job made my pulse beat in my temples and behind my eyes. The prospect of a big job always got my blood up.

We headed across the desert toward a clump of rocks to the east that now looked like an island as the sun set behind us and shadowed the ground around it. The rocks grew larger and at the same time slowly sank into the gloom of dusk.

The other jobs had been closer to civilization. All of a sudden I thought maybe he was taking me out to "bumfuck Egypt," a place he described when taking someone no longer useful off the board. I was a witness to his criminal activity, all felonies, and unlike me with one strike, he had two. I'd made him a lot of money in the last four weeks. Maybe it was time to clear the boards. What better place to do it than in the desert? Now I wished I'd taken the pear's gun.

Just before we started to pass the large rocks, Jumbo stopped, the red brake lights overly bright in the gathering gloom.

We waited. He finally rolled his window down, stuck his arm out, and waved me forward. He wanted me to walk up and get in his car. I stayed put. After a time, he got out, a smile on his little ferret face. He stood six-foot tall and weighed a buck seventy. Thin, rail thin. John Ahern. They called him Jumbo because of his big floppy ears. The story goes that someone made the mistake of calling him Dumbo, a name he took exception to, not wise with a psychotic sociopath. The next time someone with any real balls called him Jumbo, he allowed it, and it stuck. He had on a black Tommy Bahama shirt, black slacks with a gold earring and matching bracelet, classy, unlike most thugs of his rank. He had little hands and held them open away from his body and said, "Hey?"

I checked the terrain one more time, got out, and walked up to him. "What's with all the sand this time?"

"It's the big one I told you about. It's got to be a long ride. I got triple the crew catching for you."

This time I held up my hands. "Where? I don't see 'em."

"They're up ahead. I didn't want them to see you. It's better that way."

I looked around again, not sure I believed him.

He cracked a small smile, "Why? You gettin' sketchy on me?"

"Jumbo, if you haven't noticed, we are out in the middle of nowhere."

"Ease up on it, bad boy."

"I told you not to call me that."

He smiled broader. "You're right. I'm sorry."

"I'm going to need a hundred thousand this time."

The smile disappeared. "I was going to be generous and double what I gave you the last time, give you fifty, out of the kindness of my heart. But a hunert, no, you can't call the game like that, not after I already got this thing rolling. I could've got someone else for your part."

"I don't understand why you want me to begin with. But I'm here, and my price is a hundred. You said it was a big score."

"I told ya before. It's because no one else has the balls. They get up in the car, panic, and just start tossin', breakin' everything. You're cool, take your time, treat the shit like it's yours, and our recovery rate is higher. But this time there's going to be a lot of loss no matter how gentle you are."

"What's the load?"

He squirmed a little, so I knew the next thing out of his mouth was going to be a lie. "Computer towers."

"Bullshit."

His eyes went hard. "Don't push me, big man."

"What's the load?"

He hesitated, his mouth a straight line, "Computer chips."

"Computer chips?"

Now, all the other times made sense. They were dry runs, training for this one. That nonsense about soft hands was just that, there was going to be heavy security. Heisting computer chips had become big business. They were small and valuable and easier to handle than gold bars. The computer companies had taken to delivering them in armored cars with escorts.

I smiled at him. "How much security?"

He nodded his head, smiled back, "Piece of cake, really. Four guards, two up front and two in the back. If you do it right, like you have in the past, they'll never tumble to it."

I tried to calculate the odds in my head. This changed the whole scenario. No one had hit them like this before. This was virgin territory for something of this magnitude. We were kicking over a hornet's nest, and folks were going to be beyond pissed off. "What's the take going to be?"

"None of your damn business. You in or you out?"

"Out." I turned and headed to my car.

"Bruno! Bruno!"

The sand swished as he ran around me to be seen, a small gun in one small hand, the other up against my chest.

Chapter Ten

I looked down at the hand on my chest, "You better think twice about shooting me with that popgun. Sure, you'll hit me with it. And I'll probably eventually bleed out. But I'll rip your head off first. And you know I'm telling it straight."

He looked down at the gun in his hand, thought about it for a long second. "It's too late to get someone else. You have to do it or you're hanging my ass out here. I paid out the ass just for the information on this load and timetables for this gig."

"What's your end?"

He took the hand from my chest reached into his pocket. "Here." He slapped the bundle of currency against my chest. I let it fall to the warm sand and ignored it.

He said, "Here's seventy-five. I brought twenty-five extra just in case you tried to hold me up like this. Seventy-five, that's even twenty-five more, that's triple what you got before. Take it."

"The deal's changed. After the fence takes his cut, you'll clear a couple million on this, won't you? Even after you pay all your guys off, you get a cool couple of million. Fact is, your hooligans probably don't even know what a computer chip is. They're probably doing this for the same chicken-shit little price as last time.

"I'm taking all the risk. No. Now my price is two hundred thousand."

His mouth dropped open.

I stooped and picked up the seventy-five. The money, cool to the touch, was compressed and bound tight. Still, it barely fit in Chantal's sugar daddy's pants pocket. "What's two hundred to you when you're looking at an easy two mil? And that's two million tax free." He didn't say anything. I smiled, "It's more than two mil, isn't it?"

"Okay, okay then, two hundred K, that's what you said. We got a deal. That seventy-five's all I got on me, but you know I'm good for it."

I moved right up close. I could smell his Doublemint breath. His teeth gnashed away a hundred miles per hour. "And you also know I'm good for coming for you if you try and gyp me out of it. I won't be happy."

He held out his hand. "You got Jumbo's word."

I took his hand and gave it a good squeeze, gave the bones a little grind. He maintained his smile. It looked like he'd just pulled one over on me. Like he knew it would go this way all along. Jumbo never played the dummy, never. He had something else lined up. I'd played right into him. I would have to keep my eyes open. "Where do I get on?"

"Gyp, and hooligans, what kind of words are those? You slay me, you know that, you really slay me."

I waited.

His grin lost some its shine. "Okay, continue on down this road until it veers right. Stay on it another mile and three-tenths. There's an orange cone in the road by some juniper trees at the base of the grade."

"Where do I get off?"

"Same as before."

"You got to be kidding me, that's an extra sixty or seventy miles."

"Eighty-eight, that'll give you another hour and ten for the job. I'm paying you two hundred big ones. Don't start your bellyaching now. You're going to have to earn your money this time. Get going. You got," he looked at his watch, "twenty-one minutes to get set up."

I hesitated, again thinking something was wrong. I had somehow walked right in and got blindsided. It scared the hell out of me. He stood facing the west. The dying sunlight turned his face orange and contrasted greatly with his jet-black hair. He waited, comfortable, knowing no matter what, he had me. I would do it the way he wanted. I got in the car and headed out, going around his Beemer, spinning sand in a rooster tail. He scrambled out of the way. In the rearview, he brushed sand off his Tommy Bahama, mad enough to stomp his feet and kick at imaginary minions. I couldn't put it from my mind. I couldn't help thinking like a two-bit sneak thief. I imagined all the money before I even had it in my hand. Enough money to do it all the right way. I couldn't wait to tell Marie, show her, and watch her eyes light up. Not from greed but from what the money could do for the children.

I passed the rock-strewn mountain and looked to the right. In a little rock alcove were fifteen or twenty four-wheel-drive vehicles, with three to four men each, a small army of thieves to support me in my endeavor to make Jumbo a kingpin thug. They all stood ready, overly animated in their anticipation. They stopped talking and watched as I kept going on by, their faces too far away to distinguish features. Jumbo was right, I didn't want them to see me.

I drove. Just as he'd said, I came upon an orange cone. I turned and followed the railroad tracks south. I came to a bunch of salt cedars as the sun switched off all the yellow, the ground turned red, then quickly into long shadow. In the head-

lights, on a branch among a clump of salt cedar, hung a canvas
bag weighted down with heavy tools. I didn't have to check
my watch. The bright light from the train to the north heading
south cut through the clear night air, through the vacant desert
all the way to where I sat watching. I shut off the headlights
and pulled in behind the salt cedar. I didn't have time to con-
template the act. Jumbo planned it this way. I got out, pulled
the bag of tools from the branch. I scrambled along the right-
of-way a hundred yards to the base of the grade where the
train would have to slow. I found a good place just off the
right-of-way, and lay down among some sage. As the massive
freight approached, the ground started a soft rumble and grew
as the behemoth rose up larger. I should've been scared, but
I'd done this before and knew how it would play out. I opened
the canvas bag, took out the cotton work gloves, put them on,
and then took out the small set of bolt cutters. I put the powerful flashlight in my back pocket and the pry bar in the back
of my belt.

The long, black train engine roared by at fifty miles per
hour as it tried to gain enough momentum to climb the grade.
I watched the cars. This time Jumbo didn't say anything about
the markings. I assumed it would be obvious. The cars were
all transport car carriers, sea containers, and tankers with
chemicals, all with bright paints of local gangs from across the
country. Mobile billboards tagged with graffiti as it came
through their town. All the cars except one, a newer cargo car.

The speed of the train bled off as more of the long train hit
the grade. In no time the train was down to a crawl. The
wheels clanged over the tracks.

The boxcar I waited for came chugging along in the moon-
less twilight. I started to get up to make my move when a dark
figure jumped off from in between two cars and landed on the

ground without falling. He'd done this sort of thing before. Many times. It had been a dangerous place to ride unless he'd been on the roof of the car carrier and had climbed down. He was security, a train bull who knew the train's cargo was the most vulnerable on the grade. He was there for no other reason than to check for the likes of me.

Chapter Eleven

He looked up and down the desert on my side. I ducked, face planted in the sand. No way was I going to get caught. Too bad, Jumbo. The money in my pocket had already turned warm and comfortable against my leg. If I didn't earn it, I'd have to give it back.

I cautiously took a peek. The boxcar went by. The security man scrutinized the lock and seal with a bright light, then reached up and tugged on it. He walked alongside of the slow-moving train and checked the empty desert again one more time, a mother hen protecting its chick from all the evils of the outside world. When a break in the cars caught up to him, he climbed up in between. This was strictly against railroad policy. I knew this because I had researched everything about cargo trains before pulling the first job. The computer chip or insurance company was paying the security folks a lot of money for this sort of service, the reason Jumbo wanted me for the job.

The train was still climbing the grade. Three more boxcars and the one carrying the train bull would go past and then it would be too late.

I thought about the money in my pocket I would have to give back, and the other hundred and twenty-five grand, how useful it would be. I got up and ran in the sand alongside the train. Not in the cinders where it would make noise. I hoped the train bull didn't stick his head out from between the cars to look.

I caught up with the boxcar as it started to gain speed. I entered onto the cinder and ran alongside juggling the bolt cutters, tripped, and almost went down. I regained my balance and got the bolt cutter teeth on the lock, but the speed of the train was almost too fast for me to keep up and manipulate the handles at the same time. This lock was the same sort I encountered before and not a beefed-up one. They didn't want to point out the value of the cargo with fancy hardware. The lock snapped.

The train continued to gain speed, going faster and faster. I was out of shape and had already gone two or three hundred yards. I tossed the bolt cutters. I didn't have much left. I grabbed the handle and pulled, my legs a blur, moving quicker than they were made for, the handle dragging me along. If I let go, it was going to be ugly. The door wouldn't budge. The other times it had come right open. In the dark, I had forgotten the small lead seal. I pulled the pry bar and raked the lead seal off. My lungs burning, I was light-headed to the point of going down. One last effort was all I had left. I yanked the handle. The door squeaked and slid open. I hung on, stunned. The boxcar was loaded floor to ceiling with wooden crates. There wasn't any room at all to climb in. I jumped up on the foothold and grabbed onto the crates. The timing was off. The crews wouldn't be in place to recover the load so I couldn't throw them off yet. And the train was still too slow. There stood too great of a chance of being seen. I hugged the wood crates in a precarious perch and tried to catch my breath.

The boxcar this full, Jumbo would make a fortune, two mil easy, closer to four or five. He'd make enough from this one haul to retire. No wonder he didn't balk at the two hundred K.

Up ahead the front of the train hit the summit and started down. My half of the train was still going up but the weight on the other side of the mountain pulled the train along faster. The cool wind dried my sweat-soaked shirt. I shouldn't have looked down at the passing cinders that now turned into a blur as I clung like an insect, my nails digging into the wood. If I fell, I'd break too many bones to walk out.

I reached as high as I could and pulled on a wood handle of a crate. There were too many crates stacked on top of it. I pulled myself up until my toes were on the boxcar floor's edge. My forearms swelled as I held on with fingertips. With one hand I reached higher for a handle farther up, got it, and yanked. This time, one moved. I yanked again. It moved a little more.

My boxcar made the crest and started down. The black night whirled by. I yanked hard one more time. All of a sudden the crate came free and damn near jerked me off the boxcar with it. I swung back too fast and banged my face. I clung there for a long moment thinking that if I had fallen, what would Marie have thought? After all I had promised her. How would she feel when she was told I died committing a burglary?

My face flushed with anger. From the now open slot, I pulled off crates fast and furious until a spot opened up for me to climb up and rest. This train was picking up speed, faster than the others I had worked. Another facet of security. I had to get going.

I pulled crates and tossed them out, aiming past the cinder right-of-way, trying for the desert sand dunes. It felt as if hours had passed. I had not completed half the car yet. My shirt, soaked, stuck to my skin, my muscles screamed for let up. The sutures in my hands under the bandages ached. I took a breather, walked to the door, tried to get my bearings, and checked my watch. I'd been at it thirty-three minutes, so I figured we'd be just outside Barstow. I went back at the stack again, this time not worrying so much about where the crates were landing, shoveling them out like cordwood. There wasn't time for finesse. With a load this large and the train's speed, Jumbo was going to have some breakage; the cost of doing business.

At my next breather, it looked as if the train had made it through Victorville. An hour had passed. Only another twenty minutes remained before the train hit the Cajon Pass. I wasn't going to make the entire load. If I didn't shag ass, a full third would be left behind. I went at the stack again. I wanted the whole hundred and twenty-five thousand and didn't want Jumbo to have any recourse to say otherwise.

I started checking the open door as the train approached the jumping off point. The backup thieves in their four-wheel drives were only going to drive so close to civilization before they pulled off. My back hurt, my hands ached, and I was out of breath the same as if I'd run a marathon. Ten more, then I'd go. Ten crates flashed out the door. Ten more after that went out.

And then ten more after that.

Only one row remained against the back wall. I was fast approaching where I needed to disembark. I went to the open door, climbed down on the foothold and hung on watching for my point to bail. I was about to jump when up ahead I caught a glimpse of something, a reflector to a taillight, right where'd I normally jump. I swung back and held on, the wind drying my hair. The train passed the reflector that belonged to a car. A '63 lowrider with a lot of chrome. A car I recognized.

It belonged to Crazy Ned Bressler, Jumbo's main man, his

enforcer. He waited at the spot to reclaim Jumbo's seventy-five thousand dollars. Not his primary goal. He would also silence the star crook who could put Jumbo away forever.

I waved as the train flashed by him.

Chapter Twelve

I grabbed a few minutes' sleep behind a dumpster at an AM/PM market on Denker Avenue off of Santa Barbara and made it to court the next day, banged up and so fatigued I had to fight the urge to lay down on the wooden bench and nap. Court got underway, the cases called. To watch as a bystander and not as a cop gave me a new perspective on the judicial process. The court setting gave off an air of pretentious arrogance. When I'd been on the other side of the banister, in the "good guy chair," I was a part of their little performance—the DA, Public Defender, the judge—as they bandied back-and-forth. All the while the poor slob whose life hung in the balance, stood by, hands crossed at the waist, watching his future wander around the room in the form of words he didn't understand. Today, I again realized how intimidating it could be as a bystander in the audience—until the bailiff brought out Johnny Wayne Bascombe. Then I just didn't care about anything else.

Johnny Wayne Bascombe wore all orange, with "LA COUNTY" in large, white block letters across his back. His hands were shackled to his waist, and the leg irons forced him to shuffle. His arm was in a cast up to his shoulder, and his face was under reconstruction in various shades of swollen purple and reds in between railroad tracks of sutures. He stood there as a sawed-off version of Doctor Frankenstein's monster.

They kept him in the partitioned-off section of the court, behind bulletproof glass. Not because he was so damn dangerous and a threat to public safety, but for his own protection from that same public, who if given the opportunity, would tear him apart. I forgot about my fatigue, sat up straight, and thought about the overwhelming satisfaction I would derive from five minutes alone with him. I'd do more than rearrange his face like the last lucky guy. I began to glare, trying to get him to look my way, to give him the stink-eye treatment, scare him, make him realize he had nowhere to hide, inside or out of his barred walls.

The judge called the case, the DA announced she was ready.

A hand on my shoulder startled me. I jumped and turned. Robby Wicks stood in the aisle, suit coat rumpled, tired, a smile on his haggard face. "Hey, Bruno. What the hell you doing here?"

He must have followed me. He knew all about the caper in the desert, probably saw the whole thing from the air with infrared and was laughing at the irony of taking me down in a courtroom.

"I . . . I . . . wanted to talk to you about something," I said, quickly, with nothing else ready to feed him.

His smile faded, making him look older. He didn't buy my weak excuse, again patted my shoulder. "Ah—sure, sure. I was going to look you up anyway. Wait around, this won't take long. Let me test-a-lie and we'll grab a bite to eat." Test-a-lie, one of the words used by the BMFs.

He'd caught me off guard. I hadn't expected to see him in Compton court, especially on this sort of case. "You're on this?" I said. "Really? Ah, yeah, I mean, lunch sounds good." So he wasn't on the prowl, ready to make an arrest after all.

He smiled, figuring this was a scam and I was in court for an entirely different reason, like a pending case under an aka—also known as. That's what I would have thought.

He walked up, raised his right hand, and was sworn in.

The Deputy DA, a Ms. Hosseni, a Middle Eastern gal, dark complexion, with black hair pulled back from her face, held by two abalone barrettes, stood at the podium. "Lieutenant Wicks, by whom are you employed?"

"Los Angeles County Sheriff's Department."

"How long have you been a peace officer?"

"Twenty-eight and a half years."

"What is your current assignment?"

"I'm temporarily assigned to a task force attached to Homicide."

"Were you working as a peace officer on September fifteenth of this year, in the county of Los Angeles, state of California?"

"Yes."

"Can you tell us what happened?"

This was a prelim with no jury, a prelim that had been put over again and again for one reason or another mostly because there was really no reason to rush it. And from the looks of him, until recently, the defendant hadn't been up to it physically. The judge was going to determine if there was probable cause to bind the defendant, Johnny Wayne Bascombe, over for trial.

Wicks looked to the judge. "At the time I was working in my regular assignment out of narcotics assisting in a search warrant service on Nord Avenue in the county area of Los Angeles. As a supervisor, I was only there to observe. My guys deployed on a house while I watched from my unit in the street. That's when a Rocky Mountain Spring water guy came up to me and said that he had just delivered some bottled water to a house five doors down and across the street. He said he went in the back door because there was a pit bull chained up out front. On a daybed at the back of the house he saw a child hog-tied. That's the way he put it, 'hog-tied'."

Chapter Thirteen

The blood started to pound behind my eyes. I looked over at Johnny Wayne. His chin was up as if proud of all the attention he now received, as if he were some sort of Al Capone who derived respect from his criminality.

"His hands and feet were bound together behind his back. He was facedown on a dirty sheet that was bloody. The Rocky Mountain Water guy said it was real hot inside, and he didn't know if the kid was even breathing.

"Because there was a dire threat to a human life, I immediately advised dispatch, asked for a patrol unit to assist code-three, and went to the house."

"Lieutenant, did you go by yourself?"

"Yes."

"Why didn't you alert some of your men?"

I knew why. Robby also carried the BMF tattoo and he knew it was going to get ugly. He knew he wasn't going to want witnesses.

"There wasn't time to alert my men. From the description the bottle water guy gave me, the child was in imminent danger. Besides, my men were still securing the house for the high-risk dope search warrant. To pull even one of them away would have jeopardized the operation and their safety."

"What did you do next?"

"I went to the location. And because there was a threat to

the safety of a child, I didn't knock. I drew my service weapon and went in the back door."

"And what did you find?"

"A six-year-old boy hog-tied facedown in a stifling room. It was at least a hundred and twenty inside the house. He was bleeding profusely from his mouth and nose. It looked like his arm was broken, and he was in shock."

"What happened next?"

"The defendant," Robby pointed to Johnny Wayne, "without provocation charged me. I was forced to defend myself."

"He's a liar!" Two pews back a sketchy speed-freak woman in a dingy-white tank top and greasy jeans, stood up. I knew her as Dora Bascombe. "He's a liar. He attacked my Johnny and beat the livin' shit out of him. Pistol-whipped his ass until he was a bloody pulp. Look at his face, Judge. Christ, look at his face."

The judge banged his gavel. The bailiff moved into the audience, took the screaming woman by the arm, and tugged and pulled her out of the courtroom.

I looked back at Johnny Wayne. He smiled, happy that his woman had stood up for him. Her misplaced loyalty meant a lot in his world. Johnny didn't have any front teeth, courtesy of Robby Wicks, which gave his smile a sunken look, as if the vacant space where his brain should have been sucked and puckered his lips and skin into an empty vortex.

When the courtroom was again under control, the deputy DA turned back to Robby, "Please, Lieutenant, continue."

"Like I said, before I could render aid to the child, the defendant attacked me. I had no alternative but to use the force necessary to subdue and take the suspect into custody."

"Thank you, Lieutenant. Now, I would like to show you some photos of—"

"Your Honor," the public defender stood and spoke for the

first time, a diminutive man dressed in a worn JCPenney's suit. "For the purposes of this hearing we will stipulate to the injuries of the child." He sat back down.

The judge looked at the Deputy DA. "Do you have anything further?"

"Prosecution rests."

"Mr. Howard."

The public defender again stood and moved to the podium. "Your Honor, the State has not proved that my client was the one who committed these crimes. The mere fact that he was present does not prove he was involved."

The public defender knew the whole story. The woman hauled out of the room had broken the little guy's arm, but Johnny Wayne was just as culpable. He was the one who'd tied the child up, slugged him in the mouth, gave him fifteen sutures in his lips, and had broken his nose. My Marie had gotten the whole story out of the child when they brought him into Killer King to be treated.

"Further, the felonious assault on a peace officer charge should be dropped because the officer did —"

The judge interrupted him. "Counselor, are you going to cross examine the witness or go right into your closing argument?"

Howard paused, turned back to Robby, "Officer, did you have a warrant to enter the residence?"

"No."

"Did you . . . no, strike that. What were you wearing?"

"A suit and tie."

"At any time did you announce that you were a police officer?"

"Yes, as Mr. Bascombe was charging me I yelled, 'Stop, police.'"

I looked over at Johnny who knew enough from past court

encounters where cops were involved to keep his mouth shut concerning this lie and only shook his head no.

"Officer, was there anyone else in the house that witnessed this, that heard you identify yourself?"

Robby lost his professional demeanor. "Yes, there was, the poor little defenseless kid who was damn near beat to death."

The judge looked at him as if about to issue an admonishment and changed his mind. "Anything else, Counselor?"

Howard shook his head and sat down.

"Ms. Hosseni?"

She stood. "Yes, Your Honor, we believe there is sufficient evidence to hold the defendant, on the charges PC 273d, 236, PC69, and PC 243b."

"Mr. Howard?"

"Your Honor, the officer entered without cause and—"

"Mr. Howard, that belongs in a 1538.5 motion. Anything else?"

"The officer did not identify himself, and the defendant believed his residence was being burglarized and defended himself."

The judge waited for more, and when Howard didn't continue, the judge looked down at his papers, "The court finds there is sufficient evidence that a crime of 273d, 236, and PC69 did occur, and that there is probable cause to believe the defendant, if tried, would be found guilty. As for the charge of 243b, the State did not prove to this court that the officer sustained any injuries during the assault." He rapped his gavel. "Let's set this for December fifteenth. Are there any problems with that date?" Both attorneys were busy logging the information in their files.

"No, Your Honor."

"No, Your Honor."

"Next case."

I got up and hustled to the door.

Robby came down off the stand, and patted the DA on the shoulder as he passed on his way out. She stood. "Detective Wicks?"

I stopped at the door to observe.

Robby turned, went back, lowered his head. They both smiled as they spoke in low tones. Robby nodded, took hold of her shoulder, and gave it a squeeze.

Out in the hall, the elevator was too slow; Robby caught up to me.

Chapter Fourteen

"Hey," Robby said, "I thought I was going to buy you some lunch."

"Yeah, sure, that'd be great."

"Whatta ya say, since we're so close, for old times, we run up to Stops for a hot link?"

I didn't have much choice. The entire purpose of the court appearance was to follow Dora Bascombe when she left the courthouse. Now she was nowhere to be seen. Robby had already cheesed that. I'd have to get the information I needed another way, which meant I had to tell Marie all about what I was doing. She wasn't going to be happy.

We walked in silence out to his car, the same one he'd given me a ride in to Killer King the night the Violent Crime Team killed the kid out in front of Mr. Cho's. We got in, he started up.

He put his arm over the seat to back out, his face close to mine, "What was it that you were going to talk to me about?"

I was tired and my mind felt full of sludge. "I need your help." I never intended on telling him, but there was nothing else I could say that he would believe or at least not see right through.

"I'm here for you, man. You know that," he said.

He steered the car over to Willowbrook Avenue and headed north in the late morning traffic.

"Well, you gonna tell me or sit there like a bump on a log?"

"Detective Mack paid me a visit."

"Ah, shit. I thought I had that fixed. I'm sorry, man, really. You can bet your ass it won't happen again. Not after I get through with that little son of a bitch."

"I've been thinking about it. If he came at me after you talked to him, talking to him a second time is only going to make things worse. I'd appreciate it if you'd just lay off him. Maybe he'll cool out all on his own." I knew that wasn't going to happen, but all I had to do was dodge Mack for another week, and then it just wouldn't matter anymore.

Robby shook his head in disgust. "You know his kind. He's not working the Violent Crimes Team because he shies away from trouble."

"I know, but I think I can duck him long enough that he'll forget about me."

"It really pisses me off he went against my orders. I'll go along with you, but only on one condition."

"What's that?"

"If he catches up to you on some lonely dark street, you leave enough of him for us to identify."

I smiled. Robby still had far too much confidence in me. I was nothing more than a broken-down, wrong-side-of-forty ex-con.

Before I could say anything in response, he said. "I need your help. I'm just going to lay it out. I haven't slept in thirty-six hours and I'm dead on my feet."

"Help you how?"

"Like the old days. I need the best of the best to shut down this asshole who's torching everyone, and you're it. He hit again last night, fried another one. He's doing it more frequently now."

"How can I help? I'm on parole."

"I can call in a favor, fix it with your PO. I'm calling in a lot of favors on this one. All I got."

"I can't help you, Lieutenant, it would only get us both in trouble and you know it."

"Like I told you, I'm so tired I can't see straight. I don't have time to stroke your ego or pat you on the head. You owe me, and I'm calling in your marker. You know I never intended to do it, but this situation is getting real shitty. You can't imagine the pressure they're putting on me."

I did owe him. Going back a long time. He was a patrol sergeant, and I was new to the streets pushing a radio car in South Central. It was something I didn't want to ever think about, the images of that night. Just the thought of it—her name—I'd pushed her name out of my memory and wouldn't let it back in.

Robby stopped at a red signal at Compton Avenue. "Say something, Bruno. You know that if you and I team up like the old days, we'd have this son of a bitch all grappled up inside a week. That's all I want from you is one week. One week, pays you up in full."

On second thought, I really didn't owe him, not after he shot me, though independent of his argument, I did feel the tug of morality, to do what was right.

The signal turned green. We sat at the light. Cars behind us honked. He waited.

I looked at his haggard face, his bloodshot eyes. He looked a thousand years old. Maybe I did owe him for all the times he did what was right to shut down a violent offender in the ghetto. And beyond that, he had done what was right when he went alone in the back door of the house and saved the kid from Johnny Wayne Bascombe. I hadn't known he'd been the one. Why wouldn't it be him? He had always championed the underdog, walked the line, often venturing into the gray area of the law to throw assholes in jail. He'd taught me to do the same. For that and nothing else I knew I was going to help him. Before I could form the words, he said her name before I could stop him. "I'm calling in your marker, pal, for the little girl twenty years ago. You owe me for Jenny."

Chapter Fifteen

That night, I had been assigned code-three to a traffic accident, car vs. pedestrian. I beat the paramedics and other patrol cars. Jenny was down in the street, knocked right out of the crosswalk, knocked right out of her shiny black patent leather shoes.

The night was hot. Groups of people clustered on the sidewalk, quiet, pointing, as if I wouldn't see Jenny.

At first I thought Jenny was some little girl's doll tossed haphazardly from a passing car.

No first aid or medical attention was going to help her.

Half her face was mashed, the other half was perfect, angelic in the scant aura of the streetlight.

There was very little blood.

Mercifully, she died on impact.

Her blue gingham dress masked the horror underneath.

Sweaty Marty said later he came up and spoke to me but I was "zoned out," that "I had the blood spore with my nose to the ground."

From the debris field, the bits of headlight glass and aluminum trim knocked off the car on impact, I knew the car was old and large. Then I noticed the asshole had hit poor Jenny hard enough that her little body ruptured the radiator. I started following the water trail in the street, a trail that would be gone in minutes, evaporated into the hot summer night. The swath started out large and wide and narrowed as the murderer picked up speed as the coward fled.

I ran.

The water narrowed further and then turned to sporadic blotches.

Then, to droplets.

At an intersection, I lost it entirely. He'd caught the green, only I didn't know which way he went. I ran in a big arc, cars skidded to a stop to avoid the tall, black uniformed deputy who'd lost his head and ran in a circle in the middle of a busy intersection.

My flashlight dimmed as it started to fail.

I thought I picked up the trail headed north that meant a left turn. I got down on one knee and still wasn't sure. I got down, in a prone position, and sniffed. I then got up and ran in a full sprint, fighting the heat that now helped the suspect to escape, drying up the evidence.

The foot race worked.

At the next intersection the murderer caught the red and left behind a puddle. He continued on through, went two blocks, and turned on Spring Street. He'd been close to home, a mile and half away when he ran Jenny down.

The water turned rusty and led up a concrete drive to a garage door closed and padlocked. I took a minute to catch my breath and tried to shove back the lion that wanted to get even, to make things right.

In the academy they called it "your professional face." No matter what happened, you had to put aside your personal feelings and be professional.

I went up to the door, sweat stinging my eyes, my uniform wet under the arms. I wiped my eyes clear on my short sleeve that left a sweat smudge.

I knocked.

The door opened immediately. The room on the inside was dark, the screen door between us. I couldn't see him and didn't know if this man, who without conscience, ran down a defenseless little girl in the crosswalk, had a weapon.

His rich and deep timbre voice said, "Can I help you, Officer?"

"Yes, I would like you to come out here and open your garage door."

Silence for a long moment. "Heh, heh, I don't think so, Officer. You don't have a search warrant."

I carefully, with as little movement as possible, reached up and tried the screen door.

Locked.

He started to close the inside door.

"Wait."

"Yes, is there something else, Uncle Tom? Something you want to do for your whitie, the people you serve?" He didn't try to mask the anger and hate in his tone. He was safe and he knew it, swaddled, nice and comfortable, in the shroud of the law.

The next second I sniffed it.

Alcohol.

A drunk driver.

The scent of metabolized alcohol set something off inside me, snapping the last straw. The professional face came off.

I roared.

With both hands I clawed through the screen, reached in and took hold of the enigma, a large, black man wearing a white Stetson hat. I pulled him through the screen door and out onto the ground.

"I caught that last signal," Robby said. "You remember? By the time I turned on Spring and found the house you had that old man down in his front yard and was putting the boot to him."

Robby had pulled me off. He had to slug me in the stomach to bring me out of the blind rage. That wasn't how he'd saved my bacon, though. As a supervisor, he had witnessed a crime I'd perpetrated when I took the cowboy into custody with excessive force. Robby was obligated to stop me. Then turn me in for felony prosecution.

No, the way he'd really saved me came after he got everything calmed down with med aid responding for the suspect. He told me I'd done a hell of a job tracking the car, that he'd never seen anything like it, the tenacity, the perseverance. Then he helped with the story, the way it would be written, the way the courts would accept it, and at the same time save my career. Get at least some token of justice for Jenny. Six months later, Robby was transferred to run the newly formed Violent Crimes Task Force and specifically asked for me to be on his team. So started the genesis of the BMFs.

I owed him.

The name Jenny brought it all flooding back, the hot night, the sweat, the odors, the images of shiny patent leather and blue gingham.

"Yes, I'll help you, but only for a week. One week."

Chapter Sixteen

Robby smiled as he wheeled into Stops and parked among the derelict vehicles belonging to other customers. Stops had been at the corner of Wilmington and Imperial Highway forever. Right across the street was Nickerson Gardens, a city housing project that the city had finally fenced in with ten-foot-high wrought iron. Most places turned the curved pointed tops outward to keep the riffraff from entering. With the Nickerson, the wrought iron points were turned inward to keep the animals from escaping the zoo. Stops served hot link sausages on a bun smothered in barbeque sauce and chili fries so thick with grease they'd lie in your stomach for days. Cleevon Tuttle, a rotund black man in white apron with red barbeque sauce smeared in splotches all down the front, set a tray down on the counter with two hot links and chili fries. "Good to see ya, Bruno."

Robby, his money clip out, peeled off some bills. Cleevon lost his smile, "Man, don't you dare insult me."

Robby put his money away and took up the tray.

Cleevon looked back at me. I'd had a great deal of respect for this man, that's why I hadn't come around. I broke eye contact and lowered my head.

"Don't you be that way, Bruno. We was all pullin' for ya. And if Johnny Cocoran hadn't gone and died, you woulda got off just like O.J." He leaned over the counter and took hold of my hand. "You stop that now. Listen to me, you been out a while, come around when you get hungry, anytime. It's on me. You hear? You got nothin' to be ashamed of. That sombitch had it comin'. He needed killin'. Everyone knows it."

"Thanks, Cleevon." All the help behind the counter stopped and watched. My new self-image, the crazy emotional old man thing, had me by the throat, sparking tears. "Doesn't matter," I said, "I still killed a man and I had to pay my dues."

Robby saw my dilemma and nudged my shoulder. "Come on, let's eat. Thanks, Cleevon."

I followed Robby over to an outside table so we could keep an eye on his car and the thugs across the street on the other side of the wrought iron fence who milled about in gang attire, watching our every move. Robby took off his suit coat, which exposed his shoulder holster, let the thugs see it. He also didn't want to get the messy chili on it.

The smell of the spicy food made my stomach growl. I'd been so busy, I couldn't remember when I'd eaten last. Robby was always hungry and never put on an extra pound. He had that kind of metabolism. We ate in silence. He finished off his link and half the fries before he pushed them away and took up his Coke.

We'd missed the rush. Inside at the counter the line grew until it snaked out the door.

Without preamble, Robby started in. "The first victim was a good-for-nothing coke whore over off of Long Beach and Elizabeth Ave. The patrol deputy heard what he described as screeching. He turned the corner and saw Keeshawn Wilkins burning like a fresh-lit match, writhing in the street. When she saw the patrol car she yelled, "Help me." That was it. She collapsed and burned out. I talked to the deputy personally.

He admitted to me he was shook by it and all he saw was the burning woman. If there were wits in the area, he wasn't aware, couldn't remember. He said he never felt so helpless. I think it actually fucked him up in the head. He put in for a transfer to Malibu station."

Barbeque hot link was a poor choice for lunch. But then anything would have been a bad choice. I pushed my half-eaten sandwich aside and washed it down with a lot of Coke.

"The next one, Devon Sherman, he was already a smolder-ing heap on the sidewalk when someone, an anonymous tip, called it in. That one was right out in front of the church over off Aranbe, you know the one. The press got a hold of it and tried to make it look like some kind of hate crime. We weath-ered it pretty well until the third one. Rasheen Patel, a motel owner over on Atlantic Avenue just north of Taco Quickie. He was robbed. And if you ask me, it looked like a copycat, which is going to make things more complicated when we do catch the guy.

"The fourth one, you're really going to like this one. Late last night, not even in this area, up north of here, Central and Twentieth Street. Same MO, only this time it was the field representative for County Board of Supervisor Kendrick, name of McWhorter. You can imagine what a circus that turned this thing into."

The tables around us started filling up, and Robby felt un-comfortable talking about the sensitive case. He looked around. "Let's get out of here."

Back in the car, he took out a pack of Dentyne from over the visor, unwrapped a piece, put it in his mouth, then offered me the pack. I waved him off.

He chewed and looked at me. "Well, what do you think?"

"When you first told me about this the other night, you said the guy used a coffee can to hold the gas, tossed the gas, held up a lighter, and demanded money."

Robby smiled, reaching over to lightly punch my arm. "That's why I need you on this. You don't miss a thing. Rasheen Patel was braced by the suspect out on the side of his motel when he was taking the trash out."

"Which motel?"

"The Sands."

"You have a witness from the second story who was looking out the window."

This time it shocked him. "How did you know that?"

"How else would you have that kind of detail without a witness? The suspect wouldn't do it with anyone standing close. And I know the Sands and where the dumpster is around back. Why do you think this one's a copycat?"

"Because the first two had their money still in their pockets, burnt, but it was still there."

"And the field rep for Kendrick?"

"His money was missing. Kendrick said McWhorter carried about a grand around all the time and liked to flash it. He was bold, into the power thing."

"Where's your witness?"

"We have her stashed. No one knows about her, especially the press. You can talk to her tonight. Right now, I need some sleep or I'm going to doze off standing up. You don't look so hot yourself. I'd ask what you've been doing, but I know it's something I don't to want to know about. Am I right?"

I ignored the last part. "Can you drop me at my pad?"

"Sure." He started up and turned north. He'd read my file and knew my residence of record. Had he not been so fatigued, he would've asked me where I was staying instead of tipping his hand.

He talked the entire way in order to stay awake, inane chatter about bygone days. For the most part, I tuned it out. I had
more important things to think about. The foremost of which
was whether or not someone saw me burying 75K behind the
burnt-out apartment complex on Alabama and 117th. When
you're so tired the paranoia gets a good foothold, it plays
havoc with your logic. My imagination had bulldozers knocking down the burnt-out apartments, churning up my hard-
earned cash, the wind picking it up and blowing it down the
boulevard.

He pulled up in front of Chantal's apartment on Crenshaw.
"I'll pick you up right here in six hours. Then you can talk to
our one and only witness."

I nodded. "Right." Which meant only three hours' sleep. I
had to track down Jumbo to get the rest of my money before
he had time to change his mind. I watched Robby drive away.

I knocked on the door. Chantal opened it. She was dressed
in Chinese silk pajamas. Her hair was mussed and she didn't
have on any makeup. I'd never seen her this way. She looked
ten years older, the youthful girl gone.

"I'm going to have a key made for you. This is ridiculous
getting up to let you in. I was dead to the world."

"Sorry."

She wandered down the hall and stopped. "Some guy was
here looking for you. I think he was a cop. Good-looking guy.
For his age, I mean."

"You got a name?"

"I think it was Wicks. What kind a name is Wicks? You in
trouble, Bruno?" She stopped at her bedroom door.

"No. Well, not anymore than usual."

"Since you woke me, maybe you could rub my back until
I fall asleep." She turned around and pulled up her pajama top

to reveal a lean sexy back, the little bumps of her spine, the dimples above her rounded bottom, the smooth, unblemished mocha skin.

"Maybe another time," I said as I hustled into the spare bedroom and closed the door.

Chapter Seventeen

When I half stumbled from the bedroom, sleep still thick in my eyes, muted-orange filled the living room window, the sun low on the horizon, the last remnants of a dying day. Three hours' sleep wasn't near enough. My body ached and begged for more. Anxiety to have it all over was too strong a stimulant. I went to the phone and dialed Jumbo's number for the third time. No answer. He was dodging me. I'd have to go after him. The anger that he was going to cheat me cleared the rest of the sleepy cobwebs from my mind. The task ahead wouldn't be an easy one, getting him to turn loose that kind of cash.

We didn't have to have the money, it wasn't part of the plan, but now that I had earned it, the amount would make things a lot easier later on. Jumbo would be at his pad laying low while his number-one thug, nasty Crazy Ned Bressler, searched for me.

I leaned over to the window and pulled the sheer away to look out, something I did a lot since my release from Chino, let out of that six-by-eight barred chamber. I had an itch, reached back and scratched a butt cheek.

"Those aren't your boxer shorts."

I jumped, spun around, hands coming around front—an involuntary modesty instinct. Chantal sat unmoving on the couch in the shadowy recess of the living room. On the table, strewn haphazardly, lay a syringe, rubber tie-off, a spoon, and a couple of balled-up red toy balloons—her outfit along with Mexican brown heroin. Tears rolled down her cheeks. I went over and sat next to her. She wore an eggshell chiffon blouse with Kelly green slacks, her feet naked. The big toe on her right foot sported a slim, gold ring.

I took her hand. "What's the matter, kid?"

Her eyes large and brown, the kind you could get lost in if you stared too long. This evening they didn't have the usual spunky bring-it-on look. They were soft and vulnerable. Scared.

She scooted over, put her hip up against me, her hands grabbed mine. "I'm scared, Bruno. I'm scared to death."

"Of what? What's the matter?"

The fear in her eyes flamed bright, then extinguished as quickly as she changed her mind about the truth she wouldn't reveal. She looked away. "I . . . I found another wrinkle today. Bruno, what am I going to do when I get old?" She pointed to the corner of her left eye. "What's going to happen to me when I can't live this life anymore?"

Her hesitation said aging wasn't the real problem. Something was up. Her outfit on the table lay unused. Her hands were cold and shook with an alcoholic's palsy. She released my hands, reached up, and put her arms around my neck. She smelled of lilac and Colgate toothpaste. She put her head on my shoulder in an awkward position. I was too tall. I scrunched down and put one hand on the side of her face and gently stroked it. "Tell me, kid, what's up?"

Her body started to shake as she wept. I turned and took her in my arms. Gooseflesh rippled across her back, coarse enough to be felt through the thin satin material.

"He's going to dump me. I know he is. Then what's going

to happen? He was the best, the — " She buried her face in my chest and let out a muffled wail.

I felt helpless and sorry for her at the same time as my t-shirt turned wet. "You'll be all right. You have some money put away, don't you? You do, don't you?"

She pulled back, her eyes angry. "Not that kind of money. Not enough to live like this, not forever."

Right then I saw it. It flashed big as life like a hungry animal in the back of her eyes. "You're in love with him, aren't you?"

Before she could catch herself, her mouth sagged a little. "That's not fair." She balled up a little fist and socked me in the chest, not nearly as hard as Marie. "The ex-cop in you lets you interrogate people when they don't know they're being interrogated. Yes, for your information, I am very fond of the gentleman. I'm not totally materialistic, you know. I do have emotions."

"Never said you didn't. You have a fight with him?"

"No, I just sense things. I'm a woman, but you wouldn't know anything about that, would you?"

Boy-howdy did I know. She was pure, one hundred percent woman, but I wasn't going to throw my dog into that fight. I knew women well enough to stay out of it.

"Bruno, will you do me a favor?"

"Anything. Name it."

"My hands are too shaky. Will you shoot me up?"

"Anything but that. I won't be a party to something so detrimental to such a beautiful young woman."

"You really think I'm beautiful?"

"Babe, you are absolutely gorgeous."

She sat back and primped her hair, carefully wiped her wet cheeks with the backs of her wrists to avoid smearing makeup, most of which had already transferred to my t-shirt. "Then how come you won't—" She brought her hand down to my thigh. I saw it coming and jumped up. " 'Cause I'm a one-horse kinda guy." I headed for the safety of the hall.

"Those aren't your boxer shorts."

Once I was safe out of view, I slipped off the boxer shorts and flung them around the corner at her. She giggled.

I dressed in more of the pear's clothes and got out of the apartment. I couldn't stay cooped up, even though I needed the sleep. I missed Marie something fierce. She was like a narcotic. I jonesed for her if I stayed away too long.

Chapter Eighteen

Marie walked up Wilmington Avenue to the bus stop and waited. The urge to see her, to hold her, was all but impossible to suppress. I told myself I wasn't some kind of obsessing creep and was only checking for surveillance that might be on her tail, trying to get at me through her. I loved her so. I was scared to death something might happen to her.

I sat up against a wall across the street in a wool, full-length green army surplus dress coat with red corporal stripes and a black beanie next to a rogue Mexican palm tree, a volunteer that grew without irrigation in a barren parkway the county chose not to maintain. Off to the right, on a dark-brown telephone pole spotted with acne of a hundred tacks and nails from garage sale and lost dogs and cats signs, I recognized another poster, one of thousands of Wally Kim distributed widely throughout South Central Los Angeles. The image of the missing child was faded, but the fifty-thousand-dollar reward stood out in sharp contrast, a reward that added a lot of pressure to keep our kids out of sight. Folks in the ghetto sold out for a lot less, tens of thousands less. Below the reward was a police sketch artist version of the man who'd walked into the crack house in fruit town and snatched Wally up. The rendering of the suspect didn't much resemble me. Even so, a Korean kid with a black man for a kidnapper stood out the same as a salt-and-pepper bank robber team.

If you read in between the lines of the numerous *L.A. Times* stories, Mr. Kim, a South Korean businessman—diplomat of sorts—had hooked up with an escort while visiting the US. Nine months later, said escort contacted him in Korea to extort child support. Mr. Kim, smart in business and the ways of the world, demanded a paternity test. The test was completed and proved positive. The woman had not lied. In between time, during the wait for the test, the mother of his child discovered the evils of rock cocaine. When Mr. Kim went to find her, she'd fled. Mr. Kim used a great deal of money and influence to track her down and find her in the same rock coke crash pad that I took Wally out of a week prior. Who would have known? Bad luck for us. To hand him over now would jeopardize our plan. When we got to where we were going, Marie and I had agreed we would contact Mr. Kim and arrange for Wally to reunite with his father. Of course, we would decline the reward.

In the short time we knew Wally, we fell in love with him. He was a great little kid and it would be very difficult to give him up, but we would.

At the bus stop, Marie wore her raven hair down around her shoulders. I didn't like it that way. I liked it up, pulled back tight, like the first time I saw her the night the cops brought me in to have the bullet they put in me removed. In all the years as a cop, the nurses and doctors always treated the crooks brought to them with strict professionalism but never meted out the compassion, the TLC reserved for the victims of the same crooks. That night Marie was different. She was gentle and genuinely cared, even though I was a murderer. She saw something in me, Lord only knows what. She followed the court case, wrote to me in the joint. At first I felt like slime, that to correspond with her might in some way corrupt her. She stayed with it until one day she came to visit. I took the visit to tell her to leave me alone and half expected her to be weepy and sad that I hadn't responded to her long, awe-inspiring letters. Instead, when I came into the visiting area with the thick glass between us, she stood with her arms across her chest, her eyes fierce, angry. She wore a classy red dress and black high heels. I sat down and pointed to the phone. Instead of picking it up, she started to jump around, yelling and screaming, shaking her fists. The guard came in and told her to calm down. She gave him a piece of her mind as well. The guard left and came back with another. They took hold of her arms. She kicked and screamed, her rants muffled by the barrier as they dragged her out.

I stood there a long time, stunned. Then, after I thought about it, I started to chuckle, then laugh out loud. The first time I'd laughed in forever.

Now she stood at the bus stop moving her feet back and forth to stay warm. It was cold but not that cold. She always had to have the heater on, an extra blanket, or a hot drink. She frequently talked about moving to warmer climes with palm trees and a balmy breeze. What she really liked best was when I climbed into bed, and I took my warm socks off. She wanted me to put them on her feet. I had to do it for her or it wasn't the same. For some strange reason it acted as an aphrodisiac. The memory made me ache for her.

I got up and crossed the street without staring at her so I didn't draw her attention. I wanted to keep her in sight as long as I could. Tomorrow, no matter what, I'd go see her. By tomorrow, if nothing changed, I felt sure it would be okay. I only had an hour and a half before I had to be back out in front of Chantal's apartment where Robby was supposed to pick me up.

The bus slowed, stopped, the doors opened. My Marie was first to get on but had to back out to let the passengers getting off pass first. I saw her expression change to surprise, and it scared me. I took a quick step, looked to see what had caused her reaction, to identify any threat.

Sometimes there was a God who looked after the little children. Dora Bascombe was exiting the bus with little Tommy Bascombe in tow. His tear-streaked face, dirty denim pants worn with holes in the knees hung from his too-skinny body. And, of course, he was barefooted. His broken arm with the cast should've been in a sling but swung back and forth banging against his chest as she jerked his other arm. Dora got off the bus to take him to Killer King for his follow-up. According to Marie, Dora had missed two appointments, and if she missed another, Child Protective Services told her they would take Tommy and put him in a foster home. The threat of a foster home wasn't what motivated Dora. If she didn't have Tommy, the state money would dry up. She was forced to take heed of CPS and protect her little golden goose.

The mother and child moved down the street toward the hospital as Marie stood on the first step of doorway of the bus. Her head whipped around wildly, not knowing what to do, helpless to do anything. She wanted to act, to run and "sock the livin' shit out of the bitch" but thought better of it. As I watched, I loved her even more. If that were possible.

Finally, she got on the bus. The doors closed and the bus moved off down Wilmington. She stood in the window and watched as the bus zipped past mother and child and then faded off into traffic. I walked along behind Dora and Tommy, seething at her abusive language to the boy who wouldn't walk fast enough, his dirty bare feet a blur, getting air every time she jerked his arm. I looked around for a rock or even a bottle to bash her head, but, like Marie, knew that would solve nothing. I'd have to bide my time, play it smart.

Dora didn't know me, never saw me before, and if she did

recognize me from court, it would mean nothing. She would have merely thought I was someone else in the audience watching court cases like she'd been doing, waiting for an unfair justice system to screw over a loved one. I followed her close behind into the out-patient wing of Killer King. She waited in line a long time. I stood off to the side, back against the wall, and couldn't quite catch all her vulgar language as she chastised the receptionist in a lengthy tirade for the long wait. She took it out on Tommy, yanked his arm so hard he screamed. I clenched my fists. Not yet. Not yet.

She went over to the U-shaped waiting area filled with chairs all occupied with indigents seeking medical attention. She looked around shaking her head in wonder, then said, "Fuck all this." She towed Tommy out the door. I recognized her thought process, had heard it before. When the welfare caseworker asked her how come she didn't take her injured child in for a follow-up, she would say that she checked in and waited for hours and hours, something that could now be verified, the check-in part. They never called her name, so she left. She'd be given another chance. Too bad for Tommy.

Up close, I got a good look at Tommy's feet. They were blue from the cold. They had not been inside long enough for him to thaw out, not on the cold floor, not before they were on the move again. Dora lived immersed in the tweaker life and only cared about one thing, rock cocaine. Tweakers thought of nothing else but their glass maiden, the pipe.

She walked south on Wilmington, her head spinning on her shoulders. She searched for someone to give them a ride. If that happened, I'd be out of luck. I easily stayed with them, past 121st Street, 122nd and at 124th where she turned west. After one block on 124th I figured out her destination, it made my blood boil. I again wished I'd snatched the pear's automatic from his sock drawer, because if I was right, I was going to need it.

We passed a lookout, a preteen black kid who sat on a broken-down cinder block wall in his designer kicks and his Raiders jacket, who watched, ready at any moment to give the alert, a long whistle. I knew their routine, nothing had changed since I'd left. I pulled the knit beanie down further until it covered my eyebrows. As I walked, I reached into my pocket for the Band-Aids. I peeled them open, put one across the bridge of my nose and one on the cheek under my left eye, an old armed robber's trick. The victims key in on the Band-Aids and never peep the person beneath. When interviewed, they promptly say it was some big black dude with Band-Aids on his face. The problem was I knew the area, had worked it before, and if I knew the area, the area knew me. Band-Aids or no Band-Aids, if someone said, "Hey, that's Bruno Johnson," the jig would be up.

Chapter Nineteen

We crossed another street that bisected 124th and headed into a cul-de-sac filled with apartment buildings. Thugs sat in groups on the hoods of their highly polished hoopties, with red bandanas folded and tied around their foreheads. They wanted all who came onto the block to know the block belonged to the Bloods, the Playboys, Pimps, and Gangsters clique. They had their gats—guns—stashed close at hand ready to go to guns at a moment's notice.

They whistled at the white woman with her child and made lewd gestures with their hands, some grabbing their crotch. I kept my head down, watching the sidewalk and the gangsters out of my peripheral vision. I increased speed, caught up with Dora, to let them think we were together, then backed off a little before she turned and said, "Hey, what the—?"

I was in, past their main defenses. Getting out would be another problem.

She knew exactly where to go. She followed the walkway between two apartments, made a left, went around a derelict pool filled with dirt and weeds and surrounded by rusted chain-link that sagged in places. She stopped at an open apartment door and peered in. She bounced from foot to foot as if her bladder were about to burst. "Q? Q, are you in there?"

She looked back over her shoulder, sensing my presence.

Our eyes locked for a long second before her need for meth again took control.

Q? Maybe the kid's luck was holding out. Q was Quentin Bridges, Q-Ball, a nickel-and-dime street dealer I'd known personally and had gotten up close and personal with on two occasions, laced his head with the barrel of my .357 for dealing crack to the neighborhood junior high school kids.

The first time it happened when my team was executing a search warrant. We rolled up Trojan horse-style—the entire team in a van jumped out and deployed on an apartment complex on El Segundo Boulevard. I carried the door ram. When we rounded the corner, Q-Ball stood at his apartment door with a line of poor folks who hardly had enough money to eat, waiting to buy his rock cocaine.

He saw me and slammed the door. The line scattered. Some screamed when they recognized the Los Angeles County Sheriff's green raid jackets. "Grab yo babies. Grab yo babies."

I threw the ram through the door just as it latched closed. It sprung open so hard the knob imbedded in the wall. Inside, Q-Ball ran up the stairs. I chased him, clubbing him over the head with my gun.

The second time, out on bail, he was back at it in the same apartment. I wrote another warrant and we hit it again. This time he'd changed his MO and thought he was safe. With the front door locked and barred, the line of customers ran out from under the second-story window. Q-Ball hung precariously out his second-story window, his heels locked under his bed to keep from falling. He dropped a fistful of money when he saw the team deploy on his apartment. He yelped, struggled to pull back in as I rammed the door barricaded on the other side. It took ten or fifteen strikes, putting everything I had into it. The door came down. I ran up the same stairs and found him lying on his bed, feigning sleep, his head bandaged from our first encounter. What else could he do? On the floor, piled two feet high were the wadded-up greenbacks he'd been throwing back into the bedroom from his perch dangling precariously out the window. I said, "Peekaboo, asshole," a saying that became immortalized in the BMFs, and fell on him with both knees, the barrel of my gun again educating his noggin in how it was not a good thing to sell dope to kids.

Dora Bascombe didn't venture in without permission. She'd been on the street long enough to know better. Q-Ball came to the open door, a big smile on his ferret face. He knew what stood before him. Bascombe didn't have any money. There was only one thing he'd take in trade. I only hoped she wouldn't do it in front of Tommy.

Out front on the street, gunfire erupted, sounding like popcorn in a microwave, a common occurrence this side of Central Avenue.

Q-Ball paid it no mind, put his arm around Dora's shoulders, and with his other arm outstretched, ushered her in. He hesitated, looked over at me, trying to remember where he'd seen me before, the Band-Aids doing their job. I didn't look away and held his glare for several long seconds before he took out a cell phone, dialed, and spoke. They went inside, all of them.

Even Tommy.

I knew I didn't have much time to do what had to be done. He'd just called in his ghetto dogs.

Chapter Twenty

Q was bold and left the door wide open. He'd moved up in the world he'd chosen. He was now a VP, head of a district, probably five square blocks.

Just before I got to the doorway, he reappeared, gun in hand, his eyes locked on mine. I continued to move toward him as he brought the gun up, pointed right at my belly, a pistol barrel, large and round, one I knew from experience could wink fire and pain. His smile dropped. His expression transformed to fear as recognition set in and stole his common sense and false bravado.

Because he recognized me, the caper wasn't going to be a clandestine snatch. The loss of the element of surprise turned into a real problem that in the end would jeopardize everything we'd worked for. Nothing I could do about it. I couldn't leave Tommy to the life he'd been dealt. No way.

Pale and quaking, with his free hand, Q reached over, took hold of the door, and slammed it shut. Before he had time to throw the deadbolt, I rose up on the ball of my left foot, at the same time bringing my knee up to my chest, and kicked as hard as I could. The door banged open a second after it closed. The edge caught Q in the face. It mashed his nose flat. His raggedy ass flew back against the wall where he slid down with a sappy expression on his blood-smeared face.

Inside, Dora held Tommy up in front of her as she backed up. Using him as a shield.

"Put the boy down."

"Get away from me."

Tommy caught his mother's terror and began to cry, a long, slow wail.

"Now you've gone and scared the kid. Just put him down and go in the other room."

"What? You going to take my boy? Is that it? You some kind of baby raper?"

"Put him down, now," I said through clenched teeth, the thought of her accusation, the nerve.

She set him down on the floor, but held on to his shoulders. "Okay, okay, gimme five hundred dollars, and you can have him."

She read my mind, saw the sharp edge of hate in my eyes. "Okay, okay, three hundred."

I squatted. "Tommy, I'm your friend. You don't have to worry about me. I won't hurt you. I won't ever hurt you." I reached out a hand. "I promise. I only want to be your friend."

Unafraid, he stopped crying, toned it down to a whimper, and stared me right in the eye. He had a lot of grit. Out of the corner of my eye, I saw mama back up, her hand going behind her, searching for a weapon. I couldn't break the contact too soon, not and have him on my side. His small hand came out slowly reaching for my big mitt. "That's a boy. You're a brave little man."

Outside the apartment I heard footsteps. The ghetto dogs trailed in to protect their master.

Tommy's hand was ice cold. I noticed his lips were tinged blue. He shivered from fear and cold.

Dora found her weapon. Her hand wrapped around a heavy, green glass ashtray. I stood in one long fluid motion so it wouldn't spook Tommy and stepped around him as his mother pulled back with everything she had and swung. I ducked my head and took the blow on the shoulder. The frightful pain rippled up and down my spine. With my left hand, I tucked little Tommy inside my great coat, covered him up. At the same time, I swung a right fist backward at his mother's face. My fist connected solid to her forehead. Her body let out an involuntary sigh as she wilted to the floor, unconscious. Tommy, on the other side of me, never saw it. His body an ice cube, burrowed into the heat of my body, his little arms going around my chest, as I squatted, the arm with the cast a little awkward.

There wasn't time. Q's crew would be coming to back him up. I stepped over to the moaning Q, his eyes now wide with fright, leaned down, and took the Colt .45 from his limp hand. Too much gun for a punk like him to accurately control.

The doorway shadowed with a throng of Blood gang members. In an after-action, beer drinking tailgate party, the BMFs would have called it a "blood clot." I automatically turned my shoulder away from them, putting my body in between the threat and Tommy.

"Step out of the way, boys. I got no beef with you."

Four of them, just outside the door, backed up almost to the chain-link fence that surrounded the defunct pool. Only one held a gun, a sawed-off double-barrel twelve-gauge. Enough fire power to cut me right in half. The largest by far of the thugs had on a red tank top. His thickly muscled right bicep wept blood from a fresh bullet wound, the result of the earlier gunshots, a drive-by. Fearless, loyal, and brave, he said, "Where's Q-Ball?"

I kept the gun down by my side, half looking at them over my shoulder. "You don't want any part of this. Back on out and —"

"I said, where's Q?"

Behind me on the floor, Q said, "Man, are you crazy? Doan you know who dat is? Dat's Bruno Johnson, the poooleeese. Let him go 'fore he kills all've us." Q's voice rose as he spoke until it was almost a screech. He crab-crawled deeper into the apartment. On the top of his head, ropy strips of scalp laid bare where the hair never grew back from when I had tried to educate him in the ills of drug dealing. I guess I'd been a poor teacher.

The four thugs looked at one another. The big, mean one with the fresh bullet hole in his arm remained undeterred. "Fuck this punk, man, dere are fo' of us and only one a 'm."

Q screeched from deep in the dim apartment. "Dint you hear what I said? Dat's Bruno, The Bad Boy Johnson, and I swear to gawd, he'll kill us all. Let him go, let him go, let him get his sorry ass outta here."

Maybe he had learned a little something from our prior lessons after all.

Q's hysteria turned contagious. The big thug broke eye contact, looked at his friends who continued to back up. They all shifted and moved off around the dirt pool, slowly at first, then in a big hurry, cowardly curs with their tails between their legs.

I put the Colt in the pocket of the army coat and picked Tommy up, his rib bones hard against my hands, he was so damn skinny. He wrapped his legs around my waist. I buttoned the coat around him. He'd stopped shivering.

I went back into the foul-smelling apartment only dim enough to show the outline of furniture, found Q huddled in the kitchen, next to the wall and fridge, his arms over his head. "Whatta ya want? Whatever it is take it. Take it and go."

His plea stopped me short and gave me an idea. I nudged him with my foot. "You know damn well why I'm here, asshole."

"No, I don't, swear to gawd I don't."

"I want my money."

"What gawd damn money's dat?" His head came up, indignant. Money was his life and easily superseded his fear.

I kicked him, but not hard. "Don't you play dumb with me, you candy-ass punk, I'll shoot you right here. You know me. You know I'll do it and not think twice about it."

"Aw'ite, aw'ite, doan shoot. All the green I gots is in a bag behind the vent, behind the vent under the water heater."

I kicked him again. "Get it and hurry up."

I followed as he crab-crawled quickly through the living room area, down a short hall to a closet. Tommy's legs had relaxed, his whole body limp. The comfortable heat after the constant cold put him right to sleep.

At the end of the hall, Q started to open the door. I kicked it closed. "You come out with a gun it'll be your last conscious act. You understand me?"

"I ain't no fool."

"Get it then and make it snappy."

He opened the closet. Inside sat a fat water heater just like he said. He fumbled in his pocket and came out with a slot screwdriver, the key to his riches. His hands shook. Blood dripped from his broken nose onto his wrist as he fumbled with the four nearly stripped screws. When the vent came off, I grabbed him by the shoulder and pulled him away with my free hand. I reached inside and felt a Mac-10 submachine gun on top of a nylon gym bag. I pulled the bag out.

"How much is in there?"

"Dere's forty-five."

"Forty-five, that means you can tell Jumbo he still owes me another — no, you tell Jumbo this is interest only. You tell him he still owes me the entire one-twenty-five. You got it?"

"Jumbo? I doan know no —"

I shoved him with my foot, then put it on his chest pinning him. "Don't even try to tell me you don't know Jumbo."

"Awite, awite, I knows him. But all dat money ain't his. Some've it's mine."

"You can work it out with him. This is your boy, isn't it?" I said, indicating Tommy Bascombe under my jacket.

"Hell, no, that ain't my boy."

I put more weight on his chest.

"Awite, awite, he's my lil rugrat, whatever you say, awite."

"I'm taking him, holding him ransom until I get the rest of my money. You understand? You want your kid back, you better tell Jumbo to pay up. And I don't have to tell you what will happen if you go to the cops. You or your woman out there."

The idea came to me all of a sudden, some smoke to cover for the taking of Tommy.

"We won't rat to no cops, dat's for damn sure."

"Now get up. You're going to walk me out of here just in case some of your homies think they can take me on."

"Aw, man."

Outside on the sidewalk, night had slammed down without fair warning. Tommy still slept against my chest and grew heavier with each step. I tried to hold him up with one arm the other in my pocket holding the Colt against Q's spine. He carried the bag of money.

"Where's your hooptie?"

"I ain't got no ride."

"I'm not going to steal your car. You're going to drive us out of here."

"Right dere." He pointed to a Cadillac Escalade, Kelly green with twenties on the wheels. He'd moved up the food chain, an aberration for such a weak-kneed, pencil-neck geek.

"Get in."

Chapter Twenty-One

He drove us east on 124th Street with the heater on full, then over to Alameda northbound to Imperial Highway. I started to sweat. "Pull in right here."

I pointed to a no-name tire shop. Mexicans inside hard at work, long after dark, finishing up their twelve-hour day, with four cars up on lifts, a couple still in queue waiting. He didn't question, but pulled right over, anxious to get rid of me. I opened the door and hesitated. "Don't you want to say good-bye to your son?"

"Ya, ya, bye, kid, doan you worry none. I'll git yo sorry ass back."

I found it difficult to stifle a smile. "Don't forget, tell Jumbo, no cops. And keep that woman in enough dope she doesn't cause a problem. You hear?"

I got out. He gunned it before the door closed, pulled right out in traffic without looking. A Bimbo bread truck slammed into the side of his perfectly kept Caddy with enough force to slew it sideways over the curb and into a power pole. The crash startled Tommy who jumped. He rose up like a prairie dog over the vee at the top of the jacket. "Wow."

I walked down along the side of the tire shop, Tommy in one arm, the bag slung over my shoulder.

"You hungry?"

He looked up at me his eyes large and wet. "Where's my

mama? I want my mama." He put his head back against my chest. It never ceased to amaze me how a parent could abuse a child, starve him, torture him, and the child continued a rabid loyalty.

"She'll be along soon. She told me to get you something to eat, said that you haven't eaten in a good long while. What do you like best to eat? Hot dogs, hamburgers, French fries, vanilla malts?"

"I want my mama."

We continued through a field onto the next street. "Okay, how about an ice cream? My boy always likes ice cream after we have dinner."

"You gotta boy?"

"Yep, just about your age. He loves ice cream."

He hesitated. "Chocolate ice cream with hot fudge?"

I thought about it, not wanting to lie. Where would I get chocolate ice cream and hot fudge? "Yep, we could do that. First, your mama said to get some good food in your belly before the sweets. You know the rules. So what'll it be?"

He brought his head up, looked around. "Go left here over to Lucy's, they have great taquitos with real guacamole. Whenever Mama gets a little extra money, she takes us out for a treat, Lucy's for the real guacamole."

The word guacamole didn't fit with someone so young, and it would've been cute the way he'd said it had he not been too anxious to defend the witch of a woman who had mistreated him, the woman who so readily agreed to sell him off like so much chattel.

I knew Lucy's and they knew me. I'd have to chance it. Three blocks later we walked into the sit-down part of the walk-up restaurant. People lined up outside and on the inside waiting their turn for dinner. I went right to the door off to the side like in the old days and looked over the tops of the folks' heads at the girls behind the window taking orders and serving the food. I didn't see who recognized me, but the door's solenoid automatic lock buzzed. I pulled. We were in. The door closed automatically behind us. The warm, sweet aroma inside smelled of fresh cooked tortilla, carnitas, and cilantro. My stomach growled. Not so many years ago, years that now felt like decades, I stood in the back by the same stainless steel table and ate all the free food Lucy's owners put down in front of us, patrol cops who kept the restaurant safe for the inexpensive price of a little food.

I let Tommy down on the floor. He didn't flinch at the cold. He was a tough kid. A fat woman I didn't recognize came over with a tray of tacos, beans, and rice, and chips with salsa. She looked us over, my battered face, dirty bandaged hands, and Tommy's naked feet. She shook her head and started to leave.

"Excuse me," I said, "Can we please have some guacamole?"

She nodded and headed for the large walk-in refrigerator. Tommy didn't wait, he went up on tiptoes, grabbed a taco and took a bite too large for his mouth. The office door opened. Out waddled Ramon Gutierrez, the son of the owner. "Bruno, my man, long time no see." He held out his hand. I shook it. "Good to see you, too. I didn't expect this kind of service."

He smiled with his eyes, his grin wide enough it looked like it hurt.

It made me uncomfortable. "I'm not with the cops anymore."

He waved a hand in dismissal. "I know that. I saw you come in on the surveillance cameras and popped the door for you."

"I pay my own way, Ramon." I put a hundred down on the stainless steel table, the smallest bill I had.

He pointed a finger. "Your money's no good here. And that's disrespectful. Put it away."

When I looked back the hundred was gone. Tommy busied himself eating another taco as if nothing out of the ordinary happened. His mom had turned him into a sneak thief, a thief of opportunity.

Ramon chuckled, "That kid's got a real appetite and fast hands." The fat Mexican lady came out of the walk-in with a plastic tub of fresh guacamole big enough for four people. She set it down in front of Tommy who groaned in satisfaction and immediately dipped his taco.

Ramon nodded his head toward the office. "Can I talk to you for a minute?"

I looked at Tommy, not knowing what to do about him. Ramon read the play. "Rosy," referring to the fat Mexican lady, "will watch the boy." He gave her some rapid-fire Spanish. She nodded and took a position right beside Tommy. Ramon led the way into the office cluttered with stacks of invoices on the desk and boxes of overflow paper stock stacked clear to the ceiling. I stood in the open doorway watching the aisle in case Tommy decided to take it on the lam and juke the rotund Rosy.

"Come in, sit down."

"No, thanks, I think I'll stand."

Ramon hesitated, uncomfortable in what he was about to say.

Years ago, 18th Street Hispanic gang members came around and threatened him and his family with great bodily injury if they didn't pay a neighborhood tax for protection. They paid it for a while until the amount kept going up and up, an amount that threatened to take the business to its knees. Like most all cops in the area, I ate on the cuff, unaware of the tyranny right under our noses. One busy night on patrol, I didn't have time to stop to eat, the in-progress calls came too thick. I got to Lucy's so late they'd already closed. But not too late to find two gang members, shaved headed, tattooed soldiers for the Mexican Mafia who had Ramon up against the wall around back of the restaurant. They had already stabbed him once and were about to gut him. I'd seen his car out front and walked around to see if he'd answer the back door. The two soldiers let him slide to the ground and immediately squared off with me. I could've legally shot them both, pulled my .357, and without checking for witnesses, gunned them right where they stood. Only I was angry and wanted a little get-even time. Back alley, no witnesses, no lights, classic curbside justice BMF style. I drew my mahogany straight stick baton and for two months, while in intensive care, they wished I had used my .357.

Even severely stabbed, in fear for his family, Ramon remained reluctant to tell the story about the protection he paid. All the deputies and cops from the surrounding area loved Ramon and his family. They put enough heat on the 18th Street gang members that a truce was called. Mad Dog MacDonald from the Lynwood Sheriff Station gang unit brought the news to the family that Lucy's was off limits to all cliques associated with the Mexican Mafia.

Now in his office, Ramon looked torn.

"It's okay," I said. "I understand. I won't come back anymore."

"No, no, that's not it at all." He broke eye contact.

I took a step toward him. "What then?"

"Robby Wicks is a friend of yours, right? I know he is. You used to be thick as thieves, coming here to eat all the time when you were a detective."

I felt a little weak in the knees, backed up, and grabbed hold of the doorway. "What? Tell me?"

"It might be nothing. But, well, he came in two weeks ago, like old times, like he had never missed a week in all the time he'd been gone, at least two years now. Came right in, asked for me. I wasn't here, so my guys called me. He wanted them to call me. When I showed up, he acted like it was no big deal, like this was just a social visit. You know what I mean?"

My mouth went dry. "And?"

"Well—"

"Come on, Ramon."

"Wicks tried to cover it but he finally got around to the reason he came. He asked about you."

"He asked about me?" That wasn't so bad, he was just checking up to see how I was doing. That wasn't it at all. Not judging by Ramon's expression.

"What? Give me the rest of it."

"He wasn't alone."

"Who was with him?"

"A guy who wasn't like other cops. His hair was—" Ramon put his hands up to his own semibald pate. "You know, perfect, his clothes were pressed and new."

"Who was he, Ramon?" I already knew the answer.

"He had a little gold badge hooked to his belt next to his gun. I saw it when his blue suit coat came open. He wouldn't take a free meal. The guy insisted on paying. The badge, I seen it before. It was FBI."

Chapter Twenty-Two

Tommy ate tacos until his stomach bulged round and hard. My appetite was suddenly gone.

Ramon patted Tommy's head. "Where's this niño's shoes?"

"It's a long story. I'm watching him for his mama who had to go out of town." Tommy looked up at me at this news regarding his mama.

Ramon got down on one knee. "Chiquito hombre, how did you break your arm? Did you fall off a wild bucking bronco?"

Tommy looked away, hesitated, then looked right in Ramon's eye. "I fell off the back porch while I was playing. My mama told me not to play there." The coached lie hung heavy in the air.

The kid covered for his parents. The experts had ruled the break as a spiral fracture only accomplished by a child abuser who yanked and twisted at the same time.

"My mama really went out of town?"

I nodded, the lie stuck in my throat. Right now this was the only way for his own good. "Come on, kid, we have to roll."

"Don't forget the ice cream. You promised chocolate ice cream with hot fudge."

Ramon chuckled. "Wait a minute." He disappeared back in his office and rummaged around. He came back with a pair of shoes, stylish shoes still in the box, the kind with the skates in the heel. When Tommy saw them his eyes went round as saucers and his mouth into a little *O*.

"I hope these fit. I got them for my nephew, but never got around to giving them to him before his own grandmama beat me to it and bought a pair."

Tommy grabbed the box and sat down on the floor. "They'll fit. They'll fit." His pure delight warmed my heart.

I could see they were a little too big. I got down on the spotless floor to help him. I wadded up some of the tissue paper from in the box and put it in the toes. His legs wouldn't stop moving as I tried to lace them up. I tied the last bow. He jumped up and skated around the small kitchen area. I held my breath. If he fell—

"We have to get going. Thanks, amigo. And don't worry about that other thing with Robby. I already knew all about it. It's no big deal, okay?"

"Sure, sure, Bruno. Don't be a stranger." He put his warm hand on my arm. The man was street-smart. He knew I was in way over my head. I'd put it out of my mind, tried not think about it until I got Tommy to Dad's safe and sound. I had to focus on one thing. The alternative was far too ugly.

Tommy insisted that he walk and wouldn't let me carry him. We took Long Beach down to Mr. Cho's and went in. Cho stood behind the counter. He started yelling as soon as we came in. "Get out, get out. I call poleese."

We ignored him and went to the chest freezer where he kept the ice cream and then over to the aisle where he kept the jars of marshmallow and chocolate syrup. Mr. Cho followed along yelling. Tommy didn't seem to mind. He must've grown accustomed to a similar environment.

"All they got is chocolate syrup and no hot fudge. Is chocolate syrup going to be good enough?" Tommy put his hand to his mouth and burped. The thought of more food took him to the edge. He nodded and skated away down the aisle.

"Where's my last paycheck? You owe me for two weeks."

"They say, you come back I call. Get out. Get out. I call right now." He went to the phone on the counter and dialed.

"Okay, forget the check. I'm taking the ice cream instead."

"Hello, poleese." I snatched the phone from his hand and listened, heard the dial tone. He didn't want any more trouble and tried to bluff. I yanked the phone from the wall. "Have a good life, Mr. Cho."

Outside, I again averted my eyes from the spot where the kid had fallen, not wanting to see the dried blood if it was still there. I ran to catch up to Tommy who rolled off down the street riding on the heel skates.

I'd been wrong or right, really, the first time I assessed the situation. The surveillance had been for me, and the robbery was collateral damage. Robby had not been there by coincidence, his team was watching me. But then what about the murders with the gasoline? Was it just a cover? He hadn't made it up. The murders were really happening. The story was all over the papers and TV news.

I caught up to Tommy and guided him around the corner. I'd been right about that night. My internal radar had been right-on after all. I didn't feel any eyes on us now, but wasn't going to take the chance. I used a preplanned escape route I'd set up far in advance. If they were watching, the plan would only work once. We went on down to Washington Avenue and turned west. Tommy's stomach was full. He'd had a little nap and now he had some shoe skates. The ice cream made my hands ache from the cold and acted as a good prop. The bag of cash hung off my shoulder. I took Tommy by the shoulder and guided him down a long path to an old, tired manse. In its day, Lynwood was an upper-middle-class neighborhood, labeled The All American City. The south side had huge houses on big lots. Los Angeles, the city on the west border, put in vast blocks of public housing—Imperial Courts, Nickerson Gardens, and Jordan Downs. Crime raged in all the nearby cities: Compton, the gateway to Los Angeles, and Bell Gardens, and South Gate. Eventually, the good folks moved out and left the zoo to the animals. Some stayed and fought the good fight. This house was one of them.

I knocked on the solid oak door. Mr. Howard Marks, a wrinkled, white-haired old gentleman, who should've been long dead from old age, opened the door. The skin under his watery blue eyes sagged, displaying little pink half moons. His entire body shook from the effort to stay on his feet. He smiled, knew the reason for the preplanned visit, put a hand on my arm, and ushered us in. He closed the door. I took Tommy right through the house and out the back door into a huge one-acre lot overgrown with what had once been a world-class garden. I picked up Tommy because his skates wouldn't roll on the dirt path with all the vines and overgrowth. We went right out into an alley where a car was parked. We got in and started up. Mr. Howard Marks was a friend of Marie's. He agreed a long time ago to help out.

I drove down the alley, made a right, did a couple more counter moves, checked the mirrors for a tail. We were in the clear. I headed for Dad's. I was late for the meeting with Robby. No way was I going to see him now. Fate had interceded and saved my ass.

Chapter Twenty-Three

This time Junior caught our scent and came up, his hind end waggled with his tail. Tommy clung to me tighter when he saw the dog and buried his head in my chest. "It's okay, little guy, this is a nice dog. Here, look."

Tommy would have none of it. He started to whimper.

It was still early. The interior lights lit up the house. The door was locked this time, like it was supposed to be. I knocked quietly. Nothing. On the other side came the noise from the Game Boy, a trade-off to keep the kids quiet inside the house where no one could see them. I knocked again, a little louder, and looked back over my shoulder. The backyard was long and deep with overgrown shrubs. No one could see. Dad opened the door with a big smile. I handed him the ice cream and chocolate syrup. I left the black gym bag with the money on the porch. The bag represented something corrupt and filthy, the idea of bringing it inside where the kids played would pollute their innocence.

Dad didn't falter at the sight of another child, this one not in the plan. He smiled and rubbed Tommy's head, didn't ask any questions. His eyes smiled at me.

"I couldn't walk away and leave him, not—"

"I didn't say a word. Come on, let's get some of this ice cream dished up, whatta ya say?" With his free hand, he pried Tommy off my chest and took him over to the kitchen table and sat down. He was going to talk to Tommy a good long time, like he did with the others. When he finished talking, Tommy would call him Grandpa and feel like he'd known Dad all his life.

The house was too hot. I took off the army coat and put the ice cream in the freezer. Then I peeked around the corner into the living room where the make-believe battle raged on the television screen. Four boys, Ricky, Toby, Randy, and Wally with controllers in hand juked and ducked, playing the game. Alonzo was too young. He marveled at the action. Two others, Sonny and Marvin, lay on the floor playing the board game Chutes and Ladders.

Alonzo's eyes were bright, his smile heartwarming. He reminded me of my daughter who reminded me of my dear wife, God rest their souls. Alonzo sensed a change in the environment and looked up. When he saw me, he leapt up, came right off the floor as if propelled out of a cannon. "Daddy."

I wasn't his daddy. He'd taken to calling me that. And who was I to correct him? The other boys hesitated, looked up, only the game was too enticing, and they went back to their controllers.

Alonzo all but bowled me over. I backed up several steps, regained my balance, scooped him up, and swung him in the air, hugging him so hard I caught myself, the little voice inside my head reminding me he was only three and terribly fragile. He'd put on even more weight. He'd been skin and bone two years ago, now Dad had gone the other way feeding him. I'd have to have a talk with him about feeding the kids too much. What was I thinking? We were done, officially on the lam. Tomorrow we'd all be in Costa Rica, or at least too far into the journey for anyone to pull us back.

Costa Rica.

Alonzo giggled and hugged my neck with his little pudgy

arms. The thought of leaving elated me and at the same time scared the hell out of me. I looked over at Dad who sat at the table talking quietly to Tommy, the new family addition. Dad looked up, our eyes met. He read me like a book, saw it was all over for him. He was going to have to give up his kids and never see them again. I felt as if someone had socked me in the stomach. I closed my eyes and hugged Alonzo, kissed the top of his head. Dad continued on in a low murmur to Tommy, the kids always came first.

I took out eight bowls, used up the whole half gallon of chocolate ice cream and most of the bottle of syrup. I knew it probably wasn't the healthiest diet and recognized that it was the guilt making me do it. I set Alonzo down and carried three bowls into the living room, then another three. The dessert was enough motivation. They put the games on hold and dug in. Spoons clanged on glass bowls. I went back in the kitchen, gave Tommy his bowl while Dad continued to talk to him. He spooned chocolate ice cream into the boy's mouth as the child nodded. I took the last bowl into the living room with Alonzo, sat in Dad's chair and watched my grandson eat. A great weight lifted off me. Even though it was earlier than we planned, the idea of leaving, escaping before getting caught let me breathe in a full lung of air for the first time in months. I sat with Alonzo a long time, rocking, and stroking his hair. Dad came in with Tommy asleep in his arms and carried him down the hall to a bedroom. When he returned empty handed, he said to the boys in a quiet voice, "Time for bed."

They didn't argue, they turned off the TV, put up the controllers, came over and carefully gave me a kiss on the cheek without disturbing Alonzo, and went off to bed.

I started to get up. Dad waved me back down. He sat on the couch, one too low and difficult for him to extricate himself with his bad knees. He stared at me. I didn't want to look at him. There was no alternative. Finally, I said, "Tomorrow, five o'clock. Marie will be here at three to help get things ready."

Saying the words made it real.

My mind spun out far ahead, categorizing and prioritizing all the things that had to be done. I had to go back to the house on Alabama and 117th to dig up the money. Track down Jumbo for the balance. The latter might take more time than I had available. We would need the money. How could we house and clothe and feed eight kids without it? Marie knew nothing about the money and planned on living by both of us getting jobs. But then who would watch the kids? No, I wouldn't leave without the money.

Dad's eyes welled with tears, a sight that kick-started my waterworks as well. We'd talked and talked about it before. I wanted him to follow along in a year or so when the heat died down. But he was the one against it. He said it was too dangerous, and if the Feds ever discovered where we were, the kids would be in jeopardy of going back to where they'd come from, an absolutely untenable environment. "Besides," he'd said, "I'll be dead and gone long before all the hubbub dies down." Something I didn't want to believe. Dad had always been there for me, to imagine him gone, well, it just wouldn't be the same world.

At the same time, I knew these kids had been keeping him going, keeping him alive. Take them away and he'd wither like a flower without water.

I got up, went over, and offered him my hand. He took it. I pulled him up and hugged him with Alonzo between us. After a long time I stepped back and handed him Alonzo, kissed them both, turned, and left.

Chapter Twenty-Four

I'd made one pass on Alabama to check for problems, like extra eyes that didn't belong. The red light from a patrol car came on in the rearview at Mona Boulevard and Imperial Highway. For a brief second I thought, no, that can't be for me, that if I just gingerly pull over, they'd go on by. It can't be for me. Not now. It would ruin every damn thing. The next thought was to run. Push the accelerator to the floor. Hit it. Drive it like I'd stolen it. I'd been there before on the other side, and knew that I might be able to outrun the cop car. But not their radio, not their helicopter. I pulled over and hoped I could bullshit my way out of it. Time rolled by in long successive increments as I waited for the cops to approach. They were running a make on the car that was cold. I'd paid cash for it and made sure everything on it was in good working order before I'd laid it off in the back of the manse. The only thing they could've pulled me over for was DWB, driving while black. They say it didn't ever happen. I knew better and had done it myself while on the prowl for crooks.

Finally, the strong spotlight beam broke, it shadowed as the cops approached, one on each side, standard procedure. The one on the passenger side knocked on the window. I leaned over and rolled it down. "License and registration."

I opened the glove box and took out the registration. "Officer, I think I left my wallet at home. The car's registered to me though."

He looked at the registration with his powerful flashlight. "Mr. Norbert, could you please step out of your car?"

"Sure."

I started to get out on the driver's side.

"Hold it, get out on this side. Slide over."

I did as I was told. When I got out, my eyes adjusted. They were blue bellies, LAPD, and not Sheriff's deputies. I had a chance. He put me against the car and patted me down.

The officer had his notebook out, "What's your full name and date of birth and if you know your driver's license number?"

"Jonathon Delbert Norbert." It was the name on the registration when I bought it and it sounded made up. "DOB is 10-15-60, and I'm sorry I don't remember my driver's license number."

He left, went back to his car to run the information. By the time he came back, sweat beaded on my forehead in the cold night air.

"Couldn't find you in the computer."

"Yeah, that's happened before. Sometimes it hits on my mom's maiden name."

"That right? What's your mama's name?"

"Aretha Jackson."

"Jackson? That's the same as Smith. There'll be a thousand hits on it."

I shrugged, too scared to smile.

"You got anything illegal in the car?"

"No, not at all. I was just going out to get some milk for my babies."

"Then you don't mind if we search?"

"No, not at all. Go ahead."

The one cop nodded to his partner, who immediately went

over to the car and opened the door. The inside of the car was, "clean as a Safeway chicken," as Robby would've said. The searching cop worked over the inside for about ten minutes then came out with the ignition keys in his hand, headed for the trunk. The trunk contained the black bag with Q-Ball's money, 45K, and the gun. It wasn't against the law, under normal circumstances, to have that kind of money, but a black man at night in the ghetto was a sure call for the narcs to respond. If they put a narc dog on it, he'd sure as hell key on that dope money. After that, they'd eventually find out my real name. Game over.

The cop tinkered with the keys trying to find the right one. "Come on, show me which key opens the trunk."

The car was an early model Plymouth, root beer-brown with a black stripe. As a precaution, I'd taken the trunk key off and put it in my shoe. "Oh, I lost that key a long time ago. But you can pull the backseat off, and if you're real small, you can crawl into the trunk."

The one cop looked at his partner, as if asking what they should do next. Time hung in the misty night air.

"Screw it. Let's go." He turned to me, "I'm going to let you off with a warning this time. Get a driver's license. I stop you again, I'm going to run you in."

"Yes, sir. Thank you, sir."

The night was suddenly lit up with a bright spotlight from a slow-moving sheriff's patrol car eastbound on Imperial Highway. I brought my arm up to shield my eyes, my face from recognition.

"Hey, look what we have here." Said a voice from the slow moving car. The car squeaked against the curb. "It's Bad Boy Bruno Johnson."

Chapter Twenty-Five

The two blue bellies jumped me, took me to the ground hard. One gave me a cheap shot, a fist to the back of the head. The other hit me with a flashlight across the back of my legs. I roared and came up with them on my back, in a push-up position. There was nothing else to lose. They had me. The blue bellies quickly figured they'd grabbed a tiger by the tail.

I would have taken them and gotten away if the two sheriff's deputies hadn't joined in.

Dog pile on the black man.

The deputy who'd identified me, Good Johnson, no relation, laughed his coffee-sour breath right in my face as they got the handcuffs on. He'd been at Lynwood Station for at least fifteen years. The kind of deputy too cynical and callous, a violent-tempered ghetto deputy no other station or division would have. He was stuck, destined to do his entire career at the same place, festering, getting meaner and meaner until he'd eventually implode; take a lead pellet in the mouth to end his, sad, pitiful life.

The tag "Good" wasn't earned out of job performance. It came up out of necessity when I first arrived at the station, a boot deputy. Two Johnsons became a problem. A white Johnson and a black Johnson like in the westerns with the cowboy hats. They called him the Good Johnson and me the Bad.

Good added the "Boy" to mine, a derogatory reference to race and it stuck. Bruno The Bad Boy Johnson.

One blue belly stayed with his knees on my back, making it difficult to breathe, pinning me to the dirt. The others stood and brushed off their uniforms.

Good said to his trainee, "Get on the radio, advise 60L8 we have his package." He turned to the blue bellies. "Nice stop. This guy's wanted. There's a BOLO out for him from our homicide division." He kicked my hip. "He's a real piece of shit. Used to be one of us, believe it or not. You guys can clear. We'll handle it from here."

I was on the ground again, handcuffed with white cops standing over me, deciding my fate. I didn't like it, not one damn bit.

Down Imperial Highway came a screaming police car running the red signals, braking hard and accelerating, his engine winding out in a roar in between each stop. The blue bellies stepped back in the shadows, sensing something was about to happen. Good put his foot on my head in a pose, the great white hunter.

The car slid to the curb.

Robby Wicks jumped out, came up, and shoved Good. "Get the fuck off him. What the hell's wrong with you?"

Robby stood me up and brushed me off. The coincidence that this was the second time it happened was not lost on me.

I looked him in the eye. "This is getting to be a habit with you."

"You were late for our meet. I thought you might be jacking me off. I put out the call. Just to make sure you knew how serious I am about you helping on this thing."

"So you're not arresting me?"

"No. Have you done something I don't know about?" He'd

said it purely for the benefit of his audience. A question he'd never ask, not wanting to know the answer.

"Come on, take the cuffs off."

"I don't think so, not after what happened the last time." He escorted me over to his car, hands still cuffed behind my back.

Johnson yelled, "You're welcome. Those are my cuffs. I want 'em back."

Robby turned, smiled, "Okay. For your own safety, get in your car and lock the door. I'll bring them to you."

He started to take the cuffs off. "You be cool, we have too much to do tonight for any more bullshit. You already put me behind the eight ball being late like this." I nodded. I rubbed my wrists. He walked over and tossed the cuffs in onto Johnson's lap. Johnson peeled out, tires spinning. The blue bellies quietly walked over to their car, got in, and left.

Robby waited until they were out of sight, saw me looking at my car. "You can't drive. You don't have a driver's license. It's a parole violation."

"How am I supposed to get around?"

"Last I heard, you were laying your head in that burnt-out derelict apartment house over on 117th and walking or taking the bus to the liquor store."

How'd he know about the pad on Alabama? "I don't work there anymore."

"Don't dodge the question."

"All of a sudden you know a great deal about me."

"I told you, I want you to help me out with this thing. When you FTA-ed I gotta come look for you. Why all of a sudden are you driving a car? And whose car is it?"

"Okay, truce. I can't leave my car here. I'll follow you. Where're we going?"

He hesitated, thinking it through. He knew I wouldn't run,

not with him following. "We got the witness stashed over at
the Shamrock on Atlantic." He looked at my car and thought
some more. I didn't give him a chance and headed back, got
in, started up.

He wandered to his car, checked over his shoulder one last
time before he got in, and fell in behind as I pulled out.

How did he know about my place on 117th and Alabama?
That was supposed to be a cold pad. My residence of record
was Chantal's on Crenshaw. What else did he know? How
long had the FBI been on me? Two weeks prior was when I'd
first sensed I was being watched and didn't trust my instincts.
The money Jumbo paid me, the cash I buried out back of
117th, did they know about that too? Was the whole deal
blown?

I was going to have to play along until I found out.

We stayed on Imperial Highway all the way east until Atlantic and turned south. He pulled into Taco Quicky, a joint
owned and operated by a reserve deputy. Like Lucy's, the cops
from all around came to eat for free. The parking lot was an
absolute safe zone that crooks walked a wide path around. He
rolled down his window. "Leave that heap and get in."

I locked up and did as he asked. We pulled a U-turn in the
parking lot and came right back into the drive-thru. Robby
said, "I gotta get something in my stomach. I got a bleeding
ulcer from all this stress. You want something?"

"No."

He ordered two tacos and a cup of joe.

"That's not exactly the best food to put down on top of an
ulcer."

His head jerked around about to spit fire and realized he
was better off with the you catch-more-with-honey approach.
He opened his mouth then shut it.

We pulled up further in line, two more cars before our

turn. "I heard you came over and talked with Chantal."

"Nice gal, great equipment. You tapping that? I know I would."

He spoke too fast, covering for being found out.

I almost told him about Marie but didn't want to give him anything he didn't already have, especially if the FBI was onto our rescue operation. "How's Barbara?"

The smile left his eyes, "She's still the same old Babs. You know what I'm sayin'?"

I'd tossed back many a beer and had more than a few barbeques with Robby and his wife Barbara. He met her when he was a detective in narcs. She was a police officer working patrol for the city of Montclair when she pulled him over one night on the freeway doing a hundred and ten. They both loved to tell the story. She walked up and asked for his license and reg. He flashed his star, told her he was en route to a two-kilo coke deal in East L.A., and had twenty minutes to get there. She said, "License and registration."

"If I have to get out of this car," Robby told her, "I'm going to handcuff you to your bumper." He drove off and left her standing in the oscillating red light of her cop car, cite book in hand. It ate at him all night. He sent her red roses the next day. A month later they were married in Vegas and had been together ever since, close to two decades.

I needed to pump him for information without him knowing. He was playing me, and I didn't have a clue why. "Who's the witness at the Shamrock?"

He pulled up to the window and like a gentleman tried to pay for the food with a tattered twenty. The clerk recognized the car as on the job and waved off the money. He reached into his ashtray, dug out a handful of change and put it up on the counter as a tip before he drove off. He parked in the parking lot not far from my Plymouth, unwrapped a taco, and took a bite. I fought the urge to look at the Plymouth and wonder if the money in the trunk would be there when I got back. We needed that money, the kids, Marie.

"You going to tell me the name of the wit or is it some big secret?"

"It's Chocolate."

"Debbie Brown?" That at least made a little sense. She had been my snitch when I worked the street, a beautiful street-walker, and after the first toke, a slave to the glass pipe. She would only talk to me. No matter what kind of information, dope, stolen cars, or murder, she'd only give it up to me.

He took a bite of taco and a sip of coffee. After he swallowed he winced, put his hand on his stomach and burped. He dropped the taco in the box and dumped the coffee out the window.

"Don't you say a thing." He put it reverse and we drove.

Chapter Twenty-Six

The stench was the first thing that hit me when the night clerk buzzed the glass entry door to the Shamrock. It smelled as if a hundred soaked St. Bernards had been let in to roll on the tattered carpet. Inside, the narrow hall led past the window where a disinterred skeleton of a night clerk sat. Robby held up the room key. The night man behind the bulletproof glass couldn't care less. He glanced over then went right back to his *Hustler* magazine, a glossy page with lots of skin color.

The Shamrock was a rent by the week or month or hour kind of place. Some of the doors on the ground floor had hasps above the door knobs with large padlocks, extra security for the meth-fried speed freaks who thought everyone was out to get them. We took the stairs to the second floor, the stairwell too narrow for fire code.

The second floor wasn't any different than the first with the exception of the odor. Here, it was warm and sour, like thrown-up milk. Robby stopped, listened, and looked. His paranoia made me reach down and touch the place on my hip where I used to carry my gun, back when we rolled as a team, rolling hot, chasing violent fugitives.

Robby put the key in the door, hesitated, knocked quietly, turned the key, eased the door open a crack, and said, "It's me." He waited a beat and went in. The room was dark with an orange cast from a t-shirt hanging over the end table lamp. The

Mötley Crüe emblem on the tee threw an eerie shadow. I entered, button-hooked left out of habit, and kept my back to the wall while my eyes adjusted. Off in the center of the ten-foot-square pleasure palace, stood a shadow, a figured obscured by thick clothing that gave an image of a robed monk. "Bruno?" Her voice, disguised with a heavy rasp of a smoker. I didn't recognize it.

Robby moved to the right over to the end table. "I told you, I don't like the room dark." He yanked off the Crüe shirt.

Chocolate flung up an arm to cover her face. In the brief glimpse it afforded, I didn't recognize Chocolate. Robby tricked me. This was some old crone at least seventy years old, wrinkled, slump-shouldered, dressed in panhandler rags.

She slowly brought her arm down, her expression yearning for approval. A smile, concave from no teeth, added to the haggard image.

Her eyes suddenly stood out, brown and youthful yet over-tired. Right then it clicked in, an old memory. This was Chocolate. The street had been horribly unkind. It never was kind to anyone wedded to the glass pipe. It stole thirty years of her life, probably more because she would never recall the first thirty, her memory a blur, having lived fast and loose way out on the fringe. I tried to remember how old she should be. Twenty-eight. My God, twenty-eight.

I couldn't keep the shock out of my expression. Her smile fell. She covered her face with her hands and ran to the bathroom. "Chocolate, wait." I went after her, got to the door before she could close it. She didn't fight and stepped back, her face turned down, hands up for cover.

I stepped in and closed the door. The room turned to pure blackness. We waited, her breathing the only sound. "I'm sorry. I . . . I—"

"You don't have to explain. I know."

I stepped over, hands out in the dark reaching for her. I touched her. She backed off a step. I moved in and took hold of her, hugged her frailness. She shook as she wept.

The first time I came across her was on Long Beach Boulevard during a call of an armed robbery.

The white-haired diminutive old man, the victim who'd called, stood out in front of the motel waiting for me. He couldn't have weighed more than a hundred pounds. I pulled into the driveway, rolled the window down. The night was cold. "Are you the one who called?"

He nodded.

"What happened?"

"She took my car. I want my car back."

"Who took your car?"

"A hooker."

This was odd. Usually the johns made up some story as a cover for their extramarital vice gone wrong. This one held his head up, proud.

"Who took it and what kind of car was it?" I wanted to get out a broadcast right away. "She was an African goddess. The most beautiful woman you ever did see. You'd have to look a long time —"

"Sir, what kind of car was it and what kind of weapon did she use?"

"As soon as we got in the room, she said, 'Give me the keys, ol' man.' I didn't even have time to reach in my pocket. I'd have given her anything just to see her naked, just to see that beauty in its natural state. Deputy, she's that beautiful. Then she —" he laughed, then said, "she grabbed hold of me, picked me up, turned me upside down, and shook me until my keys fell out of my pocket. The way she touched me, wrapped her arms right around me, turned me upside down, my God, it was sensual. Worth every penny of the two hundred dollars in my wallet. I don't care about the money, honestly, I don't. I just want my car back. It's a brand-new Lincoln Mark IV, green with soft, butter-cream leather interior."

Chocolate never wanted to hurt anyone, at least not at first. Later on, the street put the finishing touches on her. With her corruption complete, she did a year and a half in the joint for stabbing John Ahern, aka Jumbo. In reality, it was self-defense.

I caught up with her a few days later, still driving the old man's car, the Lincoln. The old man was right, she was an absolute beauty, the kind of young girl you wanted to just look at, her youth, her vibrancy, the wildness in her eyes. She was a gorgeous seventeen-year-old hooker, new to the street, tall, five eleven, a hundred and forty-five pounds. Her weight in all the right places, hips and breasts, muscular arms and long, well-defined legs.

She looked at me strangely when I didn't handcuff her. I gave her what I called my Father Willy speech about the life she'd chosen and how she was on the wrong path. No one had ever done that for her, especially not a cop who should've been taking her to jail. I'd passed the test. Two weeks later, she called me at the station and gave up a mid-level rock coke dealer, Q-Ball. When I didn't give her up in court, she grew to trust me. Her beauty opened every door on the street, the lowlife slime and the corrupt upper class let her pass, told her about their robberies, the molestation, where they kept their stash. Together we threw a lot of bad folks in jail. I'd lost touch with her, my life overcrowded with my obsession, working on the Violent Crimes Team.

Chocolate was content to stay just the way we were in the quiet, dark bathroom that smelled of urine and mold and soured plastic. We stayed for a long time. I couldn't help thinking how everyone involved in this thing: Robby, Jumbo, Q-

Ball, and now Chocolate were linked to and through me to everything going on. Sure, everything on the street was connected one way or another. With the regular Joe Citizens there's six degrees of separation. With crooks, since they only make up five percent of the population, there was only two degrees. This wasn't Robby's street doctrine, it was mine.

Jumbo ran a big section of South Central Los Angeles, which meant everyone on his turf he controlled or at least influenced. Everyone swirled around the same toilet bowl, never leaving, never changing.

Finally, I whispered, "Did you see what happened? Did you see who threw the gas and lit the fire that burnt that poor soul?"

She shook her head no.

Chapter Twenty-Seven

I pulled her away, reached back for the switch on the wall.

"No, please, leave it off."

I stopped just as my hand found it. "Then why are we here like this?"

When she hesitated, I knew it was going to be the truth. "The cops, they kicked in my door, threw me to da ground, and found my stash, what little there was. They said dey wouldn't take me to jail if I cooperated and told them what I saw outside my window. I didn't know what to do. I couldn't go in on another possession. I'm on probation already. I'm lookin' at five years. I saw that asshole Wicks come up. So I told the cop I wanted to talk to Wicks and then I told Wicks I'd only talk to you. You gotta help me, Bruno, I can't do another day in the joint."

"That's not going to happen. I promise."

"Thanks, Bruno." She clung a little tighter. "You think you could spot me a twenty?"

"You know better than that. I'll buy you some food, but I won't give you money for any rock."

"I know. I had to try. I thought maybe, after all these years, you know, after you went inside, maybe you'd've changed."

Robby knocked on the door. "You two about finished with the reunion and with your little slap and tickle?" He chuckled, a lewd one I would jump him about later, maybe knock a few of his teeth down his throat. "Back off, Robby."

I moved Chocolate farther from the door so he couldn't hear with his ear up against the thin wood. Her back bumped against the sink, my hips bumped against hers in the perfect dark. My mind, all on its own, flashed back to the image from the past, the "African goddess." I became aroused. She nuzzled closer, "You're a good man, Bruno Johnson. Thank you for that. Thank you."

"I'll tell Robby something to get him off your back. But when you get a chance, you're going to have to go to ground. Hide out for a while until things cool off."

"I got no money. And . . . and from what you saw, no means to make any. No one wants what I've turned into."

I wanted to ask her what she'd been doing to survive and, instead, reached into my pocket. She knew what I was going to do. "You're a good man. You're a good man."

I peeled off five one hundred dollar bills, enough money for a slave to the pipe to kill herself. "I have to trust you." I put the money in her hand. "I know you're going to use some of it for rock, but use the rest for food and a place to lay your head. I'm not kidding, Chocolate. I'm trusting you."

"Sure, Bruno, thank you, thank you."

"Go someplace where you don't usually go. Go up north instead of south. Up Atlantic into South Gate, lay low over at the Grover Hotel. You know the place."

"Really, thanks a lot. I promise I won't buy any rock. A hundred bucks won't go far on rock, but it'll buy food and a place at the Grover."

In pitch blackness, she thought the bills I'd handed over were five twenties. I held her a little longer, then pulled away. Her body like an oven, I instantly missed the warmth, the comfort. It made me think of Marie. I decided life was too short. FBI or no FBI, I was going to see her.

"Chocolate," I whispered, "I need a favor."

"Anything you want."

Robby knocked on the door, "Come on. We haven't got all night."

I moved back over, moved my lips close to her ear. "You know about me going to prison, right?"

She hesitated, nodded. "It wasn't right. Ask anyone, it jus' wasn't right. Anyone would have done what you did. Swear to gawd, Bruno, anyone."

"Just listen. I'm in a real jam. A bad one. They're trying to send me back. I need your help."

She nodded again.

"If you get caught, it's going to go down real bad for you."

This time she didn't speak or nod.

I took out the last five hundred in my pocket.

"No," she said, "you helped me enough."

I took her hand and forced the money into it. "Go to Killer King tonight before midnight, find a woman in the emergency room named Marie Santiago and tell her, code red, south side rumba. You got that?"

"Code red, south side rumba."

"Right. Tell her two o'clock, okay? That's two o'clock in the morning."

"Code red, south side rumba, two o'clock in the morning. How am I going to get out of here? They're watching the motel."

"I'll take care of that."

"You sure? I'm gonna owe ya big this time."

"Stay in here. Then wait five minutes after we're gone and go through the fence out back. I'll make sure all the cops are pulled off. Just make sure to go out the back, through the fence and south to Platt Avenue. You understand?"

"I know the way. You don't have to tell me."

I squeezed her shoulder, turned, and went to the door. "Remember, five minutes and then hustle over to Killer King. I'm counting on you."

"Don't worry about me."

I opened the door, then shut it again, asked, "Hey, you know where I can find Jumbo?"

"Ah, Bruno, don't go messin' with that trash. He's the devil. You're crazy to even think about gettin' hooked up with him."

"Chocolate?"

She took a deep breath, "He's got hisself a big pad over in Downey. Looks like an apartment building right in the middle of a neighborhood. It's on two or three lots. It's huge. North of Rosecrans, four or five blocks from the river. You can't miss it."

I opened the door again, the light made me squint.

Behind me Chocolate yelped, said, "My God, Bruno, these aren't twent—" I closed the door. Her words drowned out behind the wood.

"Well?" Robby said, "Was it as good as it used to be?"

I stepped over and gave him a left jab to the jaw then an uppercut to the gut. He was soft, too many years as a supervisor. He went to his knees.

Chapter Twenty-Eight

He pulled his gun, something he never did lightly. He stopped short of aiming it at me. "What the fuck's the matter with you?" His words came out in a groan, his face a shade paler.

"You, man. What's the matter with you? You were never like this before, crude and crass, uncaring about the other person. What the hell happened to you?"

"Life, asshole. It's what happens to everyone. Did the bitch tell you or not?"

I wanted to sock him again. I turned and went down the hall, down the stairs, and out into the cool of the evening, the entire time thinking how to turn the thing around. At the car I waited. Robby didn't follow right behind. I waited. He didn't show. Did he go back and bat Chocolate around? I took a step toward the entrance just when he came out. He banged the door shut, his arm holding his stomach, his shoulders slightly hunched. He went around to the passenger side where I stood. I thought about backing up a step beyond his wrath.

"I lost my lunch. Thanks a lot."

I didn't feel sorry, not after the way he talked around Chocolate.

"What did she tell you?"

"She said the dude who threw the gas and lit the guy up was wearing purple."

"That's it? Purple? That's all she's got? We put her up, fed her, and that's all she's got? Purple?" He put his arm on the car, leaned over until his forehead touched the cold metal of the hood, and let out another long, sad groan.

The man was chasing me, making my life miserable, and I still felt sorry for him. And at the same time guilt for what I was about to do.

I was facing the motel, Robby facing me. A figure, concealed in shadows came out into the light. Chocolate. She held her hand up to her ear, index and thumb extended, the sign for a phone. Then she pointed at Robby. She melted back into the dark, back into the street. She was trying to warn me. She'd seen Robby on the cell phone after he left her and in between the time he came back to the car. He hadn't lost his lunch, it was a crummy little alibi for a crummy little man. What had happened to the great Robby Wicks?

Why would he have to make a call without me hearing? Especially, before I told him what Chocolate had told me?

I held out my hand for the keys. "Hey, man, if you're sick, let me drive."

He kept his head on his arm and didn't look up. "Drive where, asshole? That was our last lead. We're through until he does it again. When he does, hope he makes a mistake and leaves us something this time."

"He?" I asked.

Robby froze. Slowly he looked up.

I said, "I never said he. I did, but didn't mean it that way. It's they."

For a moment he looked scared. It didn't match the reaction he should've had. Fear flashed for a microsecond. Again, had I not known him so well, I might've missed it. He recovered. "They? What the hell you talking about, they? There's more than one suspect?"

"I told you purple. That's Grape Street. She said Grape

Street Crips had a new initiation." This was all the lie I needed. He took it from there. His eyes grew big. "You're shittin' me, right? We got all of Operation Safe Streets and the Gang Enforcement Team, working on this, and they couldn't come up with that kind of intel. Some street ho—"

"Careful." I pointed a finger at him, at the same time felt a surge of guilt for what I just put into motion, the pain, the carnage. Grape Street was a notoriously violent street gang that needed a little extra attention. Justification for my sins.

He took his cell phone out of his suit coat pocket, then handed me the keys. "Here, you drive. And don't you dare crash. I'd never be able to explain it." We got into the car. I reached under the seat to let the seat back for my long legs and felt a crumpled paper bag with a pint bottle.

He dialed his phone. "This is Wicks. Put it out to everyone and I mean everyone. I want every swingin' dick in Nickerson Gardens, who's wearing purple, brought in. Now. I mean right now. Call in whoever you have to, to get it done. Call Century Station and tell them they're about to be inundated with assholes. I'll call the chief and get it cleared." He snapped his phone shut, put it inside one breast pocket, and reached into the other side where he pulled out a silver flask. Robby never drank on the job. Things sure had changed in the three and half years I was gone; a year and a half to fight the case and two years of a four-year sentence in the joint.

He unscrewed the cap, tilted it back, and took a long slug. I didn't know why I hadn't smelled it on him until now. My partner, my friend had turned into a juicer. He pulled the flask down and wiped his mouth with the back of his hand. In the day, we drank quite a bit off duty, mostly beer to celebrate great accomplishments—crooks no longer prowling streets, put away for long stretches, bank robbers, murderers, some put down hard—but we never drank the hard stuff. The day before I surrendered for my stint, I got stinking-assed drunk on twelve-year-old bourbon and felt the shame of it the next day. Dad drilled it into me not to drink at all.

Robby looked over at me with genuine elation. As far as he knew, the key to his difficult case was on the table. All he had to do was reach out and touch it. I just didn't know what it had to do with me or why I was being followed. Not for real, not that I wanted to give credence to anyway.

I felt worse.

Then I thought about what Ramon, the owner of Lucy's, had said, that Robby was asking about me with the FBI standing right there beside him. That meant federal time. And that, I didn't really want to think about. The Feebs, one of the crimes they investigated was kidnapping. Not that I looked at what I was doing as a crime; saving these kids wasn't kidnapping, not morally it wasn't. Other people would see it differently, especially since some of the kids were white. No, the guilt didn't last very long.

Robby's wide smile filled his entire face. He might make captain out of this. Hell, if he took me down, recovered the kids, and the murder suspect, he could make deputy chief. He handed me the flask. I sat entranced with his eyes. Would he turn on a friend? Especially the kind of friends we'd been. All that had obviously changed. I just couldn't get my mind around it. I would never have turned on him, not for any enticement. Yet, in a way, I just had. My stomach rumbled. Soon I'd have his ulcer.

I didn't smile back, couldn't, but I could take the flask and drink from it to deaden some of the pain brought on by the loss of a friend. I tilted it back, not knowing what to expect. Vodka. The odorless drink of a drunk.

Two and a half years without a drop. The liquor burnt all the way down, warming my stomach, and seconds later my blood and lungs, rekindling that hint of shame. To drink right now dulled the senses. Not a smart move when so many people depended upon me. I breathed fire, took a breath, and another long slug, finishing the flask.

"Hey, hey, buddy, don't Bogart the whole thing." Robby took the flask, tipped it back empty in his mouth. "Not to worry." He reached into the glove box and pulled out another one, then turned on the unit radio to channel 22. It immediately lit up with chatter.

"Jesus, listen to all that. We have unleashed a shit storm like those punks have never seen."

I backed out. I drove under the speed limit. He probably thought it cautious. I needed the time to think.

"Pick it up, man, pick it up. Once our thugs hit the street, and the Crips figure out what's going down, they'll all go to ground, and we'll have to dig 'em out with shovels. I wanna catch one or two ourselves, you know, like the old days. Here, take a right on Imperial. Come on, you haven't been gone that long. You know the way."

Some of his excitement came my way, contagious, infectious excitement I so dearly missed. The way it felt when we rode together and were close to uncovering someone's hidey-hole.

At Alameda Avenue, not far from the Imperial Courts housing project, a couple of miles from Nickerson Gardens, a male black on a bike rode like hell right at us. He wore a white football jersey dyed purple with the name Montana on the back. The Grape Street Crips never ventured this far east. At least not alone. Something had spooked him. It was Gang Enforcement Team and Operation Safe Streets hitting Nickerson hard.

"There. There." Robby pointed, as if I hadn't spotted him. "Get over there and cut his ass off."

I went across the lanes of traffic, the bike rider still looking back, not watching where he was going. I braked, thinking he would look up in time. He crashed into the side of Robby's county ride and flipped over on his back onto the hood. His black bowler hat snugged down on his head stayed that way.

Chapter Twenty-Nine

Robby jumped, dragged him off, put him facedown in a wrist-lock, and was taking out the cuffs before I got around the nose of the car to help. The crook gasped for air. I looked down the road toward Nickerson. It wouldn't be long before Operation Safe Street interrogated a few and figured out my game. I didn't have much time.

Robby picked the guy up. He was an OG, an Original Gangster, someone older than twenty-one, still alive, and not in prison. He tried to talk, but the words wouldn't come, the air still had not returned to his lungs. I got a closer look. "I know you. You're Jesse Cole's nephew. I thought you moved to Rialto?"

"What'd I do?" The first words he could utter.

Robby laughed, "Well, obviously you're driving that bike on the street without a light because you crashed right into the side of my hooptie."

"Man, that ain't right and you know it."

"Why you ridin' like that, lookin' over your shoulder?"

"You know why. The sheriff's in the hood ridin' deep. Jackin' all the homeboys for nuthin'. Nuthin', man."

Robby reached up and took a joint from behind the guy's ear and put it behind his own. "Now we're going to add a Primo to the charge."

"Dey ain't any rock in dere, it's pure weed."

"We'll just send it to the lab and find out. Until then we're going to put you on ice. Unless you want to make a deal."

Even if the game was correct and Grape Street was at the bottom of it, Robby was moving too fast. Under normal circumstances, we'd have taken him in and put him in a cell, let him fester while we grabbed a cup of joe. Robby wanted this too badly.

"I ain't got nuthin'."

Someone on the radio said, "Ten-thirty-three." The code for emergency traffic.

Robby yanked on the dude's arm, "Come on, get him in the car."

A panicked voice on the radio said, "My partner's in foot pursuit, Nickerson Gardens, east side, south of 115th." Deputies from all over came up on the air advising they were en route.

Robby yelled, "Come on, come on. Get his ass in the car we gotta get over there."

We shoved the Crip in the back. I got in and put the pedal to the floor, burning rubber, leaving the Crip's bike back in the street. He didn't seem to care.

The deputy came back up on the air screaming, "Shots fired. Shots fired."

Robby spun in the seat. "This is going to be better than I thought. We just kicked over a hornet's nest."

"Man, let me out." The Crip in the back said, "Doan take me in dere inta that."

He knew in situations where deputies get in over their heads, the responding units don't differentiate the good and bad and beat down anything that moves.

Robby reached over with his foot and slammed it down on top of mine holding it to the floor after I'd eased off a little. The car leapt out, grabbing asphalt faster and faster.

"It's going to be crazy when we get there," Robby said. "Here, take this." He handed me his sheriff's gold star on a chain and I put it around my neck. It felt strange, warm to the touch as if a religious medallion. I didn't want it, not at all. There had been a time when I worshipped the fraternity. He was right though, without it I became fair game.

Ten years ago we would've just driven over the curb and into the projects. Nickerson was now surrounded by ten-foot wrought iron and could now only be accessed by a few streets.

I took a couple of fast corners, the tires squealing, the passengers inside getting batted around. It didn't stop Robby. "Tell me who's throwing gas and lightin' up the people for initiation."

"Man, what the fuck are you talkin' about? Is this what all this shit's about? You're crazy. Swear to gawd, you're off your rock."

"Gimme something good and I'll let you go. We know it's Grape Street doin' it."

"Someone's playin' you a fool. You got it all wrong."

Robby leaned over and punched the Crip right in the chest. The thump sounded hollow and was followed by a long groan. The Crip lay across the backseat.

We were in the Nickerson driving west on 115th.

"There. There." Robby yelled and pointed to a throng of blacks moving toward two deputies with their guns out, a suspect down at their feet. They stood back to back right in the center of a quad area. I went over the curb and headed right toward them, fishtailing, kicking up grass clods. Robby reached under his dash, down by my right leg, and hit the siren to disperse the crowd and to keep the deputies from misinterpreting who we were and opening up on us. A half-empty forty-ounce beer bottle bounced off our car. Yellow foam rolled down across the windshield.

Robby said, "This is going to get real shitty before it's over."

The crowd moved out of the way for us. The deputies held their guns at the ready. They would shoot into the crowd if it got any worse. I recognized Carter Bingham, a good old white boy transplanted from Tennessee who'd finally made it off of patrol and into the Gang Enforcement Team. They called him Pig Farmer because of his faint accent. He wouldn't let the mob overrun them, not without taking a few with them.

The guy on the ground was shot in the back. He was dressed in denim pants and a Raiders jacket with a purple rag tied to his belt. He didn't look too hurt the way he thrashed around in the handcuffs, screaming bloody murder how he was shot in the back and that he was going to sue.

Robby popped the trunk button, jumped out, pulled a riot gun from the back, and racked it. The loud, metallic noise made everyone in the crowd moving toward us freeze. "Get his ass in the car. Let's get the hell out of here." Half a red brick hit the windshield and shattered it. Red grit mixed with yellow beer foam and clung to the spiderweb damage. The Gang Enforcement Team deputies didn't have to be told twice. They each grabbed an arm of their victim, drag-carried him over to the car, and threw him in on top of the other guy. Then Robby got in standing on the running board with his door open. The deputies followed suit in the back doors. I gunned it, spinning a brodie. The crowd took their cue. Rocks and bottles rained down. As we bounced back onto the street in our headlong flight, LAPD rolled in six cars deep. Behind them came all of Century Station Patrol, their heads large in the windshields from riot helmets. All of them braked, pulled U-turns, and exited. We met up in the shopping center parking lot on Wilmington where the ambulance came to tend to the wounded Crip gang member bleeding in the backseat. They put him on a gurney and rolled him out.

I stood by the car watching the other crook while Robby met with some of the Operation Safe Streets guys wearing jeans and green raid jackets. I was close enough to see the LAPD guys staring at Robby as he talked animatedly with his hands. I cringed at what they might be telling him and confirmed it when his hands froze in mid-explanation. He slowly turned to look over at me. OSS was a tough, well-organized group. They had their informants. They gleaned the intel fast, told Robby his info was bad. Robby figured it out, how I had stabbed him in the back, made him a horse's ass in front of everyone. Mobilized half the department, got a gang member shot, and almost started a full-blown riot. I held his gaze until he broke and gave his men additional instructions. He would try to bolster his position, bully his way out of the embarrassing situation, insist he wasn't wrong.

Other LAPD officers joined the group staring at Robby. Some pointed at him.

OSS and GET started to break up and head for their cars when a string of unmarked cars slid into the parking area. Unmarked with tinted windows. The way they rolled in told it all, the elite Violent Crimes Team. They pulled up in adjoining parking slots and stopped in unison, one after the other as if they had choreographed the maneuver. The men were the same from the other night at Mr. Cho's. Mack, in Levi's, t-shirt, his shoulder holster with a large-framed automatic, got out and swaggered over, not with the rest, but over to Robby who stood alone, not taking his eyes off of me, waiting. When he came in range, Robby made a quick-step over to Mack and with one hand grabbed him behind the neck and escorted him away from the others, away from their ears. Mack hunched his thick shoulders and knew better than to resist, even though Robby was no match for him. Mack, if he put his mind to it, could break off Robby's arms one at a time and beat him senseless.

The throng of LAPD officers watched with an unusual intensity.

Mack finally had enough and shrugged Robby off. They were far enough away. Their words, though loud, were still indiscernible.

The urge to hop in Robby's unmarked car with the Crip still in the back was almost too strong to suppress.

Robby pulled back to strike Mack. Mack brought his arm up to block. Robby stopped himself before he let the genie out of the bottle, one he could never put back. Not with all the LAPD witnesses. Robby and Mack both took some deep breaths and calmed down. More words were exchanged, Mack doing most of the listening. Then they turned, looked at me, and smiled.

Time to go. I turned to get in Robby's car, make a wild dash for it, but had waited too long. My attention had been focused on Robby while the other members of the Violent Crimes Team casually, instinctively, deployed in easy striking range. They crowded all around, their arms folded across their chests, leaning up against both sides of the car where I stood.

Robby shook Mack's hand. They both walked over, their path right by the LAPD officers who had just started to disband now that all the action was over. They stopped to take a close look at Robby. After Robby passed, they moved on, talking in low whispers, shaking their heads.

Robby stopped in front of me, his eyes angry. He didn't take them off of me as Mack came around and took the crook out of the backseat, took the cuffs off, and let him go. The other members without prompting went back to their cars, got in, and left.

Robby and I were alone in the vacant parking lot. He continued to stare.

"What?" I said.

"This what you learn in the joint? How to fuck over your friend? A friend who has gone out of his way to help you?"

His words hurt. I wanted to throw my ace, the fact that his real motivation was to find the kids I had stashed, that he was working with the FBI, and if successful, he'd put me away for the rest of my life. Tell him to kiss my black ass. Instead, I stood and gave back his stare.

He shook his head. "The bitch didn't know a thing, did she? You fed me a woof cookie that I gobbled up and went off half-cocked, without covering her because I trusted the information."

I said nothing.

"You let her get away."

I walked from the car, leaving him, waiting for him to draw a blackjack or a gun. Come up on me fast, jack me in the head, take me in. Give me the BMF treatment, get me to talk, tell him what he really wanted to know, where the kids were. But that was the point of this whole charade. I knew where they were, and they didn't, and nothing they could do to me could make me tell him. Robby, more than anyone else, knew that. I didn't know how they had gotten on to me, but somehow they had.

I'd made a slip somewhere along the way and I think I knew where. When they ran all the information in the computer, my name came up. Along with what I had done to my grandson's father, the crime that put me on the criminal path was also the last piece to the puzzle. The crime that put me in prison was the key. A blind man could've figured it out. They were only guessing, that's why they surveilled the market where I worked. All the countersurveillance I had done, the codes, and cutouts I'd put in play that Marie thought was pure paranoia had been exactly what had kept her and me and Dad out of the can. But, most important, it kept the kids safe a little longer.

Robby didn't come after me as I walked across the parking lot. He had simply put me back into play. He'd given the Violent Crimes Team a head start to get set up, ready to follow me. He had also forgiven Mack for his little transgression, coming over to Chantal's apartment. Worst of all, Robby had just unchained Mack. For a brief second I wondered if the whole thing wasn't all a setup. I looked up in the air, trying to see the cherry-red light of a helicopter and heard the careful footfalls as Robby slowly followed. He said, "I sent the team out to find her, told 'em do whatcha gotta do." Another BMF idiom that meant they were free to do what was necessary in order to make the streets safe, which included deadly force with impunity.

I stopped, wanting to turn, walk back, and beat his face in. Instead, I couldn't look at him. I said, "You know what this means, don't you?"

He said, "That it's on?"

"That's right."

"I was hoping you'd say that. You forget, I taught you everything you know."

I turned, the reflection in his eyes a strange yellow in the sodium vapor light of the parking lot. "Did you teach me to put contraband cigarettes filled with rock cocaine behind my ear and act like an out-of-control madman in front of an allied agency that will surely call Internal Affairs to report a dope-smoking lieutenant? When IA calls you in for the interview, give them my name, I'll give them a statement and character reference."

His hand jerked up to his ear as his eyes went wide with shock. He'd forgotten about it.

I walked away.

Chapter Thirty

I walked down Wilmington, wondering just how much they knew about the operation, "the life of Bruno," post Soledad Prison. I thought about hot-prowling their office. They'd have a situation board up with photos, maps, and bullets of information in order to see at a glance, "who was who in the zoo." Intelligence was power, and at the moment, I was powerless. I shifted my thoughts to the problem at hand. First things first. I had to lose them and be sure they stayed lost. Then I had to think about Chocolate, get to her before they did. I had the edge there. They'd believe her a coked-out street whore with nowhere to go. They didn't know about all the money I'd given her. She'd be laying her head in a nice warm motel in South Gate with an eight ball of rock and a bottle of sweet wine.

I sat on a bus bench and waited for the bus that now roared down the street not thirty seconds away. I didn't look for the net thrown up all around. The bus pulled over and stopped. I got up when the door hissed opened, stepped inside, the door closed. The part of the team on foot would be scrambling for their cars while the mobile units jockeyed their cars in a position to tail. The bus picked up speed. The black woman at the wheel of the bus with a pie-pan face, overflowing her seat on all sides, said, "Sit down."

I changed my mind. Can you open the door, please?"

"Sit down. You can get off at the next stop."

"Open the damn door. Do it now."

Her eyes didn't leave mine for several long beats. For a second, I wondered who was driving the bus. Then she braked hard, pulled the door handle to expel the large, angry black man who'd just scared the hell out of her.

I ran back full-tilt to the bus bench where I'd started and cut down a long dirt easement overgrown with bushes, trees, and vines. The second house in, I rolled over a fence covered with vines into a yard with an elm large enough to shield everything under its overgrown umbrella, an umbrella that kept secret three bull mastiffs. Their thick chains rattled, dragged in the dirt toward the intruder in their yard. I clapped my hands, "Manny, Moe, Jack." It paid to know the neighborhood and to make friends with its inhabitants. The closest dog bowled me over, the others jumped on, their mouths soft on my wrists and ankles as I struggled through them to their doghouse, a toolshed-size building with a low roof covered in asphalt shingles. I crawled in and curled up on top of their smelly, dirty rugs and went right into a fetal position. I tried to imitate the shape of a bull mastiff. At the same time, I worried about the spiders, the large waxy black widows with their bright-red hourglasses on their bellies, disturbed by the new presence, me. Phantoms began to crawl on my skin. The dogs bounced around, excited with the presence of a friend who wanted to play. After a while, they calmed down as the novelty wore off.

Jack, the one with a mauled ear, stayed with me, curled up close almost in a lover's spoon, his body heat a comfort.

The helicopter came in low, its spotlight searching. Its onboard Flir device displaying heat-signatures of all beasts, four legged, and otherwise. The equipment showed crooks hiding under cars, up in trees, even in houses.

Outside the large doghouse, Manny and Moe's chain rattled.

Jack's head came up. He bolted out, dragging his thick chain. When I didn't come out of the other end of the alley or pop out on to the side street, the Violent Crimes Team decided to send a man down the dirt easement to see if he could pick up my trail. Robby was right, "it was on." This was a maneuver they would never have tried had they wanted to remain strictly sub rosa in their investigation.

I didn't know the time, didn't carry a watch, one with a luminous dial or the kind with little techno-specialties that Robby called a deadman's watch. You carried one on an operation, the alarm could go off, or the luminous dial could give you away at a critical time. He was right, I had learned a lot from him. I tried to track the time in my head. I had to meet Marie at two o'clock.

How long would Robby keep his team in the area thinking I went to ground? How long to wait them out? This is where I had the upper hand. I knew him. Without someone to calm him, explain the options, he always went for the mobile search, too uptight and antsy to sit in one place. I'd always been the one to choose the more logical option for him. Without me, he would send one man to each of the locations they had me down for on his corkboard back in the office, places I'd been confirmed to frequent. Then he'd drive from each of those locations, checking up, always on the move, while his men sat static.

After an hour, all the time I could spare, I crawled out and listened. The fresh air tasted amazing, much better than confinement with Jack's hot Purina Chow breath. The wide open reminded me that under no circumstances would I ever go back to a concrete cell.

Twenty minutes later the cab dropped me three blocks from the Landmark in Huntington Park, code red rumba south side. The Landmark was in Little Cuba, the Rumba.

North of Willowbrook, which is opposite of south side, the code Marie thought I was being paranoid about making her memorize. Along with five others that would now never be used. This was it, our last day in the States. We were on our way. Not necessarily the land of milk and honey but freedom just the same, a different sort, for all of us.

The Landmark, as with most all motels in Huntington Park, was a hot-pillow fleabag, populated by the bottom rung of society. It's a mildewed structure with rotting doors and peeled dull, institutional lime-green paint that no longer wanted to stick to its corrupt walls.

If Robby and his crew had outsmarted me, it no longer mattered. I walked right up to the large, majestic queen palm with the dried out yellow uncut drooping fronds, a graceful lady too embarrassed to show her base trunk, and pulled out the green Gatorade bottle. Inside was a balled up paper that meant absolutely nothing to anyone else. Written on it was 212.

I walked up the stairs, wiping my sweaty hands on my pants. When I saw her regularly, I didn't question her love for me. The Gatorade bottle reaffirmed her desire to hang with an old, overly obsessed, broken-down black man on the run from a society he once coveted. Three weeks apart renewed the anxiety, let the insipid fear of rejection weasel-wedge into my common sense. Why would a woman of Marie's caliber even give me a second look, let alone fall in love?

At the top of the stairs a big man, a white supremacist in a white wifebeater t-shirt and broad, youthful shoulders, entered the stairwell. We both paused, enemies confronting each other, his face tattooed with AB for Aryan Brotherhood, and three teardrops at the corner of his eyes, his large arms sleeved with black ink, jailhouse tattoos touting his hate for his fellow man, the mud people. His blue eyes reminded me of Deputy Mack.

The two were one and the same, each working the opposite sides of the street yet on the same side. The man hesitated, the hate oozing from him as he decided, made a choice, the business that brought him to the Landmark was more important than the oath he'd sworn allegiance to. We passed, me going down the hall, I stepped backward, watching as he continued on down the stairs, his awful glare on me as it disappeared lower and lower with each step until he was gone. I waited by the door marked 212 until I was sure he wasn't coming back, then rapped softly, two, one then two.

"Bruno?" Her voice barely a whisper, made my heart soar.

"Babe, it's me."

The door jerked open. She froze, her soft brown eyes large and teary. The code red, the signal to drop everything and run for it, had scared the hell out of her. To talk about it was one thing; to live it was all together something else. She had not known if I was going to make it or not. A lump rose in my throat. The woman genuinely cared for me. She reached out, took my hand, and pulled me into the room. At least her brain was working on the right level, at the moment enough for the both of us. She closed the door and gently put her head against my chest. I hugged her. She felt so damn good.

She didn't complain about the tattered clothes, the bruises, scabs, dirty, bandaged hands, Jack's Purina Dog Chow breath that permeated every pore. She took hold of my sleeve, guided me into the bathroom, and shut the door, the light off. For a moment, the heat from her body moved away. I yearned for her. In the perfect dark, the water in the shower went on. Steam roiled up. I smelled it, felt it on my face and lungs, my hands reaching out for her. She was back tugging at my belt. I let her as I stroked her hair and felt her long neck, stroked her breasts, her nipples instantly hard under my fingers.

She pulled down my pants and underwear quick, took hold,

softly took hold, pulled me along to tub's edge. Both of us over and into the water jets.

"Marie." Her name came out in a rush.

I pulled her sopping top over her head and unhooked her bra. Her breasts released and moved against my arms. I buried my face in her neck and kissed her deeply. She groaned, renewed her grip, squeezing harder, tugging. With her new handle, she pulled me closer and pulled some more. She stood topless, water sluicing between her breasts, fabulous breasts; I was pantless, our clothes going hot and wet under the spray. I found her mouth with my tongue. At the same time she let go with one hand and worked the buttons of my shirt. My hands ineffectually tried to release the wet button to her pants. Her breasts pressed hard up against my stomach, her legs pushing me up against the Formica, pinning me against the wall. I was too caught up in her, her feel, her smell, her touch. I wasn't going to last, the hot water worked as a catalyst to heighten all sensation. I put my head back. "Marie." Warm water spattered my mouth.

My body convulsed.

She froze. "Bruno?"

"I love you, baby."

She giggled.

Chapter Thirty-One

We sat on the bed naked, Indian-style while she rebandaged my hands after she'd given them a thorough cleaning. She could only shake her head and wonder why infection hadn't set in. Said as much. I wasn't entirely sure myself.

The whole time I read hesitation in her eyes. She had something to say.

When she finished, I laid her back on the bed, and put my mouth on hers when she tried to talk. The next session went longer and slower with sweat, little nips with cautious teeth, kisses, and long, damp licks.

The entire time the executioner's ax hung poised over us. We both felt it. At any moment it could swing down on us in a slow arc, end it all. We'd never see each other again. Thrown down hard into the slammer. The possibility remained very distinct, thus the lovemaking all the sweeter, but a little desperate. We reveled in every stolen minute. We finished up with her on top. She dropped down, rested her cheek on my chest, her head turned away, and though I couldn't see her, I knew she gnawed on her knuckle—a nervous tic. She said, "Are we really going to do it tomorrow? Are we really finally going to go through with it? Leave here and never come back?"

"Don't be scared."

She nodded, "I'd be lying if I said I wasn't." Her voice quiet, childlike.

She hesitated. I waited for it.

"What's it like inside?"

There it was, a big ugly beast. It had sat on my subconscious feasting on my guilt, the possibility that we could fail in this mission, and she would suffer immensely for my folly.

I closed my eyes. My voice lowered, in a cracked whisper said, "I won't make it better than it is. We're talking about a small, ever-so-tiny concrete room with walls that collapse on you every night, snatch your breath away, bury you under tons and tons of invisible weight until you scream. That's the best part. Then you have the food, bland starch, pale, washed-out pastel colors that salt can't flavor. And there's an odor about the place that reeks wherever you go and penetrates your clothes and skin, sour sweat, mixed with fear and hate. But still that's not the worst. The worst is the people. These people are put there for a reason—"

Marie's fingers involuntarily dug into my chest as she braced for it.

"These people are the worst society has to offer: the malcontents, the predators, the sociopaths, and psychopaths, all churning together in one ungodly collage of putrefying corruption. But there are those few who are not absolutely corrupt when they first get there. Folks with four drunk driving arrests in five years, paperhangers with a yen for gambling, all family men, victims thrown into a sewer of humanity that will eventually eat them. You try every day to stay the same, not change and turn into one of them. It's impossible. You change or you don't make it out."

What I didn't tell her was about the nightmares that come every night to those who crossed the line of their own convictions, took the law into their own hands, and executed a fellow member of society; a man you executed who was tried and released by a biased judicial system that thrived on technicalities; a system that in the end let a man who killed twice, once with an overdose of heroin, a daughter and again a small child, a grandbaby shaken and thrown down on a hard concrete floor, while his twin brother watched, a killer the judicial system failed and let go.

Derek Sams.

He came to me every night and sat on the end of my bunk across my legs, cowboy-style. Stared at me with those glowing red eyes, the kind of eyes you sometimes see in photos. This might not be as bad if he'd just say something, anything. He'd sit there and stare. Oh, those stares. His weight on my legs, made my flesh and blood go numb from the pressure. When I did sleep, I saw it all play out again and again. Deputy Mack had been right in his description to Chantal, the way I used my experience to hunt him down, caught him in a friend's apartment, a hideout up in the high desert, Lancaster. He wept and pissed his pants. He was on the floor in front of me on hands and knees, his friends watching, not calling 911, predators themselves who understood the rules of the jungle, anxious for me to do it. Their eyes alive with the excitement of it, their breath that came in short little gasps.

I let Derek Sams look down the barrel of my gun for a long time, let him see his future, something I later regretted, again and again, as he stared at me deep into the night. At the time, all I saw was the poor broken body of Albert and how Alonzo, Albert's twin, was destined for the same treatment if I didn't intervene. The law was broken when it came to child custody. I pulled the trigger without remorse. I gave Derek Sams a third eye to help him see his way to hell.

The description of prison caused gooseflesh to rise on Marie's back, ripple under my hand as she shivered and shook.

"I'm sorry, babe. I shouldn't have been so candid."

She kept her head on my chest. Her hand came up to softly stroke my cheek. "Ssh, it's okay. I had to know."

We lay there a while, as she thought of incarceration, and I thought about what a heel I was for risking her world.

"Don't," she said, "Don't even think about it." She'd tuned into my thoughts.

We were on the same wavelength, something that will always amaze me. She read me no matter how hard I tried to conceal my thoughts. If only I'd met her a long time ago. But then she probably would've turned and ran away screaming had she met the old me, the cocky, brazen BMF, the Brutal Mother Fucker, that had inhabited my soul.

That night we'd met in the hospital, shot by my own brethren, broken in heart and soul, exposed emotionally, she stepped right in, took hold of the controls, and she'd never let go.

She said, "I made my own choice." She balled her fist and gently pounded on my chest, "Don't you dare. Don't you dare try and take all this on yourself."

I put my hand over her mouth and held it there.

She pulled it down. Her eyes softened. "Seven kids are a lot of kids."

Just like that she'd shifted gears, knew it was time to look at the silver lining, get us back on track, facing forward.

"They're great kids," I said.

She nodded as her vivacious, big browns glowed with excitement.

I couldn't help but smile and said nothing.

She said, "You remember what we talked about?"

I knew what she was going to say, but pretended I didn't. "We've talked about a lot of things. You're going to have to give me a hint."

She squirmed. "It's not right to ask. Not after all you've gone through."

"Babe, spill it."

Her eyes going large as baby brown moons. There was nothing she could ask that I wouldn't do. Nothing.

"Bruno, I saw Tommy Bascombe and — "

She didn't see me watching her on Wilmington as she got on the bus. When Dora Bascombe got off dragging Tommy by the good arm. Even after the ugly portrayal of our wonderful penal system, she was willing to step yet deeper into the quagmire of lawlessness.

Her eyes filled with tears. "You should've seen the way that evil witch treated him. It was horrible. It just tore my heart out."

When I was released from prison, she met me at the gate with Alonzo. The whole thing with Alonzo started out as a simple surprise for me. She wanted to somehow get through to me, give me something to hope for and thought if she brought Alonzo on visiting day it might help. She went over to Alonzo's paternal grandparents' house, Derek Sams's folks who had legal custody because their son was dead. "Murdered by the black bastard, the no-good bitch's father."

When she went over, she found Alonzo playing out front unsupervised in the parkway. Right next to the street as cars whizzed by on the busy boulevard not more than a couple of feet away. She said it wasn't a matter of "if" he wandered into the street, it was a matter of "when."

Marie quickly pulled up to the curb, leaned over, and opened the passenger door. She called his name, with nothing more in her mind than taking the child out of harm's way. He toddled over dressed only in a urine-soaked Huggies diaper. He tried to climb into the car, his round belly atop of thin legs wouldn't let him over the low ledge of the car's passenger footwell.

Marie looked up, her heart pounding in her throat at the thought that popped into her head. This from a physician's assistant who met a murderer while treating him for a gunshot wound inflicted by the police, corresponded with said murderer, and now contemplated "snatching" his grandbaby. That was the word she used to describe it later, "snatching." She pulled Alonzo inside and left the door open so anyone in the house could see that it was something innocent. Alonzo cooed and played with her crucifix that always hung from a gold chain between her breasts. He patted her face, his smile huge.

She waited twenty minutes, or it could have even been thirty or forty as time played tricks on her. No one missed him. The car door still open, Alonzo curled up on the seat asleep in the warmth of the heater directed on him, the sun dropping below the tops of the houses, the world turning orange and yellow. With each passing minute she wanted someone to come out. At the same time she didn't. She wanted the justification to drive off with the child, and every minute that passed reinforced her decision that continued to teeter, the battle over morally right and legal.

In court, at my trial, she'd had a firsthand look at what the grandparents were like. They attended every day of the trial, bitter and angry, full of revenge. Of course, I knew them on a more intimate level having done battle with them over custody after my daughter died of an overdose of heroin, one her common-law husband, Alonzo and Albert's natural father, Derek Sams, had given her. The day I lost the battle was the day I paid him a visit, the day I met Marie. She'd said, and I couldn't disagree, "the apple didn't fall too far from the tree." The grandparents were intent on raising him in the same manner that they'd raised their now deceased son.

Marie reached over Alonzo, pulled the door shut, and drove slowly away, ten, fifteen miles an hour, twenty, then thirty, her conscience fighting a pitched battle. It wasn't until she looked up in the rearview and saw the drunk grandfather stagger out to the sidewalk, as if he all of a sudden realized he was supposed to be babysitting instead of watching Jerry Springer and drinking Mickey's big mouth beer.

She sped up and never looked back. She didn't bring Alonzo on visiting days. She was too scared "they would be watching." If Alonzo's legal guardians reported him missing or snatched, it never made the news. She watched the six o'-clock edition, the ten, and the eleven, expecting to see footage of the cops moving up to her door with a battering ram and with their long, black guns. They never came. She kept Alonzo for the better part of two years. It was easy to say she was the one who started us down this road. But deep down, I knew I was going to snatch my grandchild and lam out, the very second parole looked the other way.

Marie couldn't tell anyone in the hospital, any of her friends. She spent all her time either working at the hospital or taking care of Alonzo. Her friends gradually faded away. She cared for Alonzo on her own, while continuing to see other needy children, repeat visitors to the ER, who, if there wasn't any serious intervention, were not going to make it in this world. She'd crossed the line and got away with it. Felt good about it, as if her life really meant something. The next most logical step was to save more.

The day I got out she waited in the parking lot standing by her little Nissan Sentra with worry lines etched in her beautiful face. When I saw Alonzo in the car seat, I cried. She drove ricky-racer-fast from the prison looking at the road and over at me, back and forth. I wept and hugged and kissed my daughter's child. I told her to pull over. Her expression one of fear made my heart rise up in my throat. Once stopped, the car in park, I said, "I just wanted to make sure you knew how much I appreciate this." I kissed her, Alonzo between us. Then I understood why she was so angry the day I finally took the visit, the day she came all dolled up in the red dress. She'd committed a major felony for me and in my ignorance I had inadvertently made it look as if I were doing her the favor by seeing her when she came to visit.

The rest of the way home she talked a mile a minute, how the taking of Alonzo had come about, happy that I wasn't angry. How could she think I'd be angry? She told me all about the other kids she'd seen and who'd needed to be saved. We didn't discuss any plans, none whatsoever. We went home and slept, well, not a lot of sleep, we had to catch up after all. The next night I just showed up with little Ricky and Toby Bixler. She didn't say anything about how I came to have them. She accepted the two into our family as if they had always belonged.

Back in the motel room, our bodies cooling, sweat drying, I put my finger to her lips, I was about to tell her how Tommy Bascombe was safe and sound at Dad's, how I had already ordered and paid for his forged passport and then watch the wonder and pleasure come over her, and as selfish as it sounded, revel in her gratitude, when a loud knock came at the door.

Chapter Thirty-Two

My nerves on edge, the knock at the motel door startled me. Marie still lay on my chest, and I all but knocked her to the floor reaching for my gun on the nightstand, a gun that wasn't there. Marie bolted up, the gold crucifix bouncing between her naked breasts, eyes wide, mouth open. I held my hand up, and with the other, I put a finger to my lips, whispered, "Does anyone know you're here?"

She shook her head no. "Of course not."

I knew she was too smart to tell anyone our plans, but I had no idea who could be knocking. Perhaps Robby. Had his team tailed me?

"Johnson?" The hard, coarse voice on the other side of the door drove a knife in my gut. Not housekeeping. This guy knew my name.

Marie waved her hands as she walked fast, back and forth along her side of the bed. Slowly, my good sense started to return. Robby wouldn't knock. He'd bust in the door, guns at the ready, with men charging in a high-risk formation.

"Johnson?" The voice again.

I jumped into my skivvies and moved to the door, listened. "Who's there?"

"Johnson, come on, man, open up. I can't be seen out here."

I glowered back at Marie, who now stood frozen in one

place. I pointed to the door to indicate that I'd be opening it. She didn't move. "Put something on, babe."

She snapped out of her trance, jumped for her abandoned clothes on the floor, and slipped into her still damp blouse and slacks.

I went to the door and put my hand on the knob. "Who is it?"

"Detective Johnson, for fuck's sake open the door. Open the damn door before someone sees me."

I didn't recognize the voice. I did, but it was way back there in the far corner of my brain and refused to come forward. A voice from long ago. I opened the door a crack and peeked out. The small man had the stature of a jockey, his head a little too big for his body. He had jet-black hair with gray wings at the temples, a neck and face pocked heavily with acne scars. I didn't recognize him in profile, but when he looked directly at me, I saw his eyes, I did know him. Jessie Vanfleet.

I flung opened the door and yanked him in. Then I eased the door closed and listened, my ear to the warped wood. After a time, I turned to see Vanfleet as he stared at Marie who stood over by the bed. Marie, in her haste, had not put on a bra, leaving her breasts barely covered by the sheer blouse. Vanfleet was an over-sexed street perv who slung rock cocaine on the side, not for the money, but for sexual access to coke whores. There had always been something creepy about him.

I took hold of the back of his collar and shook him. "What the hell are you doing here? How did you know I was here?"

"Take it easy, man. I'm here to save your ass."

Even though his words were directed at me, he still hadn't taken his lecherous ogle off Marie's breasts. I cringed as he licked his lips.

"You better talk and talk fast, little man, or I'm going to pound you into the ground."

"Okay, okay. Chocolate sent me. The dude downstairs at the desk recognized you and told me. Chocolate put the word out that she needed to talk to you bad, real bad, so here I am. It's no big mystery." He batted at my hand. "Take your big dick beaters off me."

I let him go but shoved him toward the door. I went over to the bed, yanked the top blanket off and wrapped Marie in it. On Vanfleet it had the same effect as flipping off a light switch, the lecherous leer faded simultaneously with the blanket cover. I still had the urge to knock his brown teeth down his little ferret throat.

"Is Chocolate okay?"

"Yeah, yeah, she's fine. She said there'd be a grand in it for me."

"That right? And you're a lying little piece of shit too." I looked back at Marie. I never used my street jargon around her and felt like a kid who'd just let slip a four-letter word in front of grandmum.

I looked back at Vanfleet. "You and I both know what she promised you, so don't yank on my dick." I took a couple of steps toward him.

He held up his hands, "Whoa, there cowboy. You can't fault a guy for tryin'."

"What's wrong with Chocolate? Tell me." I had an idea but didn't want to give him any more information than necessary.

"She says you're a good Joe and that you just did her a solid. Boy, she could never convince me of that. I still got the scar from when you kicked me to the curb." His hand came up subconsciously and rubbed his nose. I couldn't see any scar.

The first time I'd met the little weasel, I'd pulled up to a burglary of Radio Shack and he ran. His short legs pumping fast but no match for my long stride. I easily overtook him, ran right behind him, and told him one last time to stop. When he didn't and kept running, I jumped up and kicked him in the back. He skidded headlong into the curb, broke his nose, and lacerated his eyebrow. He went to jail for consensual sex with a fifteen-year-old, a young girl he'd gotten hooked on coke just for that purpose.

"Chocolate's fine. She kept babbling something about how you gave her a grand when she thought it was a hundred. That crazy bitch hasn't been worth a hundred, let alone a grand, since Christ was corporal. What're you doin' stickin' your dick in that when you got yourself a nice slice of Rican pussy right—"

I quick-stepped over too him, reached down, and clamped his throat. I ran him back up against the door and slammed him. The door bulged and rattled.

Marie was on my arm, yelling, "Don't. Bruno, don't."

When I came back to reality, I looked down. I had Vanfleet's feet dangling above the floor. I let go. He fell to the floor. I put my hand on Marie's chest and eased her away from the perv who writhed uncontrollably. I went over and put my right shoe on, then clumped back to where Vanfleet lay on the moldering carpet. "You tell me what I want to know right now or so help me I'll kick a lung out of you."

He stared up at me, fire in his eyes. He rubbed his throat. "She said to tell you thanks for the money. She said to tell you Five-O is all over the street raisin' hell looking for your sorry ass. She wanted me to warn you. That's what she said to tell you but, as far as I'm concerned, I hope they get your sorry ass and cap you good this time right in that fat ugly face of yours."

Chapter Thirty-Three

I was breathing too hard. I tried to slow down and think.
"What else?"

"That's it, man."

I pulled my leg back to boot him. Marie said, "Bruno, don't."

Vanfleet held up his hands to fend off the size thirteen double E. "Okay, wait, wait. The last part — the last part I could get into a lot of trouble for. Me just passing the information on to you puts my ass on the line. Just tellin' you, man. You know what I'm sayin'?"

"You think if I had any more money, I'd be in this shitbox of a motel? You made a deal with Chocolate, now tell me."

"She told me to tell you, and I don't really understand what it means, but she said to tell you it was Ruben the Cuban. She didn't tell you before and she feels real bad about it. She said to tell you that it was Ruben the Cuban and that you'd understand and she hopes you forgive her."

"What?" I said, not understanding the message, my mind too wrapped up in Robby chasing me, getting the hell out of the country with Marie and the kids. What he said didn't register. Ruben the Cuban? Then it hit me. Right. It was the guy who was lighting the people on fire with the gasoline. A name I no longer cared to know. I had no plans to do anything with the information. That last thought lasted about a second. If I knew and didn't do something about it, someone else could get torched.

"Get your ass up. Get out. Now."

Vanfleet scrambled to his feet and fumbled with the door. He got it open and lined up to make a quick exit. I gave him some help and kicked him in the butt. As he flew across the hall into the wall, I shut the door.

"Quick, get your things together, we have to leave. He'll sell us out."

Marie went into a whirlwind of activity. I could only watch. What was I going to do about Ruben the Cuban? Should I call Robby, give him Ruben's name as a suspect? To do that would jeopardize the kids.

Ruben had only been a ruse for Robby, nothing more than an excuse for Robby to watch me. Just like the dead kid out in front of the liquor store. More collateral damage. I suspected that Robby wanted Wally Kim most of all. Mr. Kim, the Korean diplomat, was putting heat on the State Department who in turn put the squeeze on the Sheriff's Department to find Wally. Every cop in Southern California, including the FBI, would be looking hard and heavy for Wally Kim. Robby and the Violent Crime Team must have been assigned to find Wally, and Robby must have then checked other missing kids during the same time period. I know I would have. Robby found the missing report on Alonzo, my grandson. From there it was easy to draw the line to me. That also meant Robby knew about all the kids. They were all now at risk.

How far would Robby go to get what he wanted? I had no doubt that he would, without hesitation, break the law and even shoot whoever got in his way. Robby didn't like to lose. If he finds Wally, he finds the other kids. Kids who didn't stand a chance unless I kept them free from the broken county Child

Protective Services system. Rick and Toby Bixler, burnt in the failed PCP lab, would go back to that same hazardous environment. Sonny Taylor, the cute hungry little kid who ate his mother's meth and then after the judge gave him back to his mother, she locked him in a closet. What chance did he have? Marvin Kelso, his mom's boyfriend the molester. I couldn't even think about that horrible scenario. And Randy Lugo with five broken bones, how long before it was his neck? No, no matter what, those kids were not going to be plugged back into that broken Child Protective Services system.

Getting Ruben would be a big feather in Robby's cap. I didn't owe Robby a thing, that was for sure. I'd only call it in because of what Ruben was doing to the people on the street. It was the right thing to do. I was torn because it would jeopardize the kids.

Marie, fully dressed with her loaded gym bag on the bed, looked at me with pleading eyes. "We'll get the kids and take off early, that's all. Right, Bruno? That's all."

I just hoped the exit strategy was still in place and viable. How much did Robby know?

She handed me the small black leather fanny pack. I unzipped it, checked the passports, the tickets for the freighter, and the sheaf of cash, ten thousand dollars. Our travel money had just turned into the whole enchilada. Not near enough to start a new life in Costa Rica. I took out a thousand and zipped it closed. "Babe, I got one more thing to do."

She froze. "No, you heard what that little SOB said. The cops are all over the place looking for you. They know you, Bruno, they know what you look like. It's too dangerous. We're going right now. No arguments. We don't go right now, we won't ever go."

I took hold of her shoulders, looked her in the eye. "You

trust me, don't you?" At that moment I realized there were two more stops I had to make. I needed to pick up Tommy Bascombe's passport.

"Don't do this, Bruno, please. Come with me right now."

I kissed her forehead, "It won't take me but an hour. An hour, that's all, I promise."

I told her to wait in the room for five minutes before she headed out. Before she started her countersurveillance on her way over to Dad's. I went first just in case Robby or his team was on to me so I could lead them away. We'd trained long hours and she was a natural, better than most surveillance cops.

Outside by the curb, Vanfleet, hand on his hip, stood in a cool-cat pose, chatting up an underage hooker. When he saw me, he sneered. I went over to him. He looked from side to side, suddenly afraid, nowhere to run.

"Don't you run. I'll kick you to the curb."

He sighed, "Now what do you want?"

"A ride. And, I have a proposition for you." I held up two of the hundred dollar bills.

His eyes went predatory. "Sure thing, my man." He looked back at the girl. "My financial situation just improved. I'll be right back. Don't go away." He subconsciously licked his lips again. He turned and headed down the street waving his hand over his shoulder like he was guiding a Boy Scout troop. I followed him over to a heap, a shot-out purple Monte Carlo. He started to get in.

"Hold it there, little man. I'm driving."

He opened his mouth to protest. I held up the two bills. He shut his mouth, smiled, went around to the passenger side, and got in.

The seats were upholstered in fake, faded purple fur, clotted together and clumpy. The interior emitted a cloyingly sweet scent, ode de carwash that after a minute could not mask the underlying sour reek of barf, sweat, and sex. I started it up with the screwdriver stuck in the ignition, put it in gear, and made a U-turn in front of a tricked-out SUV that braked hard.

"Hey, hey, man, this ride is worth more than those two Benjamins you're wavin' under my nose. Take it easy. Take it easy or the deal's off, it ain't worth it." I said nothing and drove through Huntington Park, down into South Gate, and back into Lynwood, breathing through my mouth to avoid the reek, and trying not to think about what had made the steering wheel sticky. I made two passes of Taco Quickie. Vanfleet caught on the second time around and stared at the fast-food restaurant. "What's the hap's, old man? What's the gig?"

"I need to pick up my car."

"What the hell, why don't you just pull over and get out if it's right there." He looked again trying to see into the back parking lot.

The root beer-brown Plymouth sat right where I'd left it when I got into Robby's car. In the trunk was forty-five thousand dollars and two guns. We needed that money in the worst way for our new life. We needed it bad enough to risk trying to get it back. If Robby's team was set up on it, they were good. I couldn't make them short of driving into the parking lot and checking out each and every car.

I pulled to the curb two blocks north on Atlantic Avenue. "Listen, all you have to do for the two hundred is go pick up my car, that clean, root beer-brown Plymouth and drive it down to the park at Century and Bullis. You know where that is, right?"

"Bullshit, man. Buuuuuullshit. I ain't some dumbshit pilgrim. Why you need me to do it? Why cain't you jus' drive on into the parking lot if it's your car?"

"Because that's the thing," I said handing him the keys. "You're too smart for me. It's not my car. It's hot. But either I borrow your car for a couple of weeks or you go pick my car up and take it to the park."

"Kiss my ass. This sounds like a free ride right ta the can."

I peeled off two more hundreds. "Four hundred just to drive a stolen car, what, ten, twelve blocks?"

"Four hundred ain't worth a couple days in the can and a Gee-ride case hangin' over my head. I'd have to work the case off with asshole cops like you. No, no soap. Kiss my ass, Johnson. Keep your four bills. Get the fuck outta my car."

He had a point. I showed him the entire grand, fanned them in front of his face. "Okay, but this is all I have. Don't hold out for more because there isn't any."

He stared at the money, at what it represented, and knew he could buy a lot of young tail with a thousand.

The light in his eyes started to fade. "Listen," I said, "I wasn't going to tell you this, but there's some money in that car. Five thousand dollars. I'll split it with you. This thousand plus twenty-five more, that's thirty-five hundred to drive the car ten blocks. That's worth the risk. Take it or leave it. Tell me now because I know I can drive a couple of blocks in either direction and find some other mope to take this kind of deal for half the price."

"I'm in." He grabbed at the money. I yanked it away. "Half now and half when you meet me at the park." He was about to protest when I handed him the five hundreds. The feel of the paper shut his mouth. He took the keys and got out. I watched him walk down the sidewalk among all the late-night street people going about their scandalous activity. He blended right in and checked out the area in such a casual manner that if you weren't watching for it you'd have missed it. When he was almost to Taco Quickie, I made a legal intersection U-turn and headed south.

My Plymouth was a trap.

Chapter Thirty-Four

I passed the parking lot in time to see three BMFs putting the boot to the poor pedophile. Five hundred wasn't worth a beating like that and a trip to jail to boot. I should've felt remorse and told myself Vanfleet was better off being taken out of the lineup. Better for everyone he ran with, influenced, molested, and abused.

They had the 45K I took off Q-Ball and his two guns. I didn't have too long and Vanfleet would tell them the color and make of my car and there'd be a BOLO. A calculated risk. I'd keep the car a little longer then dump it. I headed over to 117th and Alabama. The conversation with Robby suddenly popped into my head. I pulled to the curb and slugged the steering wheel. He knew about that place, he'd said as much. And if he had Taco Quickie staked out, he'd have my pad staked as well. He had me boxed. Marie was right, take the ten grand, the tickets, the kids, get on the freighter, and get out of Dodge. Bail right now before something irreversible happened. Like getting picked up.

I put the purple Monte Carlo in gear and drove. I had to think. I turned on Bullis Road, headed south. If luck had been with me, I'd have been at the park right now paying off the perv out of the 45K. I continued on south, my subconscious doing the driving. I tried to envision life in a Third World country with eight kids and a lovely wife, the hardships without any money. When I returned to reality, I was eastbound on Rosecrans Boulevard, entering the city of Downy not but a few miles away from Jumbo's pad.

Fate.

Only I knew it wasn't fate. Jumbo owed me a hundred twenty-five for the train heist. Plenty enough to start a new life, plenty enough reason to take the chance, go head-to-head with him and that Crazy Ned Bressler.

The house was just as Chocolate described, larger than all the houses around it. Easy to spot. In a time when most dope dealers were downplaying their wealth so law enforcement wouldn't tumble to them and seize it, Jumbo washed his money with auto parts stores, donut shops, and two strip joints, each of which had the ability to hide vast quantities of money. So he flaunted it. He paid all his taxes and flaunted it. He'd even, on occasion, asked me my opinion on stock investments. But the most effective method was what he called the shoebox approach.

After the first heist, I met Jumbo at Tits Up, his place on Compton Avenue, for a beer and to pick up my pay. Jumbo had thought it ironic how I'd once chased him and now worked for him. He bragged about how he'd thwarted cops' efforts. He put the US currency in shoeboxes and mailed them regular air mail to the Middle Eastern country of Jordan. The money was put in a bank and wire transferred back to him as an investment from a shell corporation. He claimed the infusion of cash on his taxes. There was more to it I was sure, but he could justify every overt penny. Hence, the large manse set in the middle of a residential neighborhood.

He knew I'd show sometime and wouldn't chance a scene at his own pad. Chances were slim that I'd find him at home.

In the long circular brick and concrete driveway, under the

portico, sat Jumbo's Beemer along with a whole mob of other expensive cars: Beemers, Lexuses, Mercedes.

The ten-foot-tall front doors were inset with clear beveled glass that gave an obscured view of the marble entry and the white carpeted spiral staircase to the second floor. The security video camera was partially camouflaged in the old Victorian gas lamp illuminating the exterior. I tried the door.

Unlocked.

Trap or overconfidence?

I went in. On an oak table just inside the door sat some sort of crystal decoration, an orb setting in a nest of icicles. I picked up the orb, the size of a cue ball, hefted it, and put it in my jacket pocket, kept my hand there.

Faint music echoed from somewhere deeper in the house. If he was running scared, he sure had balls for throwing a party.

Three steps down to the immense sunken living room, which was filled with a middle-class yuppie crowd, stood Jumbo trying to fit in, a true poseur. The group ebbed and surged around their host and the open bar, manned by two women in white see-through halter tops. I guessed this to be some sort of celebratory party.

My eyes came back to Jumbo and stayed on him until he felt their glare. When he looked over, his skin went ashen, his hand limp, dumping some of his cosmopolitan, the liquid a diluted red. He wasn't being bold after all, having the party. He'd thought I'd been taken off the board. He must have inside information. The crowd, in tune with their benevolent host, a few at a time, went quiet until the entire party stood holding their free drinks, with small plates or napkins of canapés, their eyes on me. I took the crystal orb from my pocket, pulled back and threw it with everything I had at the plate glass wall that separated the living room from the perfectly landscaped back-yard.

The crystal orb bounced off. The plate glass wall shattered into millions of tiny cubes. The crowd collectively gasped. When their amazement faded, they all looked at me, then back at their host. The glass crackled, the noise growing louder until the entire wall came down in one folding sheet. The crowd surged away in a tidal wave. Their momentum grew until they stampeded to the door, flowed around me, a pylon in a turbu-lent sea. I held Jumbo's gaze, wanting to look side to side, knowing at any moment Crazy Ned Bressler was about to sneak up with an ice pick and scramble my brain through an unsuspecting ear. Do it so quick no one would see it.

Finally, the noise subsided, the room empty. The crowd left behind broken martini and highball glasses and clear glass plates with pâté and barbequed meatballs mixed with crum-bled crackers. The two scared bartenders held their ground behind the bar. Jumbo regained some composure. "You really know how to ruin a celebration."

"That right? What're you celebrating?"

He moved to the bar, turning his back to me. In a lowered voice he asked the bartender, "Glenfiddich neat." He waited until she poured and he slugged down the amber liquid and set the glass down for a refill.

"One of your overseas companies just post a huge profit?"

He took the bottle of Glenfiddich and moved to the couch. To the ladies he said, "You girls are excused for the evening. Sorry for the short night. You'll, of course, be compensated."

He poured another. If he kept it up, he'd be pickled by morning. The girls grabbed their stylish purses from under the counter and picked their way through the debris field to the front door.

"And to answer your question, yes, an overseas corporation just posted an excellent accounting for the last quarter."

"I can imagine. What, a ten-million-dollar profit? Computer chips?"

He didn't answer and took another long pull.

I asked, "Where's Ned?"

"Don't try and play games with me. I know why you're here."

I stepped over to an end table and picked up a bronze sculpture, an abstraction of what looked like an African gazelle melded with an African tribesman, and held it down by my side. I liked the heft of it.

"Detective Johnson, you are a true thug." Now Jumbo looked really scared. Just the way I wanted him.

"What happened to calling me Bad Boy?"

"They asked me to try and get you to talk about Ned, but obviously you're too smart for that."

His words came out and entered my brain, but didn't immediately sink in. Slow motion analysis because I knew their meaning and didn't want to hear it, didn't want it to be true.

Then Jumbo said the words I knew were coming next. The words that meant the end of my world as I knew it.

The end of everything.

Chapter Thirty-Five

Jumbo smiled when he said, "Looks like some bad weather. Might even be a tornado brewing out there."

BMFs were a tight-knit team. They had to be to chase the most dangerous animals in the world. They read each other's moves, knew what each team member was thinking, and used code words to operate on a covert level that at the same time confounded their prey. Robby Wicks had used the same code words from bygone days as a matter of flaunting his ability to outmaneuver me. "Might be a tornado brewing," was the bust sign when the informant was in fear for his life and wanted the cops to swarm in and save him.

Jumbo was wearing a wire.

He was cooperating with the police.

I took a long step toward him. Before my foot had a chance to touch down, there came rapid crackling on the pool deck, storm troopers, their boots treading upon millions of little ice-cubed glass on the concrete. Behind me the thump of running feet. I was surrounded. Rage enveloped in a blanket of red. I raised the gazelle and advanced, determined to take out the rat who'd ruined everything.

"Freeze, don't move. Asshole, don't you move."

I was focused on bashing in Jumbo's head. In my peripheral vision I processed the words, the commands from Deputy Mack as he stepped into the living room, his large-caliber handgun pointed at my chest. The ugly image of the dead kid shoved up against the wall of Mr. Cho's store flashed on the wall of my brain, the unstoppable revelation of how in a couple more seconds I, too, would be posed in the same manner.

I thought: go ahead and shoot. My Marie was gone from me forever. I took another long step. Jumbo lost his arrogant smirk, tried to scramble away from me. I was too quick. I was on him, pulled back for a deadly bludgeoning.

Mack, stopped, yelled, displaying a crazy man's eyes, spittle flying, his gun, a large dark train tunnel pointed at my nose. Still undeterred, I took another step.

"Bruno, stop right there, or I'll blow your black ass right to hell."

For two years, these very same words in quiet moments alone in a cell, echoed in my brain. They triggered some kind of primordial survival instinct that froze all muscle and bone. Even if I wanted to act, I couldn't. I couldn't override the instinct put there to save my life. Those same words were said the last time a second prior to the bullet blasting through my shoulder and knocking me on my ass. The same words said by the same person. I held the gazelle cocked over my head and slowly turned my torso to where Robby stood in the entry, his gun pointed right at me, the same as the last time. Robby, my old friend and supervisor.

"Shoot me. Please shoot me."

Robby smiled. "Can't. We got video rolling. Or, believe me, I'd love to save the state all the money it's going to take to put you on death row."

I yelled and charged.

Mack tackled me from behind. Then two tons of rhinos fell on me.

I was handcuffed and hobbled, my hands behind my back, feet bound and hooked to the handcuffs, hog-tied.

One of the deputies involved in the dog pile skewered his upper thigh with the gazelle horn. He bled copiously onto Jumbo's white Berber rug. Jumbo jumped around, "Get him out of here. Get him off the rug. You're kidding me, right? Get him the fuck outside. Who's going to pay for this? Who's going to pay for the window this black bastard shattered?"

Robby stepped over to a lamp and draped a towel over it. One of the many towels a deputy retrieved from the bathroom to use as a pressure bandage on his partner's leg. A motel-like lamp that I should've immediately noticed when I walked in, should have recognized. A lamp camera, the same model we had used on other operations, the county too cheap to buy the updated version. Another in-your-face detail Robby would gloat over and tell in war stories again and again. I'd been too intent on looking for the real threat, Crazy Ned Bressler. All the people at the party a distraction as well in Jumbo's well-appointed house. Like a fool I'd been taken in by it all.

Once the camera was out of commission, Robby stepped over to Jumbo, C-clamped him with one strong hand around his throat, got up in his ear because there was still audio and whispered. Jumbo turned ashen and nodded again and again.

Paramedics clamored in with all their gear and immediately went to work on the African-gazelle-gored deputy who no longer moaned and lay absolutely still in a sea of turmoil. Two deputies leaned hard on blood-soaked towels that plugged the wounded leg.

Robby said, "Get this piece of shit out of my sight." He kicked me in the side.

Mack and two other deputies picked me up like a suitcase. My arms and legs and wrists screamed in pain.

Robby looked at his watch. "Put him in my car. Mack, you stay with him. I'll be right out." He turned to the paramedic. "How's he doing?"

The paramedic stood, his latex gloves splotched with blood and nodded his head for Robby to step aside. They moved with the group carrying me to the door. They stopped, but I heard the medic. "His femoral artery is severed. We have to scoop and run. We can't wait on the airship. Can you give us a code-three escort?"

"Shit. Shit. Hell yes. Jenkins, you and Fong, you know the routine. Call ahead, leapfrog the intersections and don't spare the horses, you understand? I mean haul ass." I was outside in the cold night air and didn't hear the response, if there was one. Robby was looking out for his own.

I didn't hurt the deputy. It was an accident. But even so, I still owned a piece of that emotion.

Chapter Thirty-Six

I was in the car facedown and still I heard Jumbo yell, "My God, look at all the blood. There's blood everywhere— There's—" His words artificially choked off with outside assistance.

Car doors slammed, tires screeched.

The earth slowed on its axis. After a long ten or fifteen minutes that could've easily been only three, the two front doors to the car opened simultaneously. Mack and Robby got in. Strangely, I thought, in another time that would've been me with Robby.

We drove in silence until Robby said, "Reach back and take that hobble off. I want him sitting up. I want him to see this."

"Pull over," Mack said. "I can't do it while we're moving."

"Cut the son of a bitch off. I'm not stopping. There isn't time."

Mack turned and leaned way over in the seat. With a razor-sharp knife he cut the nylon hobble. My legs sprang free from my hands and my feet kicked the door. My feet were still tied together and tingled as the blood returned to the nerves.

"Get him up."

Mack leaned back over and tried to grab me by my hair, only I kept it cut too close to my pate. He took hold of my shirt and yanked. It tore. With both hands he pulled on my shoulder until I sat up. There was nothing in this world I wanted to see. Not anymore. All I could think about was escape. What it would take. What I had to do. Would I go through both of these men? Yes, I would. I had until they got me behind concrete walls, then it was truly over. I made plans.

Until I recognized the narrow street Robby brought us to. We were headed down 133rd.

I couldn't breathe. The thought of what was about to happened set me firmly down in my own personal hell, one I'd have to live with for an eternity.

Four cop cars, all at the same time, pulled up out in front of our safe house. We'd made it in time all right, in time to see what Robby wanted me to see. Two plainclothes cops came over with Marie handcuffed behind her back. I was ashamed. I was emotionally bankrupt. A long, low moan slipped past my lips. Part of me wanted to slide down into a deep, dark hole and stay there until the pain went away. The other part, the controlling part of me that was still sane knew this would be the last time I would ever see Marie. I tried to etch her image into my memory, as bad as the memory was going to be, I had to have it.

Her expression was at peace. There wasn't any fear, no remorse. My brave girl. When the bright spotlights hit, she squinted, ducked her head.

Marie's expression stayed the same for a second until the light illuminated the interior of the car. She saw me and broke from the cops' grasp, screaming, keening, "Bruuunooo!"

It ripped my guts out. "Marie!"

Robby chuckled. "She's got a nice ass on her. Don't know what the hell a class act with a built-in money maker like that sees in a nigger parolee like you." He put the car in reverse

and backed down the street before the news vultures had time
to pick my bones.

I leaned forward, put my forehead against the seat. "Tell
me."

Robby smirked, "Tell you what, partner?"

"Tell me what I did to deserve this from you."

"You crossed over to the other side. You know how I operate. It's us against them. You turned into one of them. Can't
say that I blame you, enticed by a world-class Puerto Rican
piece of ass like that. I guess you might've been one of them
all the time and I was blind to it. My mistake, but I just cor-
rected that mistake. You were the best, my man, even better
than this hunk of shit sitting next to me. He's not half bad
when he's got his head outta his ass."

I let his words sink in and tried to decipher their meaning.
My voice croaked, "One of them?"

"That's right."

I looked up to see Robby smiling in the rearview. I saw an
evilness I'd never seen before. It hadn't been there. Not when
we partnered. Something had changed him.

Mack stared straight ahead. He looked at me with short,
little glances. He wouldn't let Robby see his reaction.

I said to Robby, "If I'm one of them, then so are you."

He laughed. "Now, just how do you figure? I'm not the one
going down for the last time, kidnap, murder takes you out of
the game for good, my friend. Me, I'm done. I'm taking a long,
well-deserved vacation."

"You're no different than I am. Worse maybe."

"Oh, is that right? This is rich, tell me, please."

"All those times you—we, planted evidence, lied in reports,
for what? To what purpose? To put some scumbag in the slam.
Each time we snipped off a little bit of our souls. We convinced

ourselves, each time we did it, it was for the better good. That's what we told ourselves. At first anyway, then it became as natural as any other department procedure. We committed felonies, multiple counts. How are those felonies different?"

"If you don't know, pal, I feel sorry for you."

"We were nothing but a gang of street thugs ourselves, with tattoos, guns, and initiations, who constantly conspired to commit felonies."

Mack squirmed in his seat.

"Those kids back there were in a bad place. I took them out of that place and gave them a chance. You—you—" Big hot tears blurred my vision and wet my face. "You put them right back in that hostile environment. They don't have a chance now. You're a big man, Robby Wicks, a big man. We stretched the rules to throw bad people in prison for the betterment of society. That was the theory, right? Tell me how it's different?"

We pulled up to the secure parking at the Century Station and waited for the gate to open and admit us. My last chance.

He said, "It's a lot simpler than some convoluted theory of yours. There has to be good guys and bad guys. These good guys just caught themselves a number-one bad guy, an ex-con out on parole for murder, a con who committed murder and kidnapping again for the last time. Our mission is accomplished. I'd like to say I felt sorry for what you now face. But I don't. You made your choices. It's Miller time."

The gate wasn't yet open all the way, but open enough, and he gunned the car through the narrow gap. Robby skidded to a stop, slammed the car in park, and got out. To Mack he said, "Book him. I'll see you in four weeks. I'm en route to a vacation in Jamaica, mon."

I'd been who he was after all along. I wanted to yell at him, ask him about the torch who still prowled the ghetto, dousing victims and lighting them up. How could it not matter to him? I thought I knew the man. When we worked together he would never take a vacation when a major case remained open, especially one with a psycho out on the street torching innocent folks.

Chapter Thirty-Seven

They let me cool out in an interview room, handcuffed, some of the black nylon rope from the hobble still tangled around my right ankle. The thought of my father in a cold, damp jail cell living out the last days of his life, all because of something I had done, something I had organized and put in play, made me look for a place to hang the rope. Not that it would help, as they were continually monitoring from the other room with a pinhole camera, waiting until I ripened for interrogation.

A while later Mack came in, t-shirt, Levi's, his shoulder holster empty, his hands full with two cups of coffee and a thick, brown accordion file folder he placed on the table. He did well fighting the urge to smile. They had won, brought in their prize. He'd come from the bull pen gloating over their victory. What he wanted now was a little gravy. He wanted information so he could act the big man when the FBI came in to adopt the kidnap case, take everything federal. He uncuffed one hand and secured me to the ring mounted in the table and slid the cup over. He was trying for Mr. Congeniality. Only that personality wouldn't fit, not the way I already knew him. I couldn't meet his eyes. He didn't know what to say to get it started. In the same situation I probably wouldn't either.

"You like it black?"

"That some kind of slur?"

"No, man, it's my attempt at being civil."

"How's the deputy doing, the one that hurt his leg?"

Mack grunted. "He's going to make it, no thanks to you."

"What do you want from me? You have your case. Book me and let's get it over with."

"You know the routine," he said. "I have to read you your rights."

"I'm not a fool. You're wasting your time. I'm invoking my right to remain silent." Saying the words brought me back into the real world. Far off in the back of my mind, I realized there was a chance, a slim chance with a good lawyer and a sympathetic jury that I could walk. The next logical thought popped up, I could make a deal, take all the heat of the case to get Marie and Dad off. I sat up straight.

Mack stood to leave.

"Wait. Can we deal?"

Mack couldn't help himself, he looked up to the corner of the room as if asking permission. There was nothing there, the camera lens professionally camouflaged. This was a slippery slope. I had invoked and then asked for a deal, both of which were beyond Mack's skill level and pay grade. He didn't have the ability to negotiate nor know how to take a second waiver. Even so, he sat back down.

As a sign of good faith, with my free hand I sipped the tepid, acrid coffee.

He again pulled out his waiver card. "Because you initially invoked, I have to readvise you."

"I used to be a cop. I know all about the Miranda admonishment." I looked up at the corner of the ceiling. "I know my rights and I waive them."

"Okay, then." He sipped his coffee as a stall to collect his thoughts. "What kind of deal?"

I picked my words carefully, "I want my girl and my father cut loose."

Mack waited, thinking it over. "That's a separate issue."

"What?"

"She's up on separate charges. Aiding and abetting, you know the routine. We need to talk about this other thing."

"What are you talking about? What other thing?" This was an interrogation technique, throw a little out there and let the subject wonder, and out of guilt he starts to talk.

"I can get the DA in here, but I don't think he'll deal on those charges when he's got such a strong case against you on this other thing. I'm just here to get your statement if you want to give me one. The big boys from Homicide will be here in a minute."

"What other thing? Why is Homicide involved? What am I being charged with?"

The nasty Mack returned, "Don't play dumb. It's not gonna to work."

"I'll ask you again. What am I being charged with?"

He sat back, gave the-cat-that-ate-the-canary smile. "Kidnap and murder one, multiple counts, six to be exact. And here in California it rates the death penalty."

I was numb. The revelation didn't faze me. I laughed. "Who are all these folks I am supposed to have killed?"

"Okay, we can play it your way. Ned Bressler's one. He's also the one who tripped you up on all the others."

"Ned Bressler? What are you talking about? When did I purportedly commit this heinous crime against society? Not that Bressler qualifies as a human."

Mack didn't answer, a wise move when interviewing and trying to get something, anything to get a wedge into the suspect.

"Tell me, Detective Mack, how was I supposed to commit these murders with a crack team of Sheriff's Violent Crime detectives following me twenty-four seven?"

"I'm not going to lay the entire case out. I'm not the fool you think I am. There is strong physical evidence you killed Ned Bressler. And, according to your employer and friend, John Ahern, aka Jumbo, you had plenty of motive."

"There can't be any evidence because I haven't laid eyes on Bressler for the better part of a week." I didn't want to give it to him, tell him about the train heists if they didn't already know about them. I didn't think it would bode well for my case. The murder rap was all smoke and mirrors.

"So," I said, "in the words of all the famous criminals who have gone before me, put up or shut up."

The light that ignited in Mack's eyes scared me. On his flat pie-pan face a wide, ugly smile slowly materialized. He reached over to the brown accordion file, his meaty hand disappearing inside, and came out with a gun in an evidence bag.

My mind spun trying to hook onto the possibilities. What gun could they possibly have?

Mack kept it out of reach, "It's not loaded so don't even think about it. We lifted your fingerprints off it."

The .45. It could only be the .45 I took off Q-Ball, the one in the trunk of the root beer-brown Plymouth the BMFs had staked out. The one Vanfleet took a beating over. Sure, that gun would have my prints on it. The only gun I could think of that I had touched in recent history. But I didn't kill anyone with it. But from where I sat, the distance, coupled with the plastic bag obscuring the black metal, it did look like Q's .45.

"Is that Q-Ball's gun?"

Mack's smile didn't waver. After a second, his head moved from side to side. "So you're saying you know whose gun it is? You cop an insanity plea, they might put you in the booby hatch for the rest of your life. Shooting Ned Bressler and lighting all those folks on fire, who wouldn't believe you were absolutely batshit?"

"What the hell are you talking about? I didn't burn those people. I was trying to help Robby find the guy, remember?" I had broken my cool and had said far too much. Mack knew it. He leaned forward. "Robby had an idea it might've been you firing up those poor people, burning them to the ground with a can of gas. Think about it, you even led us on a wild-goose chase, giving us the Grape Street Crips. Looks bad, real bad. You can't take this to the box, a jury will crucify you. Tell me now, and I'll do everything I can to get you the booby hatch, Patton State Hospital for the criminally insane, should be a piece of cake."

He continued to talk. I sat back and let all the events that led up to this spin around in my head. What linked me to all of these murders? The gun in the plastic bag? How so? The others were random, no links, killed with gasoline. None of it made sense.

Mack's words registered again, "Robby knew you were into those train heists. That's why we were on you. A high-profile case with a lot of heat, a lot of pressure from the FBI, the theft of interstate cargo. It was his idea to get close to you. He just didn't know how to approach you. Then the liquor store shooting, a perfect intro to present the ruse to get you to help him. He always said keep your friends close and your enemies closer. Not long after that, Robby started to put it together. That liquor store where you worked was right around the corner from one of the fire victim's. Closer if you went out the back door. Nobody would know you were gone."

Mack violated the cardinal rule of interrogation: never give more information than you receive. I let him talk.

"We ran the timeline with all the killings against our surveillance log. The times you lost us and went out of pocket, matched. For the most part anyway, each of the killings. We got you, man, we got you locked up tight."

"You don't have me. Because I didn't kill anyone."

"Bullshit, you got priors. You forget what you're on parole for?"

"I can shoot holes in your timeline. You're going to look like a bunch of buffoons. Your whole case is going to break down." His timeline would in fact break down. It had to. But to do it, I would have to come clean with every place I'd been during those times. In every instance, when I went to intense countersurveillance mode, I had been en route to a criminal caper, either taking a kid out of a hostile environment or out with Jumbo on a job or, on occasion, going to the safe house to check on Dad. To clear myself I would have to implicate and damn myself to life in prison. They had me boxed tight. I asked, "Where did you find that gun?"

"I'm not at liberty to give you that information. Homicide will be here soon."

Mack wasn't supposed to be talking to me at all, not with Homicide on the way. He thought if he broke me down, there would be something in it for him.

"What kind of gun is it and who's it registered to?"

Mack gave a little squirm as he tried to decide if it was worth giving it up. He knew it was a major interrogation point. He weighed the pros and cons.

I gave him a little nudge. "You give me something, I'll give you something."

"It's an H&K .40-cal registered to Jonathon Kendrick."

He said the name of the registered owner with emphasis like it was supposed to mean something. It did. Back in the far recesses of my brain, I knew the name, only couldn't pull it up. It was there and vitally important, and I couldn't pull it up. The anger made it worse. I tried to relax. It would come to me later. I knew the way my mind worked. In similar in-stances, out of a dead sleep, I'd sit up in bed as the answer bubbled to the surface. I needed it right away. This information was critical to what was happening now. This time he had not mentioned the kids. Why had he not thrown them into the pot to raise the stakes? Maybe he thought too many charges would spook me into silence. Why muddy the water anymore than it was. Ned Bressler, the perfect patsy nobody would miss.

"I gave you something. Now hold up your end."

"Kendrick? Who's Kendrick?"

"No. You said you'd give me something."

I needed some extra time. I needed out. Like Dad always said, never depend on anyone except yourself. And the only way to help myself was to create a little wiggle room.

I looked at Mack and said, "It's Tuesday, isn't it? I need to take a piss."

Mack looked as if I'd slapped him in the face. He sat back, his mouth opening and closing like a fish out of water.

Chapter Thirty-Eight

Being an active member of the BMFs was like being in a street gang but only more organized. Robby Wicks was the leader, the brain of the operation who thought way out ahead of everyone else. For instance, if you were on the prowl poaching in LAPD's area, in their low-income public housing projects, which was strictly forbidden by the sheriff's executive staff because, "LAPD can patrol their own shitholes," and the "shit went south," Robby had a remedy already in place.

If while in the projects, by an unlucky circumstance you became separated from your partner before you had time to confer on your fabricated probable cause, Robby's rule was simple. When asked, "why the hell were you in the projects?" you'd consider the date. On odd days you followed a blue Chevy with gang members into the projects, and on even days it was a green Ford. Once inside, something else diverted your attention. Your partner would say the same.

It wasn't really Tuesday, and I really didn't need to take a piss. The words were another code for the BMFs. It meant something critical had just come up. Either out in the field with an informant, in an interview with a crook, or while relating an incident to a boss, an incident with fabricated evidence that wasn't coming out right once exposed to the light of day. The words were an absolute code red. Cease and desist until another meeting could be reconvened to straighten it out. I was no longer a member of the elite squad and had no reason to believe Mack would honor it.

I added, "Seriously, no bullshit, you need to hear this."

Mack didn't look to the right up at the camera where his captain was watching from the other room. Mack fought the urge, and I gave him a lot of credit for it. He didn't know what to do.

The decision was taken out of his hands. The door opened and Homicide came in, a man and woman I had never seen before. Los Angeles County Sheriff's Department had nine thousand deputies. I had been out of circulation for three years. A lot could happen to an agency that size in three years: transfers, promotions, retirements, terminations.

The woman, a thin, bottle redhead, dressed in a nice black pantsuit that reeked of nicotine, said to Mack, "Thanks, Detective, we can take it from here." She shot him a put-on smile that really meant she was beyond angry for polluting her ripened interrogation subject and it would be addressed later.

Mack stared into my eyes as he got up and left.

The woman had the lead. She sat down with a notebook, held out a red box of Marlboros. "Cigarette?" It was strictly forbidden to smoke in a county building. This was another interrogation ploy, an infraction violation, that said, "See, I'm like you, I break the law." A minor violation in comparison, but it does work. And when you were talking about a case as large and as important as this one, you tried everything.

I stared at her and didn't say anything. She kept the phony smile, pulled a cigarette out of the box with her subdued red lipstick lips, but didn't light it. "So," she said, her eyes slightly pinned as if she had lit the cigarette and the smoke now wafted up, "I understand you've waived your rights."

I weighed my options: talk to this woman and make a deal or wait to see if Mack had the guts to talk to me later.

When I didn't immediately say anything, she said to her partner, a bleary-eyed red-faced man in an immaculate navy-blue suit, "John, Mr. Johnson looks uncomfortable. I think we can take the cuffs off, don't you?"

Her partner got up to take off the cuffs.

"Bruno, you mind if I call you Bruno? My name is Nancy Thorne, and I think you know why I'm here."

I rubbed my wrists and made my choice. "I would like to talk to an attorney."

There was no rush in making a deal. I could always do that later.

The sheriff long ago learned to take special care of sensational prisoners. You didn't put them in general population where another inmate with a yen for fame, a wannabe who had the desire to make a name for himself, could put a shiv between your celebrity's ribs. There was a place in the jail called Administrative Segregation. The inmates wore green jumpsuits instead of standard blues and were labeled "Keep Aways, Escort Only." I wasn't put in Ad Seg because classification labeled me based on my alleged crimes. They'd booked me for everything, the torch murders, the kidnapping, and the train robberies. They threw all the charges up against the wall to see what would stick. Can't say I wouldn't have done any different under the circumstances. Homicide Detective Thorne and her crew had forty-eight hours to file the charges.

The jail considered me a suicide risk. I was put on the third-floor hospital in a single room with a fifteen-minute observation. This meant a deputy came by every fifteen minutes and looked in the little square window in the hard steel door to confirm I was still breathing and log that fact on the chart.

Maybe I should've been suicidal, but this whole thing was too pat and obviously set up on the fly. I knew, if given the chance, there was an outside possibility I could tear it down. What didn't make sense was that Robby was smarter than all this. He had to know his house of cards would take a nosedive.

I waited for hours, counting the time off in fifteen-minute increments each time I saw the on-duty deputy put his face in the window of the door. I paced the small room and tried to stay awake by counting how many looky-loos came to my window, besides the on-duty deputy. The others wanted in to see the serial killer who was lighting people on fire, the man splashed across the TV and *Los Angeles Times*. Jail personnel, hospital staff, trustees, all came and looked in the zoo window. Gradually, the adrenaline bled off. Four hours passed. I laid down on the bed, curled up, fought sleep, prayed that the door would open, and Mack would be there. Ironically, I now depended upon him to save me.

My eyes grew heavy. The light went off and then strobed every fifteen minutes in my semidream state.

When I woke, I'd lost track of the flashes and didn't know what time it was, whether it was day or night outside in the real world. I went to the window and waited ten minutes before the deputy came by, looked, and then marked the paper. I had to yell to be heard through the door. "What time is it?"

He didn't answer and gave me the bird before he moved on. I waited. Two inmate trustees in blues pushed a noisy food cart down the hall as two others picked up empty trays. Breakfast. I'd slept longer than I thought. When I was a brand-new deputy, I only worked the hospital a couple of times on overtime and didn't remember when chow was fed in the morning. I thought it was five o'clock to facilitate preparing the inmates for court. I went back to pacing. Dust motes hung in the air. I couldn't help remembering that I had read somewhere most dust was particles of skin humans shed every day of their lives.

The activity in the hall increased, then abruptly dropped

off all together while everyone ate. The little horizontal slot
with a locked door under the window opened and a trustee put
a hot tray on the ledge. My breakfast stayed right there on the
ledge well past noon and was finally replaced with a brown-
bag lunch. I didn't eat that either, though I knew what was in
it: a white bread American cheese sandwich, a bag of chips, a
mushy apple, and a dried-out hard chocolate chip cookie.

Mack didn't come until after dinner.

Chapter Thirty-Nine

Mack didn't look in the window, the key in the door rattled the lock, the door opened, and he stepped in. His face turned red and he clenched his fists. "I'm putting my ass on the line. This better not be bullshit." He had dark half circles under his blood-shot eyes, and his hair was mussed. It looked as if he hadn't slept. He wore denim pants, a thick brown belt, a Rolling Stones t-shirt, the one with the large tongue on the front, par-tially covered by a long-sleeve, tan corduroy shirt stretched tight at the shoulders and biceps. He hadn't shaved in a couple of days, the blond hair hardly visible on his lantern jaw.

I sat up on the bed and rubbed my face and looked out the open door at freedom, a sterile institution-beige hallway. "Maybe you should close the door and lower your voice."

He hesitated.

I may have tried to take control of the meeting too quickly. He stomped over to the door and slammed it. I heard the solid steel door lock automatically. Deputy Mack was prone to those kinds of mistakes.

"You going to start talking or am I going to walk out?"

"The door's locked."

His face flushed red.

I held up my hands, "Whoa. I'm sorry, really. Don't get mad. I'm going to make you a star."

"Like hell you are. You got nothin'. I don't even know what I'm doin here."

"If that were true, you wouldn't be here at all. You know there's something terribly wrong with what's going on. More so than normal, I mean."

He calmed down, looked over his shoulder with a quick glance, and backed up to sit in a hard plastic chair.

"I know you have no reason to believe me. I didn't burn those people and I didn't shoot Crazy Ned Bressler."

He opened his mouth to speak. I cut him off. "I know who burned those people. That's why you're here. You know it's the truth."

"Why are you telling me?"

"You know why?"

He stared, thinking it over, not rising to the bait.

I leaned forward, my hands on the edge of the bed, "Why don't you tell me why I'm telling you."

His light-blue eyes were almost gray. He waited a long time, his jaw muscle knitting. Finally, he looked away as if making a confession. "I grew up in south Texas. My daddy was a lawman and so was my grandpap. I wanted to get away from being Big John Mack's little boy and make my own way."

I didn't know what this had to do with anything, but I had the time.

"I moved out here and joined the best law enforcement organization in the world. Everything was great. I loved my job. I moved up fast, made it to the shit-hot Violent Crimes Team. At first, this job—there was nothing better. It was everything I wanted and imagined. Until about two years ago."

I knew what he was talking about. I'd been there.

He paused, so I finished it for him. "Until your leader changed emotionally."

He looked back at me. "I called back to Texas and talked to my people. You know what my daddy said? He said, an Apache will ride his horse right into the ground until it dies. Then he'll eat it. Robby Wicks is an Apache."

Deputy Mack was a lot smarter than I gave him credit for.

He said, "So, asshole, if you got something to tell me you better get after it."

"I'll tell you on two conditions."

"You don't get any conditions. Look around you, you're in a world of shit right now."

"Think about this," I said, "if what I tell you is true—and you know there is better than even odds that it is or you wouldn't be sitting here—this world of shit of mine, most of it anyway, will disappear. I'm telling you, you're going to be a star."

"Knock that star shit off. All I want is to rub Robby Wicks's nose in it."

"And all I want is simple. I want to go with you." I thought he would laugh or yell, but he just looked at me as if he half expected something like this. Something more was going on. I needed to be out in the open to get at it. "And I want a face-to-face with my girl and my dad."

"Gimme the name. Tell me who you think is really burning the people."

This time I waited. If I told him, then he could go out on his own and find him. He wouldn't need me anymore. This was the only ace I had, and he knew it. I'd have to start trusting him sometime. Dad always said there was some good in everyone. I wanted in the worst way to believe that about Mack. "It's Ruben the Cuban."

Mack stood up, walked to the door, and knocked on it.

"Do we have a deal?"

He didn't turn around or answer.

"Wait. I know Ruben the Cuban. I can find him fast."

Mack said nothing.

The door rattled as the key went in the lock. My only chance was about to walk out the door never to return.

"Mack?"

The door opened. He took a step out.

"Mack?"

Mack stopped, but didn't turn around.

I said in a lower tone, "Ruben the Cuban used to work for Q-Ball—Quentin Bridges—and he used to frequent the burned-out apartment building on El Segundo where he sold rock for Q."

It was everything I had. I threw it out there to show Mack, to prove I was straight up and telling the truth.

The hard steel door swung closed and locked.

I sat on the edge of the bed, knowing I had played it wrong. Mack wasn't like me. He had the information now. He didn't need me. He'd run with it. My stomach growled. My muscles relaxed. I hadn't realized I'd been so tense. I stared at the door, at the little window until my eyes burned from not blinking.

Keys in the lock jangled. I let out a long breath.

Mack came back in with the Asian deputy from the Violent Crimes Team, the guy Robby called Fong. They closed the door. In another time and another place, I might've thought they were there for a different reason, a little get-even time for their downed comrade. Fong went to the far wall, put his back to it, crossed his arms, his almond-shaped eyes all but invisible. He was built low to the ground with stout, broad shoulders and little fat, his gleaming black hair combed straight back.

Mack said, "You only want to go along so at the first opportunity you can make a break. You got nothing to lose."

"You're wrong. I'll give you my word. And if you know anything about me, you know that it's good."

Fong smirked. "You're a serial killer. We're supposed to believe you?"

"That's the dilemma, isn't it? I'm not. You believe that I'm not or you wouldn't be here contemplating taking me out of custody for a show-and-tell." I gave them the words to make it easier for them, help with their excuse to do it. An investigator had the right, with approval of course, to take an inmate out of custody to do a show-and-tell. The inmate was to be kept under heavy guard, handcuffed and waist-chained, and was never to leave the backseat of the undercover car. The inmate then pointed out a drug house, a crash pad, where suspects were hiding or where the bodies were buried.

They looked at each other. All this had been planned beforehand or Fong wouldn't have been out in the hall waiting. When Mack had gone out, they had discussed it again, made their decision to do it. They had to be scared of losing their jobs, going to jail, and worse. They were scared of the Great Robby Wicks.

They needed a little added nudge. "Q-Ball right now is in an apartment on 124th Street right off of Wilmington in a cul-de-sac." I raised my right hand, "I swear to you." Then I remembered how Q had made the illegal U-turn in front of the Bimbo Bread truck on Long Beach Boulevard. He could be at Killer King Hospital. I also remembered about Tommy Bascombe, how he clung to me, how his head came up like a little prairie dog with the sound of the crash. How Tommy gobbled down the food at Lucy's and was now either in foster care, or worse, back with Dora. I pushed that thought back. One small step at a time.

"Here's the deal," Mack said. "I don't trust you. Not for

one second. That's why I brought Fong in. He's going to walk five paces behind with a gun in his pocket. He won't be involved in anything we do other than watching you. That's his entire focus. If you so much as take a hurried step to get out of the way of a bus that's about to hit you, he will shoot you in the back. You understand?"

"No, problem. I told you I gave you my word. My word's good as gold. You can ask Robby." I knew that wasn't going to happen.

Mack went and knocked on the steel door to call the jail deputy, then turned back and said, "You're like all the rest of those who have a higher opinion of the Great Robby Wicks. If you only knew. He always refers to you as his 'skillet.' He'd say, 'me and my skillet we did this' or 'you should've seen the skillet's eyes when I gunned him, shot his black ass off' and . . ."

The door opened, interrupting Mack. His words had done a number on me, sliced right through me, slashed open a gaping wound. Earlier Robby had hurt me with his words but I had somehow halfway justified it. Sure, I was angry, but I'd given him just cause. I'd crossed the line deep into criminal territory and allowed some of my own guilt to mask and accept his behavior. Mack's description of my friend somehow illuminated a truth that had always been there since I'd known Robby, like a bubble about to burst.

The deputy assigned to the hospital came in dragging chains. Policy for a show-and-tell was chains. No arguing this point.

Chapter Forty

The deputy locked the chain around my waist, laced the cuffs through, and then handcuffed my hands in a permanent position just above my hips. Next, he shackled my legs together at the ankles with enough slack for three-quarter's of a step. With each step, the sound and weight made me think of a chain gang.

Outside my room, all the doors were closed and the hall empty. Mack had wanted to keep the number of witnesses and involved parties to a minimum. A futile effort if the caper went south. As Robby used to say, "It is what it is."

The deputy stayed ahead of us and called the elevator, the sound of my chains the only noise in the hall, that and my heavy breathing.

The elevator door opened. I flashed on a memory from when I used to work the jail. Back when I was a new guy, "a cherry," I took my lunch break with a veteran who had all of six months at Men's Central Jail. We called for the elevator. When the doors opened, we saw an inmate all by himself, no shirt just jail-blue pants, handcuffed to the hand rail, his back to the wall, his butt on the floor. Beat to a bloody pulp, his face so swollen his features all blurred into mush. The veteran jail deputy casually reached over and pushed the elevator button. "Sorry," he said, "wrong floor." The doors closed and the inmate went on down. I stood as the veteran deputy turned to me, said, "Maybe it'd be better if we took the stairs." I never did find out the story of what happened that day, but I heard rumors that on occasion, deputies took the more obstreperous inmates for a "Disney ride, an E ticket," on the elevators to conduct an "attitude adjustment."

The doors closed. Mack and Fong stared straight ahead. The odor in the car no different from in the jail cells, a reek that permeated every inch of every jail; human sweat, mixed with spit, feces, and blood. The door opened to the basement, the odor replaced by the aroma of chicken soup. A welcome change emanating from the kitchen.

"Hey, the deal was I got to see my girl."
Fong grabbed my waist chain and shoved. He was strong. We moved into the main aisle of the kitchen. At any one time, the sheriff had twenty-five thousand, presentenced inmates in custody, a good chunk of the residents in Men's Central Jail, MCJ. To the left were rows of large cauldrons of bubbling stew, large enough to be a fat man's Jacuzzi. The inmates in blues all stopped what they were doing to watch as we ambled through. No unauthorized personnel were allowed in the kitchen. A general employee, a cook specialist II, slapped the back of the head of an inmate who stirred a cauldron of stew with a large oarlike boat paddle, snapping him to attention. The cook reached into the cauldron with two fingers and pulled out what looked like a large condom. When he shook it out, it was a latex glove mottled white and gray from the heat.

We moved on down the aisle as fast as the shackles allowed and came to a large opening. Fresh, cold night air hit my face. We turned a corner to a loading dock where a Violent Crime's undercover car was backed in.

On the dock stood a female uniformed deputy and my girl.
My Marie.

My heart soared. I hobbled faster. She broke away from her keeper. She was dressed in jail blues that hid her figure. Her hair was undone and shot out in different directions. Tears streaked her face, her eyes bloodshot from crying. We met in between. I couldn't hug her, my hands were restricted to my hips. She hugged and kissed me, her body hot, hot enough to scorch. I clung to her hips. I nuzzled her neck. Drank her in.

I said, "I'm sorry, babe. I'm so sorry. I truly don't know how they got on to us. It must've been me. They must've followed me."

"Hush, are you okay? Did they hurt you?"

"I'm fine. How are you?"

"Bruno, it's not as bad as you said it was, really, it's not."

A large ball rose up in my throat, made it difficult to talk. "You're a bad liar. Thank you for trying."

"The kids, Bruno. The poor kids. Alonzo. I can't even imagine—"

"Ssh. Kiss me."

She did long and deep.

We didn't have much time. Any second Mack was going to call time. He had already gone out of his way. And I intended to thank him later for it. Even though he'd done it for a reason. He wanted it more difficult for me to renege on our deal. He didn't know me and I couldn't blame him.

"Don't you worry," I said when I came up for air. "I got something in the works. I'm going to get you out."

Her shoulders started to shake. "Bruno, what did you do? What did you have to trade away? What makes you think these people will give us the slightest consideration for what we've done? They've got to be mad as hell. Especially about Wally Kim. Poor Mr. Kim."

"You didn't tell them anything? I mean, you invoked just like I told you, right?"

"Yes, I did just like you said. They didn't get a thing from me. What did you do? Tell me."

Mack said, "Come on, time's up."

I ignored him. "They want something only I can give them. I'm going to trade it for you and Dad."

"No, you have a record. You're on parole. They'll go easier on me. Make a deal for yourself. I'm serious, Bruno. You do it or I'm going to be mad as hell. I won't talk to you ever again."

She made me smile. "Ssh, listen, there isn't time. How's Dad? Did he take it okay?"

She looked scared.

I tried to read her eyes. "What?"

She whispered. "Did they get your dad too?"

"What do you mean?"

"I never made it to the house. They zoomed up as I was walking down the street. I saw you in the car. They already had you."

"You never got inside? Did you see the cops inside the house at all?"

"No. Do you think?"

My heart soared at the prospect. Were the cops that naïve to pick her up before she made it to where she was going? If they were so hot after the kids, they were fools for making the scoop when they did. "Robby just wanted to rub my nose in it by showing me he had you. He jumped the gun to make a point."

"That means your dad and the—" She lowered her voice to faint whisper, "and the kids are still in the house and okay. Can that be true? Is that possible?"

"Then what are they holding you on? What's going on?" I choked on the lump in my throat. "Dad's okay. Dad made it out." One of the heavy rocks lying on my chest just floated off.

Mack, behind me, tugged on the back part of my chain. "Come on, man, we been back here too long already."

I leaned down and kissed Marie, my tongue overpowering hers. I wanted to consume all of her.

They pulled us apart, my body cooler from her absence. "I love you, Marie. Always remember I love you."

"Please don't say it that way."

"Don't you worry. You won't be in long. I promise."

Overcome with emotion, she couldn't talk anymore. She wept and gulped at air. The female deputy put her in a wrist lock and tugged her along in the opposite direction. Mack gave up tugging on my chain and waited behind me until Marie was out of sight, then I let them move me to the car. I should've been ashamed at what I'd done to her. Instead I was furious. More furious than I ever remember being. Furious at Robby Wicks. He was the one who had done this. He was the one responsible. No matter what happened, I was going to make him pay.

Chapter Forty-One

Mack steered the car toward 124th Street. I sat in the passenger side of the front seat, Fong right behind me, a gun resting easy in his lap. Mack periodically stole a glance at me. "You going to be all right?"

I said nothing and continued to fume.

"Hey, man, you hear me? You going to be all right? I don't need you going supernova on me."

I didn't look at him. "You're right. He is an Apache."

In the backseat, Fong chuckled.

When the heat, the anger finally bled off, and I could see straight, I realized that we were headed down Wilmington from Imperial Highway. "Hey, pull in here. Stop in at Martin Luther King."

"Bullshit, you said 124th. That's what you said. You're trying to dick with us. It won't happen."

I calmly said, without making eye contact, "This could save us a trip. I saw him crash his car over on Long Beach Boulevard. A real slobber knocker. He's probably still in the hospital. We can go to 124th, but we might be coming right back here."

"This is bullshit." Mack whipped the steering wheel hard. The maneuver tossed Fong and me hard against the doors. The Chevy squealed into the parking lot of Killer King. Mack stopped in front of the ER, parked in the law-enforcement-only slot, put it in park, and shut her down. He turned, "If he's in here, what makes you think he's going to tell you where this Ruben the Cuban is?"

"Q-Ball and I go way back. I served paper on his pad twice. Both times he felt the barrel of my .357 across the top of his head. He sees me in these chains, though, he's just going to laugh."

"I'm not going to fall for that one. The chains stay on."

The automatic double doors to the ER hissed open when we walked in. No one paid much attention to a black man in chains. Crooks came in to be treated all the time. We went past the waiting area, past the treatment rooms, and down a long hallway, to the backside of admittance. Fong, as promised, stayed back, his hand in his jacket pocket. Mack leaned over the high counter, flashed his gold sheriff star, and whispered, then nodded as the receptionist looked up the information on the computer.

Fong and I waited.

Mack came back over a little more at ease. "You called it right. He's here, fifth floor, 513. Come on, let's take the elevator over here."

We waited for the elevator car, watching the round lights above the top edge count down. The car stopped on two. We waited some more.

Mack said, "Wicks told me a story about how you trailed a car's broke radiator on foot for five miles. The car killed a little girl. Said he never seen anything like it."

I said nothing. The light on two went off as the car came down.

Mack said, "It's one of the first times Wicks wasn't talking about himself. He said he had to pull you off the shitbag or you'd have kicked him to death."

"I never heard that," Fong said.

I looked straight ahead. "That was another time. Someone else's life."

The door opened. The car was three times the size of normal elevators. An orderly pushed out a gurney with a white-haired old woman under a thin sheet covering an emaciated frame with two IV bags hanging from an IV tree. We stepped aside, then into the car. The door closed.

Mack said, "Five miles on a summer night, in a hot wool uniform. That true? That the way it was?"

"No, it might have been two miles at best."

The lights went up the panel as we rose.

On our floor, Mack went straight to the room, hesitated at the closed door thinking something through, then led the way in. Q-Ball lay on a hospital bed one arm and one leg plastered and suspended from ropes. A jagged line across the top of his forehead pinched together with black sutures would leave a bad scar. The accident was worse than I'd thought.

He made Mack for a cop right off said, "Get the fuck outta here, I'm not gonna tell ya shit." He saw me, flinched, and grimaced with pain. His eyes went wide as he tried to get farther away. Until he saw the waist chains and shackles. His face relaxed into a smile that turned into a laugh. "Dey finally got yo number, huh, Dee-tective Johnson. Dey gonna put you where you belong."

Mack went over to the side of the bed. "We just want one thing from you."

"You kin kiss my black ass. I ain't tellin' you shit."

Mack looked back over his shoulder to Fong who took his cue, went to the door and stood close so no one could open it and come in. The other two beds were empty, one looked slept in, the patient out for tests.

"I ain't gonna buy yo hardass shit. Not in a hospital with all these witnesses."

I said, "All we want to know is where Ruben is."

He looked from Mack then back to me. "I tolt ya. You're not gettin' a motherfuckin' thing. Get the fuck outta my room 'fore I call the nurse and have 'em toss you out on yo dumb cracker asses." He reached for the hand buzzer for the nurse.

Mack was quicker, grabbed it, yanked it from the wall.

"Big man, yo cain't scare me."

Mack stepped in close, his hands moving in.

"Wait," I said. "You can get in trouble for torturing his ass. I can't. Take these off."

Fear flashed on Q's face, then quickly changed back. "Sure, you're right. I'm gonna fall for that bullshit."

Mack looked me in the eye. He was unconvinced, thought it was a bad idea. I waited him out. He finally looked back at Fong who said nothing. Q made Mack's decision for him. He pulled back his good leg and kicked Mack in the hip. Mack took two steps forward, spun, and was going after him. I intervened, bumped him with my chest. "No, do it my way."

Q put his head back and laughed. "You're gamin' me, Johnson. He cain't take dem cuffs off not when yo out on a pass. I know, I bin dere."

Mack reached into his tight jeans pocket, came out with the key. Fong, still over by the door, brought his gun out of his coat pocket held it down at his side. Q saw all of it.

"Bullshit."

Mack took hold of the waist chains. "I'm gonna trust you. You try and rush the door, Fong's gonna cap your ass. You hear that, Fong?"

"I got your back, bro."

Q watched intently, fear creeping into his expression as Mack unhooked the waist chain. Mack went down in a vulnerable position to take off the shackles. I could've taken him then, no problem, gotten his gun. But I'd given him my word.

Over at the door someone tried to come in. The door banged into Fong's back. He didn't turn to look and leaned into the door. The person on the other side said, "Hey."

Q opened his mouth to scream for help. I was on him, one hand on his mouth, the other clamped down tight on his throat. His eyes bulged white. I slowly moved my face down close to his ear, whispered, "You know what they got me on?" He had to understand I was desperate and would do anything that needed to be done.

He shook his head, no.

"Multiple counts of murder that I didn't do, multiple counts of kidnap that I did do. They booked me for kidnap and train robbery. I'm already on parole if you didn't already know. I got nothing to lose. And you know what? I'm tired of your ass slingin' rock to all the kids on the street. I'm tired in general of you as a human being. You have no redeeming value and make no contribution to the human race. The key here, if you haven't picked up on it, is that I have nothing to lose. I'll give you one chance, just one. When I take my hand away, you tell me where we can lay our hands on Ruben the Cuban, and I'll think about not snapping your neck like a pencil-necked yardbird." I kept my hand over his mouth a couple of seconds longer. I smelled urine. "You going to tell me what I want to know?"

He nodded his head. I took my hand away. Q gulped and gasped. "He layin' his head over ta Shawntay's."

"Where does this Shawntay live?"

"Two, three houses other side of Hawkin's Market. You know the place, tween hunert-and-fifteen and Avalon."

"He better be there."

"Swear to God, he stay dere. But he in and out all the time, I cain't gearuntee he gonna be dere."

"Listen to me," I said. "I'm going to the same joint you're

going to eventually end up in. If you're not straight up, I'll take care of it later." I backed up, turned, and walked to the door. Mack held up the chains. I stood between Fong and Mack. Fong brought his gun up and pointed it at my face. The threat wasn't there. I knew he wasn't going to shoot. I raised my arms so Mack could put on the waist chain. "Is this really necessary? I gave you my word."

Mack answered by swinging the chain around my waist and hooking it up. While he did, Q recovered some of his balls, said, "Why you want Ruben so bad?"

No one answered him.

"He do sumthin' real bad?"

Again, no one answered.

Chapter Forty-Two

No one spoke on the way over to Shawntay's. In the dark, the place sat steeped in a cold mist that hung in the night air. Shawntay's, like all the other homes on the street, was a mangy, broken-down, two-story craftsman that needed fresh paint and shingles and windows to replace the holes with cardboard shoved in them. The grass and shrubs and trees were in violent revolt. The only thing warm about anything in the neighborhood came from the yellow-orange glow that escaped out of slits from the window shades and meant someone was home.

Mack knew the risks of losing Ruben, especially if we just ambled up like the Avon lady and rang the bell. Someone had to cover the back. The highest percentage of chance for action always came from the back. The suspect would smell cop and flee in the opposite direction. Mack parked five houses down, turned off the headlights and the engine. We sat and listened to the car tick as it cooled, no one saying what was obviously on our minds.

"Fong, you take the back. I take the skillet with me." Fong didn't reply. They sat unmoving for a long beat. Fong and Mack had done this before. They knew how to take down an armed and dangerous without any more planning than deciding front or back. Right now what to do with their extra baggage gave them pause. They'd worked as a team for a while, so that without any cue, they opened their doors at the same time. Fong opened my door, said to Mack who came around the front of the car, "We put him in the trunk; we won't have to worry about him."

Mack grunted. "Just take the back, okay." Fong moved off into the dark a little miffed. I watched him go, waited for him to look back at us one last time. He didn't. Outside the warm car, the insidious cold seeped into muscle first, then into bone until my teeth chattered in unison with my chains.

"Come on."

I followed Mack who took several steps and then must've remembered I wasn't a member of his team. He waited for me to catch up and move ahead so he could watch. I made a hell of a noise going down the sidewalk. "This isn't a smart move. Come on, take these off. I told you I promise I won't run."

"Pull those chains in tight so they don't rattle so much." We kept moving. I tried what he said. I needed him on my side. If we caught Ruben and made him for the killings a big part of my problem would melt away.

A tall untrimmed hedge on both sides of the front walk had mostly grown together, six, eight-feet high ran right up to the front door. The unkempt center left little room to pass. The sleeves of my shirt turned wet from the dew as we passed through. Two concrete steps led up to a tired wooden stoop.

The thick front door abruptly opened. Orange light spilled out. We both stood at the bottom of the steps still in the hedge tunnel. The man coming out moved in wisps of white smoke that filled the air with a harsh chemical scent, rock coke, his back to us, his jovial mood apparent as he waved good-bye to well-wishers.

Two things happened all at once. I heard Mack's gun clear leather as he shouldered me out of the way. With nowhere to go, I got shoved into the hedge. Mack put one foot up on the second concrete step, grabbed the thin black man by the back of his neck, and pulled him down to our level. The man yelped like a kicked dog. The well-wishers inside behind the closed door missed the action outside and moved deeper into the house. They hadn't heard the snatch. Mack's latest prey was shoved into the hedge next to me, the pencil-thin light from between the window covering worked like a laser scanning the man's features. Our shoulders touched. He tried to squirm away from me, his eyes wide in terror, more afraid of me than the large handgun Mack shoved up under his chin. You would've thought I was a thirty-foot boa constrictor, maw wide about to swallow him whole.

"This him?" Mack hissed.

"No."

Mack looked back at Thin Man. "Who's in the house?"

He didn't answer, didn't look at Mack, and kept his gaze on me.

I said, "I know you, son?"

Thin Man nodded.

Mack shoved the gun upward until Thin Man's chin pointed almost straight up at the stars. "Answer me, asshole."

"Ease off him," I said.

A long couple of seconds passed. Mack backed off.

"Where do I know you from?"

"The 'hood," Thin Man's voice croaked with fear.

"I know that, son. Where? What's your name?"

"Fo' years ago August tenth, you caught me stealin' in an alley and damn near beat me ta deaf."

"That's not the whole story. What happened? I didn't just—"

"This ain't old home week," Mack said. "Tell me who's in the house."

Thin Man continued, wanting to answer anything I asked.

"Had me a slew a DVDs in a bag, in da alley. You caught me, beat the hell outta me fo being strapped."

I nodded. "Who's in the house?"

"Shawntay, Deewayne, that dumbass Franklin, and his bitch, Greta."

Mack knew better now and kept quiet.

I asked, "What about Ruben the Cuban?"

This time Thin Man stole a quick glance at Mack. Either he didn't want a rat jacket or he was more afraid of Ruben and needed the half second extra to think. "He in dere. But he ain't right in the head."

My chains rattled and startled Thin Man. He looked down, saw the restraints, and repelled away as if the chains were contagious. "You in custody, Detective Johnson?"

I continued on as if I hadn't heard. "Where's Ruben in the house?"

"He up the stairs first doe on the right."

"He armed?"

"Ruben, he always strapped. He smoked a grip of crack tonight. Damn near outta his head."

Mack yanked Thin Man out of the hedge, patted him down, found a cell phone, and tossed it up and over. No sound came from where it landed. Mack said, "You get on and keep your mouth shut, you understand?"

Thin Man took a step down the path before stopping to look back one last time. "You okay, Detective Johnson?"

I didn't remember the kid, but he'd remembered me and was asking if I wanted him to help me with Mack. The kid had a lot of nerve. Mack picked up on it and squared off with him ready to go to battle.

"No," I said, "everything's cool. You go on."

He nodded, took a couple more steps on the path that immediately enveloped him in darkness and hedge. Gone.

Mack watched, waiting for him to spring back out with a rock or war club. "By his own words, you beat the shit outta him, and he wants to help you out?"

"He knew he had it coming. You ever work the ghetto? The people are not policed, they're ruled. When I worked patrol, we fielded three two-man cars, not near enough to protect and serve. There are simple rules, you get caught with a gun, you get beat down. It's an unwritten law of the street. In California, a gun violation, all by itself, no other crime involved, like robbery or assault attached is a misdemeanor. You get your ass beat, you remember it. You only beat someone's ass when they got it coming, they respect you for it." I held my hands open, still cuffed to my waist on each side of my hips. Mack looked me in the eye for a long moment.

"There are four of them in there, and Ruben's coked out of his mind and armed."

Mack took a key from his pocket, unlocked the cuffs, unwound the chains from my waist. In the hedge, in the dark he wouldn't bend down to take off the shackles, he handed me the key. I unlocked the shackles, said, "Last I saw Ruben he was about five ten, a hundred and eighty. He's a strawberry with a gap in his two front teeth. You can't miss him."

"What's a strawberry?"

I stood, handed him the chains, "A light-skinned black with a splash of freckles under his eyes and across his nose. His hair is light brown with a red tint instead of black."

Mack nodded. "I want my hands clear." He handed me back the chains. "You carry 'em."

Mack knew he'd just put a very effective weapon in my hands. The thought to run did dash fleet-footed across my mind. It wasn't an option. "I'm not going anywhere. I want my girl out of jail."

"You help me get Ruben and he's the dude, he's good for these killings, I'll go to the wall to help you."

"That's good enough for me." I held out my hand. Mack hesitated, his stark, blue eyes locked on mine. I believed him. This was the first time Mack yielded an inch in the direction of Ruben being the killer instead of me. He took my hand and shook. His hand was stronger than I had imagined. Maybe this corn-fed cowboy from Texas would've been harder to take than I'd thought.

I wound the chains around my right hand to use like a medieval mace. Mack turned his back to me and went back up the two concrete steps. He tried the knob, when it didn't turn, he put his shoulder to the wood, put one foot back, leaned, and slowly pushed. In the dim shadow, his shoulder muscles bulged. The wood creaked, then gave.

The house had been converted into multiple rentals. Directly inside the door a flight of stairs ran along a too-narrow hall that accessed all the downstairs rooms. All the noise came from downstairs. Muffled cries from smoked-out coke freaks, creatures of the night.

Mack hesitated just inside while keeping his gaze up into the blackness of the second level, pulled his unbuttoned long-sleeve shirt back, and keyed his handie-talkie on his belt. He had an ear jack. "Mike, we're in. The primary is on the second floor. The way it's set up it looks like he's probably on the one-two side. We're going up."

The front entry of the house was always the one side. The house is numbered clockwise from there.

Mack nodded to himself as he alone heard Fong's reply then started up the stairs. Stairs always gave me the heebie-jeebies, the most dangerous part of a building search. Someone above you had total advantage and could snipe you at will,

reach a hand over the stairwell without looking, and gun whoever was dumb enough to expose themselves in that manner.
Had Mack been the asshole I'd first perceived him to be, he
would've made me go first, bait. He'd moved up a couple of
notches in my book.

The old wooden stairs with carpet worn away swayed in
the middle from decades of use. The steps didn't comply with
city code, and too narrow for the footfall, our heels hung over.
Mack ascended, his big .45 extended straight up at arm's
length, covering as best he could. I reached up and put my
hand on his back for balance, to let him know where I was
and to stay close. He didn't flinch. He kept going to the second
floor that smelled of mothballs and urine. We automatically
deployed on the first door on the right, the way Thin Man described it. I took the left side, the hinge side, Mack the right,
the knob side. Sweat ran down his forehead, his blue eyes a
fraction wider than normal. Adrenaline did that to you.

His hand went carefully to the knob, gripped, and gently
turned. Unlocked, it turned freely in his hand. He pulled his
intent gaze off the wood to look to me, as if saying, on three.
He pushed. The door only moved half an inch, then caught.
On the inside the occupant had installed a hasp. Mack was
ready for the obstruction, took it head-on as it happened,
stepped back, and booted the door. Mack rebounded from his
kick. Instinct propelled me in first. I buttoned-hooked right.
The floor was a sea of litter, trash, ratty blankets, cans. Over
by the closed window, Ruben the Cuban stood, soaked in
sweat, clad in a dirty wifebeater t-shirt, his every muscle
wound tight, ready to spring. He did. He jumped right
through the closed window. The abrupt maneuver left his shoes
on the floor in the same position. Glass shattered. Mack yelled.
I ran to the window, kicking trash.

Outside, down on the ground, Ruben rolled several times and disappeared into the gloom.

Mack yelled on his handie-talkie. "He's out. He's out on the one-two side. You got him, Mike? You got him?"

"Negative. Negative."

I didn't wait.

I leapt out the window.

Chapter Forty-Three

Freezing wind blew in my eyes and caught in my lungs for a fraction of a second before my feet jarred into the ground. I let my knees give and shoulder-rolled, as the chains clattered.

Mack yelled from above. "Stop. Johnson. Stop, you son of a bitch."

I got to my feet and went after the sound. Ruben plowed through the bushes. The window Ruben came out of had been covered. Now the light lit up a portion of the yard. Mack's gun banged loud.

Then again.

And again.

The third time cherry-hot iron slashed the top edge of my shoulder. I hit the sidewalk. Down half a block, Ruben ran full tilt, the devil chasing. "Picking 'em up and putting 'em down," as Robby would've said. I went after him. At any moment, I expected Mike Fong to step out onto the sidewalk behind me, line up for an easy shot, and put one between my shoulder blades.

Ruben cut between some houses. He knew the neighborhood. But so did I. I gained on him. No bullet caught up to me. I made the turn and was okay. I tossed the heavy chains that were slowing me down.

I lost sight of Ruben and stopped to listen for him, tried to still my rapid breath. Ruben was no fool. He quit running and now walked, hood rat silent running. The odds of catching him just diminished greatly if he no longer panicked. I went on down between the houses and into the weed-infested dirt easement that ran parallel to the street, and fought the urge to run in any direction just to be doing something. Ruben, the little weasel, jeopardized any chance I had for a deal. I waited and listened. Nothing. Fifty-fifty chance, I went right, heading south. Prey will always run downhill. This wasn't San Fran with the hills. It was South Central Los Angeles, flat as a floodplain all the way to the ocean. But maybe Ruben's survival instinct dragged him south. I walked faster and faster until I broke into a jog. Ruben could've ducked back into any one of the yards on either side of the easement, just like I had when I'd crawled in with Manny and Moe.

On the other side of the houses, a car raced, the engine winding out, tires skidding. Mack picked up Fong and was trying to set up a makeshift perimeter, a useless deployment with only one man on the perimeter especially with no bird in the air. Mack couldn't call for air support, not for an escaped inmate that he'd helped escape.

I came to the first perpendicular street, walked over to an ancient maple, stood in the shadow back by an overgrown hibiscus that smelled honey sweet and reminded me of my Marie. The thought left a hollow feeling in my chest.

Mack drove up the street, turned, and squealed around the corner. Nothing moved, not even the ghetto wolves that prowled at night in packs, looking for smaller dogs or inexperienced cats. The denizens somehow smelled danger afoot and crawled under their rocks.

I gave in to the fact we'd screwed it up and lost Ruben. It happened that way sometimes. Had we deployed an entire

Violent Crimes Team around Shawntay's house, this wouldn't have happened. You went with what you had. A crackhead wasn't hard to track down. We'd just missed him.

Headlights came north again from two streets down. I recognized the sound of the engine and stepped out into the street with my hands up, waving him down. Mack skidded to a stop. He jumped out, his hands balled in tight fists. He didn't slow as he came on. I stood up straight, closed my eyes waiting for the blow to mash my mouth, shatter my teeth.

He came right up into my face, "You lost him? What the hell's the matter with you? You were right on his ass."

I opened my eyes, his baby blues inches from mine. My mouth all on its own dropped open.

"Get your dumbass back in the car, skillet." He turned and went back to the driver's side, got in, and slammed the door. I walked stiffly to the passenger side, thinking about the bullet graze and how my knees started to complain about the second-story leap and how Mack was one difficult person to read.

I got in. He put the car in gear and chirped the tires. Two blocks over, he pulled to the side. Fong came out of the shadows from his position of ambush, got in, and closed the door. He slapped the back of my head. "How'd you lose him?"

If it wasn't happening to me, it might've been comical. I said, "Hit me again, asshole." I pointed a finger at him. When he didn't move, I said, "I heard Mack tell you to take the one-two side, the side Ruben bailed on."

Mack answered for him, "There was a cedar plank fence. He was trying to get around. It was my fault. I should've waited until he was in position before taking the door."

"Right," I said, "And cappin' my ass was just for fun?" I stuck my hand under my shirt and gently probed my shoulder. There was a narrow furrow no wider than a pencil, sticky with coagulated blood. "It wasn't anyone's fault. When you chase a crackhead, you never know what's going to happen."

Mack snickered, "Those were just warning shots to try and get Ruben to hit the dirt so you could grab him."

"My achin' ass, warning shots."

"You took us to him once, you can do it again. Where to?"

I sat back in the seat, let the adrenaline of the chase start to bleed off, and there it was, clear as day. The answer bubbled up like I'd wanted the name Kendrick to. It was hell getting old. The Thin Man's name was Alan Cole. "Alan Cole."

"What?"

"Go on down here and turn on Willowbrook."

"Who's Alan Cole?"

"The kid in front of Shawntay's. The alley I caught him in was behind Huggies off of Willowbrook. It's closed down now. A bar Ruben and Cole used to frequent. Cole had an old beat-up Bulldog .44. After I got it back to the station and got a good look at it, I didn't think it would even fire. He took his ass whuppin' without a peep."

Mack turned down Willowbrook. Huggies, two stories on the right, boarded up with weather-warped sheets of plywood painted over and over with gang graffiti stood dark against a brighter skyline.

"So your thinkin'," Fong said, "that this Cole might've been at the pad visiting Ruben?"

"Not necessarily. Cole just kick-started my memory. It's worth a check."

Mack spun the car around. "This is close, but I don't think he'd have time to get here yet. I'm going to set up down the street and code five. You give us the layout of the inside."

"You walk in the front there's a long narrow bar, real long because that's all there is. The bar goes clear back to the rear door of the place. There's one row of tables against the wall on the left with very little elbow room in between. The entire place is probably twenty, twenty-five-feet wide. Toward the back there's like this loft with stairs, but it was private, an office maybe. No one ever went up there."

"Windows?" Mack asked.

"As I remember, only on the front. The back's got a solid steel door."

Fong leaned forward. "The windows in the front are boarded up, so if he's using the place as a hidey-hole, it has to be from the back. It'll be real easy to check to see if there's any access. We could be wasting our time."

I closed my eyes and conjured up an image of the alley from all the times I prowled it at night with headlights off. "There's a steel ladder to the roof."

Chapter Forty-Four

Willowbrook, a wide boulevard with the metro rail running down the center, hardly twitched, the asphalt void of all but a few vehicles. Trees on both sides, ancient majestic peppers, had stood guard for the last century. A shadow darted from the peppers across the first street. All of us saw it at the same time and tensed. We simultaneously eased our doors open. The inside dome light had been deactivated as in all the Violent Crimes vehicles. Nobody closed their doors all the way. Mack whispered, "Let him get inside. We'll have him cornered. Fong and I will take the back. Skillet, you take the front."

This time they played it smart. The front was boarded up with little chance of any action there. We moved directly across the street to the sidewalk and tried to stay in the shadows. I brought up the rear. Up close, I could see the plywood bolted into the cinder block with heavy lag bolts and fat washers so that the night people could not penetrate without a bulldozer against it. No need for me to stay at the front. Mack and Fong went around the side. I followed. They knew, understood the dynamic, and didn't say anything. We now moved and acted like a team.

Moonlight reflected off the white paint on the walls. Chipped, peeling paint surrounding a long faded ad for Jeri Curl lit up the side of the building in an eerie, lunar glow. We moved silently to the area where the shadowy figure disappeared. The shadow could've been anyone. We came to an indentation in the wall, a door I didn't known about. The only door not boarded up. Mack and Fong pulled their guns. Mack held up his and pointed to me and then at the side of the door. I nodded. They moved off. I took up my position hyperaware of my empty-handed vulnerability. Against the white painted wall, I looked like a fly in milk.

The space between Huggies and the nail salon maybe spanned seven feet, cluttered with trash bags and discarded rotting cardboard boxes that at one time held large appliances. Mack and Fong brought their guns up to point shoulder to cover their approach to the rear of Huggies. They hesitated at the end. Fong, to the rear, nodded and tapped Mack on the shoulder. They both moved at the same time and disappeared around the corner. The night turned empty and quiet. I listened hard. Nothing moved, no sound, no wind. I held my breath.

Then I smelled it. Gasoline.

I looked around for the source. Calmed down. I took a long breath and stuck my nose in the air, moving it from one direction to the next. The reek settled all around me.

Mack, by himself, came back around the corner at the end of the building a hundred feet down. He put his gun back in his holster. I waved at him to stop. He slowed down by a washing machine carton twenty feet away but came on, too intent on his mission. "The back's secure. He must've gone in this side door and locked it from the inside. Mike's on the roo—"

The low, squat, washing machine carton shuddered then jerked to one side. Mack flinched. Gas filled the air. It landed on his face and chest. His hands went to his eyes. He screamed, windmilled, and flailed, scared to death that at any second Ruben might light him up.

Ruben stood up, laughing a psychotic, maniacal laugh. In

his hand he held a Bic lighter with a small orange flame. Mack went for his gun.

Ruben screeched, "Don't you do it. I'll torch your ass."

I moved toward Ruben who had his back to me, twenty-five or thirty feet away.

Mack froze. "Don't. I'm a cop. You burn me, and I guarantee deputies will hunt you down and make you wish you hadn't." Mack, strong, fearless, but I heard the crack in his voice.

The laugh again. Ruben was going to do it. He stalled only to savor the moment. Gasoline fumes burned before the actual liquid. Ruben just had to move the flame close to ignite the fumes, to touch it off. Mack was in a bad way. If Ruben lit him, there was no way to put him out in time. Immolation, the worst, most painful way to die.

Mack knew I was there, but couldn't see me moving because Ruben stood between us. Ruben, already too close to Mack, moved closer, inches at a time. His laugh tightened. His hand moved higher.

Ruben abruptly stopped laughing and said, "Gaily be knight, a gallant knight. In darkness and in shadow. Traveled along singing a song in search of —" His hand moved down in a slow arc.

Mack yelped. He brought his hands up.

I moved low and fast, shoulder down. I gave an Apache war cry. It came out all on its own from the bottom of my gut.

Startled, Ruben hung the flame over his head.

Mack backed up.

I hit Ruben waist high, driving my legs, feet digging in. I had to hit him hard enough to get his finger off the little paddle that kept the lighter lit.

Ruben's legs came off the ground. He grunted as I knocked the wind out of him. We plowed into Mack who couldn't move fast enough. Mack saw his death in the shape of two bodies bowling toward him, a small flame held above like the Statue of Liberty. Mack screeched like a little girl.

We hit the ground in a dog pile. Mack on the bottom. The gasoline reek strongest now. If Ruben flicked the lighter, whether it lit or not, the spark would be enough to barbeque us all. I fumbled. Looking, feeling for Ruben's hand that held the lighter. Mack yelled, "Get off. Get off."

I couldn't find Ruben's hand and out of desperation decided to go to knuckles. I slugged Ruben in the head again and again. Bare hands against thick skull. I wanted to ring his bell to daze him, make him forget the day of the week, forget his own name.

Mack grunted. Mack bench-pressed the both of us off him, tossed us aside. Mack stood, backed away, fear bright on his face. He yelled something unintelligible twice, then came in fast with a heavy boot and punted Ruben in the face. Ruben's teeth skittered against the wall of Huggies.

Mack pulled back and booted him again. Ruben had gone still. I held no love for Ruben, the way he killed five other un-deserving folks. Four years ago I might've been right there with Mack, meting out a little curbside justice, but I'd learned my lesson and changed for the better. Being inside, seeing the end result, changed me. I laid across Ruben and covered him as best I could. Mack didn't pull back on his last kick. It glanced off my back. "Hey, hey, enough. The man's down. The man's down."

Fong ran up, not knowing what happened, put his shoulder into Mack and shoved him away. My breath came hard. "Give me your cuffs." Fong tossed them to me. I climbed off of Ruben, pulled his arms behind him, and cuffed him. I rolled to my feet, stood as I tried to catch my breath.

Fong finally smelled the gas and guessed what happened.

He leaned down and picked up the Bic lighter. "Son of a bitch. Don't tell me he tried to torch you?"

Mack turned and walked away, the emotions of the event too much for him. He didn't want us to witness it. I couldn't blame him.

Fong reached into his pocket, tossed me the car keys. "Here, bring the car up to the mouth of this little alley so we can load this piece of shit."

I hesitated; I was Ruben's only advocate. If I left him alone, no telling what these angry BMFs might do.

Fong scowled. "Get your ass movin', we ain't got all night." I walked backward toward Willowbrook until it became too hazardous with all the debris. I turned and walked slowly, listening for the telltale sounds of an ass beating. At the street, I turned back and looked. Ruben still lay facedown on the ground, unmoving. Fong and Mack had their backs to me. Fong had his hand on Mack's shoulder, in close, whispering to him. Mack was more shaken than I had thought. I ran for the car to get back as soon as I could.

I opened the door and started up. I could run for it, be in Mexico in three hours, home free. Then I realized Fong, the guy who'd wanted to store me in the trunk, was the one who'd trusted me, tossed me the keys. I put it in gear and skidded up to the opening between the buildings, held my breath when I looked. Fong and Mack each held a shoulder, hands under Ruben's arms, dragging him to the car. It was over.

They opened the back door and tossed him in, an empty sack of useless humanity. Fong opened the driver's door, "Get out, skillet, I'm driving."

Mack walked by me, grabbed the driver's door before Fong closed it, "Don't call him skillet." They both stared a long time at one another. Fong nodded. "Okay. I got it."

Mack said, "Get out, I'm driving."

"Johnson, you ride up front."

Fong didn't protest. He got in the back, shoved Ruben over.

Most of the gas had already evaporated off Mack. The sour smell of barf emanated from him. Something else went missing, snuffed out in near flambé experience, something gone from his eyes. I'd seen it often in prison. That little extra spark that kept a man upright, head held high, went missing. Before now Mack had burned too bright, the odds swung in his favor. It would return. If it didn't, well, I'd ask Mr. Cho if he needed somebody to run his counter.

Chapter Forty-Five

Fong recovered, slapped Mack on the back, "We got him, bro. We did it. This is the guy. It's got to be, the way he went after you, used the same MO, the can of gas, the lighter, we got him. Can't wait to see the look on that asshole Wicks's face. Let's call him." Fong opened his cell phone, scrolled, tapped the number, and put it to his ear. "Damn. Voice mail."

In a few short hours the BMFs would gather, and over a case of beer, celebrate the taking of big game.

"That lets me out, right?" I said, "You can pull over here and put me afoot. That'd be okay by me."

Mack took his vacant eyes off the road for a second, turned. I read sadness and contrition, but I also saw his confidence ebbing back.

"Don't think so, Johnson. You still have to answer for Bressler."

"I told you the truth about torching those people and I'm telling you the truth about Bressler." I wanted to add that he owed me for the little tussle back there where I kept him from becoming a Fourth of July sparkler.

Fong fumbled around in back. He shoved Ruben the Cuban from side to side searching his pockets, a prebooking search as it were, pulling out everything in his pockets, a legal search acceptable in court. He handed the items over the seat, three books of matches with Theo's Bar on the covers, a can of butane refill for cigarette lighters, some empty Ziploc baggies with residue, a moldering wallet chocked full of moldering papers, a fat key ring with old unused antiquated keys, and five cheap cigarette lighters, all blue.

I opened the wallet, damp, still warm from his body heat, and pulled out the papers. The newest addition to the mess, a yellow copy I recognized as a booking application to Los Angeles County Jail. I unfolded it and saw John Edward Rubenstein had recently been arrested for under the influence of a controlled substance and had only just been let out on a promise-to-appear citation.

"You better have a look at this." I handed it over to Mack as he steered us toward Century Sheriff's Station on Alameda.

"Can't you see I'm driving?" His anger bled through. Transference from what happened, anger at displaying fear.

Ruben the Cuban moaned as he came around.

I took it back, "When did that last guy get torched, two nights ago? This says our friend here was in custody at the time of the last burning."

Mack yanked on the wheel, steered the car over to the curb by a vacant manufacturing building, the street dark, the streetlights all shot out. Fong reached over the seat and snatched the paper from my hand.

Every second I stayed in custody, I found it harder to breathe. Every second that passed brought us that much closer to being found out, the kids discovered, and put back in a system that let them down the first time and would do worse the second. Only because they now knew the way life was really supposed to be. It made my heart ache at the thought.

As the car slowed, I again thought about jamming out the door. I knew the area and could lose them, no problem. That left Marie holding the bag, something I could never do. At the same time, I wished for a couple of hours of freedom to pay

Jumbo a little visit, make him rue the day he ever heard my name, talk to him old BMF-style.

Fong said, "What? It can't be." He checked the wrinkled booking slip, flipped it over, not believing it genuine. "Okay then, what? What's it mean?"

Mack took it from him. "It means we got a copycat, that's what it means."

Mack possessed that innate sense needed to vault the gigantic chasm from mediocre detective to outstanding. He sprung from a family of law enforcement and probably came by it genetically. He handed it back to me, his eyes asking my opinion.

I said, "There are only two reasons for a copycat."

Mack nodded. Fong didn't catch on, he asked, "What?"

Mack said, "One is a psycho who liked the idea and wished he'd thought of it first."

"And the other?" Fong asked.

I said, "The other is someone borrowing the MO to dispose of a problem."

"Okay, so we still got this puke for the others, right?" Fong asked, missing the full ramifications of the words.

Mack said nothing and held my gaze. He put it together in his mind and didn't like the end result.

Fong leaned forward. "What? What are you guys thinking?"

I said, "I really don't like the way this is playing out."

Mack looked out the window into the dark night. "He's an asshole and I wanted to rub his face in it, but not this. The team's reputation's on the line, the entire department."

"Who?"

I turned in the seat to talk to Fong. "My car in the Taco Quickie parking lot."

Fong wasn't chosen for the Violent Crimes Team out of

ineptness. He cut me off. "What about your car? What are you trying to say?" It came together for him, only he fought it more than we did. We knew the "who," we just couldn't rectify in our minds the why.

"What did you recover out of my car?"

Fong didn't hesitate. "Dope and a gun. Rock coke, about three grams."

I didn't smile. His reply confirmed it.

Mack came out of his reverie, "What was in your car?"

Mack made the leap. I now stood as a full partner to be trusted with covering his back and more, the reputation of the Violent Crimes Team. "I had forty-five thousand cash, taken from Q-Ball Bridges, and a Smith & Wesson model 645."

Mack hit the steering wheel with the palm of his hand.

No question. He believed me.

Fong sat back. "Son of a bitch."

Ruben sputtered, "I didn't do it. I'm innocent."

"Shut up." Fong elbowed him in the chest.

"What kind of gun did you find in my trunk?"

Once I accepted the "who," truly believed it, the beauty of the flawless, perfectly executed plan, awed me.

Mack read my mind. "Something's missing. He wouldn't do it for forty-five K. No chance. If he went off the reservation, he's smarter than that. He could take down a hundred times more."

As each move fell into place, more questions popped up. I had been made a patsy to the point of comedy. It was almost funny all the crap he'd laid at my door. "Tell me about the gun. Who is Kendrick?"

Mack's head whipped back. "The last guy torched."

I stayed ahead of Mack in my thinking, not by much though. "Who found the gun in the trunk of my car?"

Fong cut in, "He did. Hey, should we be talking in front of this shitbag?" Referring to Ruben.

Mack said, "The last guy torched is the key."

When he said it, I'd already gone by that part. I'd played back all of our conversations from the very beginning. "It's not just forty-five K."

No one said anything.

I said, "How much money did you guys get from my crash pad on 117th?"

Fong said, "We haven't found any money yet."

Mack said, "How much?"

"Total? Close to two fifty."

Fong said, "Where the hell you get that kind of money?"

I didn't answer and went on. "The ballistics of the gun in my trunk matched the Bressler kill, didn't it?"

Mack nodded. "It all comes back to Ahern, doesn't it?"

"Who contacted Jumbo to set up the take-down at his house?"

Mack said nothing.

I looked at Fong. He wouldn't meet my eyes, said, "What are we going to do?"

"It's a double bind, me and Jumbo. We need to give Jumbo a visit."

Chapter Forty-Six

"No chance." Mack shook his head. "No way. What good will that do? He's too smart. Jumbo'll just lawyer up. And besides, who's he going to be more afraid of? Us or him?"

"I could talk to Jumbo. Guaranteed he won't want to see me."

Fong smirked. "You're on your way back to the can."

"Stop and think about what you just said."

"All right, I'll say it again, you're going back to the can. I'm not putting my ass on the line for you."

I didn't look at Mack and take an unfair advantage. He owed me. I let it hang in the air. When Mack didn't offer up, I spelled it out for Fong. "What did you book me on?"

"Murder, multiple counts, ex-con with a gun, possession of cocaine."

"And you base all of this on what?"

He didn't answer. He knew.

"I'll tell you what you based it on," I said. "Planted evidence in the trunk of my car. And to make matters worse, your whole team was on me during these purported murders, most of them anyway, following my every move. It would only take one instance where you had the eye on me the same time a murder went down. Just one. You'll have detailed records of your surveillance. How are you going to explain that in court? I didn't do it. You know I didn't do it."

"You admitted you had forty-five thousand and a gun in the trunk of that car, and you're on parole, that's two to five on top of the parole violation."

"Sure, you're right. Produce the gun and the money. What you got is pie in the sky."

"We booked you and took you out. We have to take you back in or it's our asses. The court'll let you out when the DA scraps the case."

"You can blue sheet me, an 849.b2."

Fong waited for Mack to ring in on the subject. When he didn't, Fong shook his head. "No, Homicide'll have our asses, making a unilateral decision like that. It's their case now, not ours."

Correct, if you wanted to follow procedure. Didn't matter if we could prove I hadn't done it. Protocol dictated Homicide handles the disposition or gets their nose bent out of shape. I had interrogated too many suspects and interviewed too many victims. Fong held something back. I opened the door.

Fong broke leather, pulled his gun. "Don't."

I put my foot out on the curb.

Fong pointed the large handgun at me.

I looked at Mack and slid out. Mack put his hand on the gun, lowered it.

Fong said nothing.

I closed the door, got down on one knee, leaned in. "What do you have my girl for?"

"Aiding and abetting a felon." Mack said in a lowered voice.

"If you no longer have the felon then how can she be abetting?" My heart started to soar upward into the cloudless night.

"There's—" Fong started to say.

Mack held up his hand to quiet him. "There's the other charge."

He yanked me back down to earth. I got up and walked around the front of the car, the headlights off. I wanted to see his eyes. He rolled down his window.

I put my hands on the ledge and got a little closer. All this time no one had mentioned the kids. They sat like the elephant in the room.

I said, "What other charge?" My throat went dry, my voice cracked.

He waited a long interminable minute. "You know, Bruno."

"Say it." I said, the bottom dropping out of my world. What did they have? Was it enough to hold her? Was it enough to hold me, and he was just going to let me walk because of what had happened between us? If so, I couldn't let it go down that way. I would have to get back in the car, take the fall with her.

"What it's always been about." His pale blue eyes, sad.

"What? Say it. I want you to say it."

"The kids."

A large knot rose up in my chest. To deny it disrespected the man, someone I had grown to like. I tried to speak, my voice sandpaper at the back of my throat. "You guys don't have a case."

He didn't move. My heart skipped. I watched his eyes.

"No, we don't have a case."

I stood and looked down the street as my eyes teared up, that old emotional man thing again. I said, "Then you're going to release her?"

"The FBI is coming down in the morning to put a hold on her. They're adopting the case."

I rode that same roller coaster back down into the basement. "You could go in and blue sheet her tonight. You could do that."

"It'd be my job."

I wanted to tell him so much. Tell him about each child, the untenable environments, the sadistic physical abuse, and the system set up to protect them that put them right back into harm's way. I couldn't help it, I threw my trump card. I leaned back in, the tears heavy in my eyes, said, "You got a cigarette?"

Mack never looked away, "Man, I'm soaked in gasoline and you wanna smoke?" He smiled. "I got to get these things off. You take care of yourself." When he put it in drive, the red brake lights lit up the dark street. He didn't move.

He finally said, "You're not going after Jumbo, are you?"

I shook my head.

He said, "I didn't think so. Tell Wicks—tell him I'm the one that let the junkyard dog loose on his ass. You got about a two-hour lead, enough for me to do the paper on this case, then I'll be right behind you."

He hit the gas. The back tires screeched.

"What about my girl?"

He didn't stop or even slow down. The purple-black night slammed down. It took my breath away. I started running.

Chapter Forty-Seven

In all the years on the street I learned one sure thing about the mind of a crook: how, when faced with adversity, a bold and brash act can pull your cookies out of the fire. I checked Wicks's house in Rosemead, burned forty minutes of the two hours Mack doled out, and found it dark and cold. If time worked for me rather than against me, I would sit and wait. Instead, I chose bold and brash.

One cold night in Compton, I stood in the parking lot of Rosco's Market sipping coffee under the eave, in the lee of the wind, along with Mark Hocks, a rookie deputy in possession of a mere six months on the street. He'd called the meet, bought the coffee, and found it difficult to ask the question, the true excuse for the get-together. He wanted to know the secret to being a good street cop, how to make not just good arrests but great arrests. Honored, I didn't know how to respond. I told him to always be suspicious and not look for the crime, don't wait for the probable cause, watch the behavior. Behavior will give it away every time. Someone looks like a crook, go up and have a chat with him. I told Mark all of this while we watched the street, the cars going by in the icy rain. A white Honda Accord pulled in and got gas just as I was about to leave. The car—I thought it the same car anyway— white Hondas in Southern California were the same as snowflakes in Aspen—had gone by on the street and now it came back to gas up.

I tossed the rest of the burnt coffee poured from the pot inside and, without telling Mark, walked over to talk to the driver. Both of our black-and-white cop cars sat in plain view to all. The driver of the white Honda got out, saw the uniform, and immediately looked around, a rabbit about to flee. I grabbed onto his open black leather jacket by the front and said, "Don't. Don't." At the same time, I felt his waistband on the right side, found a .38. I pulled his gun, slammed him on the hood of the Honda, stuck his own gun in his ear, and told him not to breathe. Mark dropped his coffee, drew his gun, and ran over to help. The Honda was stolen. Jed Ashe also carried in his right shirt pocket a half ounce of rock cocaine. When asked by Mark what the hell he thought he was doing pulling in to get gas with two cops standing in the parking lot, Jed said, "Didn't think you'd tumble to me if I acted like nothin' was wrong."

I chose bold and brash. It didn't work for Jed, but I wasn't Jed. I drove my boosted car into the parking lot of Montclair Police Station, forty miles east of Los Angeles, another forty minutes gone. It left only forty minutes to get the information I needed and get back to Los Angeles.

The little burg of Montclair sat quiet in the dark night, light from the front window warm and inviting, as a soft invitation to Joe Citizen. I walked into the front lobby, a little bebop in my step that bespoke, "nothing wrong here." I'm Joe Citizen making an inquiry. The lobby waiting area contained two gray Naugahyde couches, two glass cases with awards for the top cops, and pictures on the wall of the city council and mayor. On the other side of the counter, the blue-suited cop stood and came to the thick bulletproof Plexiglas. "Can I help you?" The sound came out metallic with some sort of audio boost.

"Yes. I would like to speak with Barbara White."

Barbara kept her own last name, a professional considera-tion. Long ago at a barbecue, she confided she didn't like the name Barbara Wicks not after being White all of her life.

"What's this in reference to?"

"It's a personal matter."

"What's your name?"

No way did I think the L.A. cops put out a BOLO for me, especially one that would reach this far out into the next county. Local maybe, not this far out. Still, I hesitated, "Can you just tell her Bruno is here to see her."

"Bruno who?"

I didn't answer.

"Have a seat." He turned, picked up the phone, dialed a number, and he watched me as he spoke. The person on the other end said something, the cop turned to reply, as if I could read his lips. I fought the urge to bolt.

He put the phone down and stared at me. My heart raced. He came over to the counter, slowly moved his hand to the edge out of view. Behind me, over at the front door a solenoid bolt shot home. He'd locked me in.

The door that led to the back of the station opened. The woman in uniform did not smile. It took a long second to re-alize Barbara had aged a great deal since our last meeting. I tried to remember how long ago and knew not enough time had passed to warrant the quick degradation of youth. She'd lost weight. Where the curves on her hips used to beckon a man, they now showed too much bone, her uniform pants cinched up with a black basket weave belt. Gray sprouted in the part of her once lustrous brown hair.

"What are you doing here, Bruno?"

I looked at the desk officer, then back at her.

"All right, come on back." She held the door open. She wore a black automatic in a pancake holster on her side, her oval badge shiny and new. I followed her into her office. She walked behind her desk and turned, "You shouldn't be here. You're putting me in a bad position."

I sat down to stop the quaking knees. "Congratulations on your promotion. Lieutenant. That's great."

She came around her desk and closed the watch commander's door. "Let's can the bullshit, huh? What do you want?"

It hurt for her to talk to me this way. I didn't know how much she knew, how much Robby told her about me, but we'd been good friends not all that long ago. I said nothing.

She went back around and sat at her desk. The only sound in the room the radio. She monitored her shift beat units answering calls for service.

I spoke first. "I thought we were friends."

"We were until you went over to the other team. What do you want, Bruno? You have thirty seconds."

"I'm looking for Robby."

"Funny, he's looking for you."

"When's the last time you saw him?"

Her hard expression cracked, it softened. "We're through. We split a couple of weeks ago."

"I'm sorry, I didn't know." They were the perfect couple. Although, I always thought she loved him more than he loved her. Now, standing on the outside looking in, seeing the past from a different perspective, I realized he may have been in love more with himself with nothing left over for her, at least not enough to hold the relationship together.

Her eyes misted. She turned, slid open the window that accessed the dispatch area, spoke to people I couldn't see, "Tell Four Paul Three, not to take code seven until he handles that missing person and then tell Four Sam One I want him to call me ASAP." She slid the window closed. The conscientious supervisor, she'd been monitoring the cop talk on the radio all the while conversing with me.

I wanted to go around and hug her to help quell her emotional pain. "What happened?"

"What always happens? He met someone else." She looked away, her chin quivered. "It's my fault."

"No it's not, Barb."

She looked back, her eyes aflame. "You don't know shit. You have no idea how I respected you, the both of you. I envied you going to work with him everyday, all the overtime, seeing him more than I did. Then you went bad, you made him shoot you. It ruined him. That's when it really started, three years ago."

Derek Sams ruined more lives than he would've ever known; my daughter, my grandson, my father, and now Wicks and his wife, Barbara. The insidious tentacles of narcotics burrow deep into the fabric of society.

I wanted to lay it all at his door, but couldn't. I had to own up to my own actions, my own choices.

Shame rose up and heated my face. I wanted to tell her I didn't ask Wicks to shoot. He didn't have to. I was going to give up. He didn't give me a chance. He never gave me the chance.

She continued her rant. "You went bad, then he followed right along behind you."

I moved to the edge of my chair. "He went bad? What happened? What're you talking about?"

"The FBI popped him, civil-rights violation. A bad shoot by one of his men. They told him they were going to go back five years to investigate his team and their cases. Look into the culture, the tattoos, a real full-court press."

"He's too good. They'd never make him on any of it."

"I told him that. He was okay for a while, until the pressure got to him. He said he was too old to start over. Even if he beat it, the department, the same people he made all those sensational cases for, demoted him to work in the jail, the watch commander at MCJ while they conducted an internal investigation. It killed him, Bruno. One week in that smelly hole and he was ready to sell out his mother."

The shame left and in sauntered fear, cold with a knife-hard edge. I saw where this was going.

"They flipped him," she said, "They flipped the great Robby Wicks. The man who knew the game better than the FBI. The FBI told him all his problems would all go away if he did one thing. Just one. Something they couldn't do themselves in eighteen months of trying with all their assets. You would have thought with all their satellites, high-tech surveillance devices, the relaxed constitution for terrorism they'd be able to follow one ex-con. Something he refused to get involved in until they played dirty pool."

She waited for me to say it.

I couldn't. I said nothing.

"Yeah," she said, "you know, it's your fault. That's why I can't believe you had the balls to come here. Say it, Bruno. You know what they want. You didn't need to come here for me to tell you. Say it."

I loved and respected her too much, I said it. My voice cracked. "Wally Kim. They want Wally Kim." The Korean kid, the diplomat's son.

Chapter Forty-Eight

She said, "That's right. Kim put a lot of pressure on the State Department, who in turn pressured the Justice Department."

"I'm sorry, Barbara; it's no longer about that. It's Robby, he—"

She turned pale, sat down, "What? What's happened?"

Of course, she still loved him and cared what happened to him. They had been together too many years. I didn't know how to say it, so I used Mack's words, "He's gone off the reservation."

"How bad?"

I couldn't answer that one. I couldn't say the words to her. She stood on the fringe about to be pulled into the vortex of this awful shit storm, one initiated by my actions. Her eyes bore right into me. The phone rang.

It rang some more.

She picked it up. "Yeah, I wanted you to call. Are you paying attention out there? Four Paul Three was about to go to dinner with a missing-person report hanging. Yeah, I know. Yeah, I understand. Just keep your crew straight, all right? That's not asking too much. Yeah. Thanks." She hung up.

She said to me, "It's the million dollars, isn't it? He killed someone for all that damn money."

She saw my expression, my jaw drop.

"What're you talking about?" My thoughts went to Jumbo and the millions wrapped up in the computer chips. He must have killed Crazy Ned Bressler, did it for money. It had not crossed my mind until that moment. If I didn't kill Bressler, then who did?

Now she mirrored my expression. She closed her mouth, stood up. She'd made a mistake, violated a cardinal rule in interrogation, she gave away more information then she received. "Time for you to leave, Bruno."

"No, this is important. What are you talking about?" She had the missing piece, the motivation. A million dollars and I needed to hear it.

"No, go. Now." She shifted her gaze to the window that opened to the hall. The uniformed desk officer appeared outside her door awaiting orders, an obedient watchdog anxious to impress his master with a thirty-inch mahogany nightstick.

"Then just tell me where I can find him."

"I honestly thought he was looking for you."

"He found me. Barbara, he said he was going on a cruise, on a long and well-deserved vacation."

The color drained from her face. "The bastard."

"Where can I find him?"

The office door opened. She waved the officer off. He closed it. "He's got his money then?"

"I'm not going to lie to you. I know nothing about a million dollars. He tried to hang a murder beef on me, locked it down tight. I only just now got out from under it. The dog team will be on him in another thirty minutes or so. I want to find him before they do. You of all people know why. If you still care for him, tell me. He might come in for me."

"I could care less what happens to the pig." Tears rolled down her cheeks. She came around her desk. I stood. She put her hand on my arm. "Looking for a little get-even time, aren't you? You've got your chance now to do to him what he did to you. Right? Is that it?"

She made me reexamine my motivation. What the hell was I doing? I wanted to track him down to help clear my name, make him talk. Mack could do the same thing, only sanctioned by the law. Robby had the money. We needed the money, money I earned. Now I sounded like a degenerate criminal justifying his criminality.

"That's it, isn't it? You want to shoot him in the back the same way he shot you."

I held my hands away from my sides. "I don't have a gun. I want to be honest with you. He has a whole lot of my money. And under normal circumstances I really wouldn't care, but there are some people very close to me who depend on that money. Please tell me where he is."

"How much are we talking?"

"Two hundred and fifty."

"Thousand?"

I nodded.

"Two hundred and fifty plus the million. That son of a bitch."

I remembered that Mack had said that Robby was smart, he'd go for a lot more. One point two was a lot more. Especially if his job went down the toilet. "Where did the million come from?"

"He talked with Mr. Kim, made a deal. Once he found Wally, he'd receive a reward."

"He doesn't have Wally." He didn't. Robby jumped the gun, took Marie down before she made it to Dad's. "You said he found someone else. Was that just a woof cookie you fed me or is it the money?"

"No, he's got both. I guess I know Robby better than any-one on this planet and knew he was stepping out the first minute he crossed the line."

"I know this is hard for you, but I need to know where she lives." Paranoia set in. I began to think maybe Robby did know where Dad lived with the kids and only waited until the time was right to make his move. I knew the location of the kids. What I didn't know was Robby's girlfriend's address.

She said, "I first suspected about six months ago. I rented a car and followed him."

Most wives hired private detectives; the dangerous part about a wife trained in narcotics surveillance is that she also carries a gun and knows how to use it.

Anxiety rose in me until I hummed like a tuning fork. I knew she would tell me and had my hand on the doorknob ready to flee, be on my way to end this thing.

"Two weeks ago, I had enough. I followed him over to an apartment, all the way over in L.A. Watched him walk up the stairs, put his own key in the door, only she'd been waiting, watching for him out the window. I loved him like that once, waited for him to come through the door, never wanted him to be away from my side. The whore opened the door for him. They kissed like there was no tomorrow. There almost wasn't."

She'd said the words in a trancelike state, now she snapped out of it. "I pulled my gun, got out of the car, and started up those same steps. They went back inside. Good thing. At the top, I realized he wasn't worth it. I was lucky. Now I'm here trying to defend him. If he did take your money like you say, then I hope you get him. When you do, tell him I helped do it."

Similar words to what Mack said. These two people who had been loved and gave their loyalty, now spurned. It struck me that everyone in his life now turned on him, his department, his team, his wife. I felt sorry for him. We'd had a lot of great times together, tight scrapes, long, hot nights, celebrations, beer drinking.

"What's the address?"

"It's a three-story walk-up over off Crenshaw and Santa Barbara."

I sat back down, the wind knocked out of me. It couldn't be. It just couldn't.

Chapter Forty-Nine

"What's her name? Do you know her name?"

She shook her head. It didn't matter. I knew.

Chantal.

Six months though? How had I not known? It made sense. He'd come up on me looking to find Wally and made contact with her, a big risk that she would rat him out to me. But he was always into big risks, they had potential to pay off in big dividends. She did what she always did, turned on the charm, offered up the only defense she possessed, she gave him a little sugar.

"I'm sorry, Barbara, I have to go." The words nothing more than a whisper. I stood and opened the door. The uniform blocked my path. I looked back at her. For a long moment I thought maybe I wouldn't leave Montclair Police Department.

"That's okay, Al," she said. "Let him go."

Al stood aside.

Thirty-five minutes to go before Mack came onto the same trail with all his resources backing him. I got in the little Toyota Camry with the punched ignition, started up, and drove to the exit watching the rearview for cop cars laying in wait to ambush me.

Too much paranoia.

I used the turn signal to pull out onto the street. A sleek black Crown Victoria came up rolling hot and squealed his tires into the Montclair Police Department parking lot. As the car passed under the streetlight, I caught a glimpse of the driver: Detective Mack from the Los Angeles County Sheriff's Department. He was early, in too big of a hurry to pay attention to an innocuous Camry with a fleeing felon in it. I saw him, but he didn't see me. I don't think he lied about the two hours. Anxiety whipped him into such a frenzy he could easily have thought he'd waited the prescribed amount of time. He drove a cop car with emergency equipment, red lights, and a siren. Once he got the same information from Barbara, he'd jump on the Pomona Freeway and scream on past me. Unless Barbara listened to what I told her, believed I was the best man to bring her husband down, if she believed in irony. If she still loved him even a little, she'd stall. I pushed the speed, as much as I dared. The trip back to the city, the freeway long and rolling ahead of me, was going to be the worst I'd ever made.

Mack must've left his partner Fong to book Ruben the Cuban. It also meant Mack had not released Marie. The bastard had the blood spoor and nothing else mattered. I unintentionally pushed on the accelerator, had the speed up to eighty. I forced myself to ease off.

Thirty-five minutes later. I pulled up a block away from Chantal's. Three floors up, the white-yellow light from her apartment spilled onto the outdoor walkway. For the last twenty miles anger rose and pulsed behind my eyes. I had no weapon. Didn't need one. I still had two hands. I had my rage. I went up the stairs intent on kicking the door.

The blinds in the window sat in the frame slightly skewed, probably from Chantal watching the street for her man to arrive home. The slot between the blinds and the frame revealed half the living room. Chantal sat naked on the couch. Her smooth, perfect cocoa skin against the butternut leather would've made a tasteful and expensive work of art. Call it Ghetto Princess. Before her on the thick glass coffee table—the subject of her full attention—lay stacks of US currency: sex and greed.

She sat perfectly still staring at the money, her eyes and facial features displaying the classic opiate droop. I stood mesmerized, stood there longer than I should've, standing right outside her window looking into her apartment. Down on the street, a random noise floated up, the acceleration of a car a block away, trying to catch an amber signal turning red. Without taking my eyes from her, my hand went to the doorknob. That's when I realized something was wrong. Chantal hadn't moved. For someone hooked on junk, sitting still for hours didn't call for panic. I guess it registered first in my subconscious. Her chest, the bellows that brought the life-giving air into the lungs, didn't move either.

My hand turned the knob. Unlocked. The little bit of pressure eased the door open. Someone had kicked it in. Splintered wood stuck out jagged in the frame. The same someone had simply pulled the door closed. I pushed it open all the way, wary of who stood behind it.

The unmistakable stink of cordite hung in the air, floating in a bank of smoke at the ceiling, too soon for it to dissipate. I walked in like an awestruck civilian. I had grown to like Chantal and saw her as a special friend. I went over and sat on the couch next to her. Her eyes stared off into oblivion, her lips were parted slightly, a narrow trickle of blood ran down the corner of her mouth. I reached up and put a gentle hand on hers; her skin still warm to the touch. Under her left breast, difficult to discern from any distance, a small red dot wept another trickle of blood. In the back of my mind I knew I should've cleared the apartment first. But I also knew this, the money on the coffee table, had not been his big payday. This whole time, he'd been after the million-dollar reward for Wally Kim. He was just tying up loose ends. Chantal.

All that money was too bulky to carry. And he was in a terrible hurry. Odds of someone finding Chantal before he got back were slim to none. That's why he'd pulled the door shut. A calculated risk. Then I realized another reason he had to come back. He'd not had time to set the scene up to frame me for her murder. No, he'd be back for the money.

The bullet must have hit a vital organ, and killed her instantly. On the table was everything he had stolen from me. The motives for murder have always been timeless: money, power, sex. Robby Wicks succumbed to all three. First, the influence of the job now lost, power. Then, the woman, sex. Then, the money, greed.

The sight of the money on the table, what it represented, what it had caused, the untimely death of this beautiful woman, made me physically ill.

Her hand moved.

"Chantal? It's okay, it's me, Bruno. I'll call 911."

I looked around for a phone. No one had landlines anymore. Everyone had cells. Where did she keep hers? "Where's your cell phone?"

Her head moved slightly from side to side, her lips moved, "No." Her eyes held that faraway gaze. Then I realized it was the heroin, an analgesic, a painkiller that also slowed down all the bodily functions. Anyone else would've already been dead. Slowly, she became more animated. She gripped my hand. "I'm sorry, Bruno. It's all my fault. Not his. It was my fault."

She spoke in short sentences, spoke around the pain, spoke around the lack of air, with small words.

I didn't want to leave her, not for a second. I ran into the bedroom, grabbed a blanket, found her phone on the nightstand and dialed 911 as I ran back into the living room. "I need medical aid at 2615 Crenshaw, number 310."

"What is the reason for your—"

I shut the phone.

Chantal's skin turned chalky in the time I was gone. I wrapped her up in the blanket and held her close. I rocked her back and forth. "It's going to be okay. I promise. You just have to hang on a little while longer. Help's on the way."

"It wasn't his fault," she said haltingly. Her eyes refocused, she came alive a little more. The blanket, the physical contact, the hope of medical aid, did it.

"I shot him."

"What?" I looked around on the table and floor for a gun.

"No, listen. I shot McWhorter. Kendrick's aide. McWhorter found out about—" She coughed. More blood rippled out of her mouth. "—me and Kendrick. My gravy train, baby. McWhorter was shutting down my gravy train. My retirement. You understand, don't you?"

Kendrick was a supervisor on the County Board of Supervisors. The pear-shaped man. The man with the clothes in the other room.

"Chantal, you have to relax. Don't move." Far off to the north, a siren started up.

"No, you have to listen. Please, Bruno.

"I shot McWhorter. I called Robby. Robby loved me. We were going to run away—" She gulped hard. "He came over, made it—He made it look like—the burning."

"It's okay, I understand. Now please, just relax, concentrate on your breathing."

The siren drew closer.

I wanted to ask her who shot her. But it didn't matter. I knew.

She convulsed. She went still. Limp.

Chapter Fifty

I stood in the shadows waiting for him. He was already there. He knew he'd erred when his team snatched up Marie seconds before she led him to the children. Then he'd driven me over there to gloat. He must've thought he'd later pit her against me in the interview and get the information that way. A critical mistake he'd rue the rest of his days.

Robby must know it had to be one of five or six houses. He, too, was there in the shadows waiting for something to give it away. A tell: father, the kids, someone going to a door with food, something out of place in the neighborhood. Wicks had never been patient. He'd wait only so long, then he'd make it happen by going door to door, force his way in, insist on searching, gun in hand without a warrant, without the shroud of law as a protective cloak. He would risk discovery to make it happen.

After I calmed down, I stood there thinking it through, about the kids, how I'd been a fool putting them second in my search for revenge, an odyssey masked by a moral obligation to make things right. I realized what I needed to do. I would miss Marie dearly. She was going to be mad.

I walked out into the street, right into the middle beneath a streetlight, stood and turned a slow circle. "I'm here. I'm right here, Robby." I searched the shadows, the overgrown trees and shrubs in untended yards, the abandoned, rusted-out cars. He could be anywhere.

"I'm alone. Now's your chance. You're a coward. Come out and face me man to man. I'm unarmed. What're you afraid of?"

Nothing.

I held my hands open, up in the air, and continued to turn. "You've always been a self-serving coward, using people, hiding behind the badge. I was a fool. I fell for your smooth talk, your words of righteousness. I let you turn my head, convince me what we did was what was necessary. You're no different than the street thugs we chased. You're worse. You're—"

I heard the shot. I didn't see the muzzle flash. The bullet bit into my ass. It spun me around, threw me facedown in the street. I flipped over, tried to get up. My body was in shock and slow to respond. I couldn't rise any higher. Hot pain shot up my spine. I reached back, my pants sopping wet. I was hit hard, losing serious blood.

"You going to finish me or let me bleed out here in the street?"

He yelled from the blackness. "You came from the street, you can go back to it. Where's the kid?"

I pivoted around to the sound of his voice. Over by a sagging box-wire fence all but obscured with a hibiscus, he stepped out.

He had someone small around the neck, the gun to the head. "Lookee what I found."

"Marie." Her name slipped past my lips in a whisper. We were lost. I didn't have a weapon and was too hurt to make a difference. He knew it. He smiled, his eyes twinkled, victory for him seconds away.

"Bruno! Bruno!"

"Shush. Shush. We were just having a discussion, you know the nice friendly kind, only she wasn't being cooperative, not in the least. Then look what shows up? The solution in the form of one dumb son of a bitch." He continued to drag her over to me. She kicked and fought. He stood a foot taller and seventy pounds more in muscle. "I gotta be honest. I don't believe Mack turned the both of you loose. If I was sticking around, I'd launch him from the team."

"Let her go."

"Which house is it?"

I said nothing.

"I gotta tell ya, Bruno, you confounded me at every turn. And what makes it worse, what really chaps my ass is that I trained you. How did you hide it from me? For months. Man, I cussed you."

"You shot me in the back just like before."

"The same I would a rabid dog. You wanted to know how I could treat you the way I did. You kept a million easy dollars from me. From me!"

"I found Chantal."

He froze.

"She told me. She told me all of it. You're worse than the worst we ever chased. She was a beautiful, kind woman. You killed her. You killed her for money."

"She was a murderer. Did she tell you that? Huh?" He took his arm from around Marie's throat, held her with one hand behind the scruff of the neck. The pressure and pain took her to her knees. The anger I caused him translated to her pain.

I whispered, "I'm sorry, baby."

She wept huge tears.

"She shot the supervisor's aide." Robby again, trying to justify his criminal intent. "She tell you that?"

"And you burned him to hide it."

"Big deal."

"Did you take out Bressler or did Jumbo?"

"Does it really matter?" Robby jerked Marie around like a misbehaving dog. "Point out the house, or I'll finish off your boyfriend. I'll pump a bullet right in his brain pan." He pointed his gun, the sight lined up between my eyes.

"Someone heard the shot. They'll call the police."

He laughed. "You know better than to try and bluff a bluffer. This is the ghetto, man. By now everyone's run up into their cribs hidin' under their beds, too afraid to get involved. You forgot who you're talking to."

"Last chance. Tell me or I will put him out of his misery."

Then someone did get involved.

Chapter Fifty-One

"Right there," the decrepit old man yelled. He came from out of the shadows the same as Robby had, only from the other side of the street. A black man with snow-white hair and cataract eyes, leaning on a spun aluminum baseball bat intended as a weapon.

"No, Dad, go back. Go back."

Robby spun Marie around to put her in between him and the approaching threat, a tired old man who didn't have the strength of a third grader. "Ho, so your old man was involved in your scandalous activities. I should've known. Who else were you going to trust?"

Dad continued to advance as fast as his tired, broken-down body allowed; a beeline right for Robby, right toward certain death.

"I saw which house you came out of, old man." In the yellow streetlight, Robby's eyes turned crazy. He shoved Marie down face-first into the pavement. She hit both hands out in front, skidding across the surface of abrasive asphalt.

"Stop, old man. Stop right there."

"Robby, don't. You don't have to shoot him. Robby, please."

Robby brought his gun up.

The gunshot echoed off the face of the quiet houses, rolled down the street until it dissipated.

A gunshot too loud for a handgun.

Robby rose up and was flung back three feet. He landed in a crumpled heap. He grunted once and lay perfectly still.

I looked back up the street. Mack walked slowly down the sidewalk, an Ithaca Deerslayer 12-gauge shotgun at port arms.

On hands and toes I scrambled over to Marie. "Marie. Marie."

She rolled over and kicked at my face. "What do you think you were doing walking out there like that? He could've killed you."

"I didn't know what else to do."

Her shoulders shook as she cried. I took her in my arms and said, "I'm sorry. It worked out. Pop, you okay?"

Dad stared down at the mortally wounded man. "What? Yes, sure."

Marie said, "Bruno, you're bleeding, you're shot."

Mack continued past us, went over to Robby. He knelt down, felt his neck. Took Robby's gun.

Sirens started up headed our way.

I told Marie, "Help me up."

I hobbled over to Robby. All the buckshot hit him in the chest, neck, and chin. The sight stunned me. I never thought I would see it. Not Robby Wicks down in the street. Dead.

"Bruno," Mack said, "we don't have a lot of time."

"Yeah, I know, we'll get off the street. Come on, Dad."

"Bruno?"

I froze. His tone told me he spoke from his official side, not out of camaraderie.

I said, "We haven't done anything wrong. You, yourself, let us go. Remember?"

He took a step back out of range of Dad's baseball bat. He let the Deerslayer hang down by his side.

Marie understood, shook her head, "No, not the kids. You

can't have the kids. Not now. Not after all we've been through. Please."

"Don't beg," I said to her. I turned to Mack. "Why?"

"I can clean it all up with the kids. You can walk clean. Think about it. If you don't give them up, they're just going to keep chasin' you and you can't keep running."

"Is that really your motivation?"

"Of course, what else?"

Sirens drew closer.

"How about a deal?"

"You have nothing to deal."

Marie said, "No, Bruno, it's all or nothing."

"It can't be—"

Mack said, "We don't have much time."

I leaned on her, growing weak, "We were going to give him up anyway once we got everyone to safety," I told Mack, "They chased us hard because of Wally. We'll give you Wally. We know he's going to a good home. But if you want the others, they won't stand a chance. You'll give them back to their people. You want them all, you'll have to gun me right here in the street."

Dad said, "Me too."

Marie said, "Make it three."

Mack looked around as he tried to decide. Way down by Wilmington, red-and-blue rotating lights turned onto our street, seconds away.

Chapter Fifty-Two

The warm Pacific breeze blew across the patio, the sun warm on my naked chest. Marie came out carrying a box under one arm and sat on the lounge next to mine. "This just came from FedEx."

My heart beat faster, my mouth went dry. "Babe, nobody knows we're down here."

"Take it easy, big fella, it's from Mack. Should be fine. Relax, the kids are all playing video games, and your dad's doing so much better with all the stress off of him. I'm really glad we took him along."

Two weeks earlier, that night right after the shooting, we'd all hobbled back to the house. When I opened the door, Marie saw little Tommy Bascombe and socked me in the stomach. I forgot to tell her about that part. She cried and kissed me like she'd never kissed me before and that's saying something.

We'd fled that night, left everything behind but the clothes we wore. We hopped into a car and hightailed it for the Mexican border. We crossed from San Diego into Tijuana, kept driving through Rosarita and down into Ensenada where we had already reserved a suite with three bedrooms. Everything prepaid in advance.

The nice thing about a woman who's a physician's assistant, she can handle most medical injuries. And, in Mexico, they sell just about anything over the counter, painkillers, antibiotics, and such.

After two weeks in the sun with three regular hot meals a day, I was healing quickly. Today was the first day I was able to sit on my butt. We were waiting for Dad's counterfeit passport to arrive from the States before we continued on. The cargo ship that would take us all to Costa Rica, would dock in Ensenada in another five days.

Now, for the first time in the two-week vacation, Marie looked a little stressed. "What's the matter?" I asked.

"Come on, Bruno, you know what's bugging me. Our finances. We're broke. We bailed so fast we couldn't get to our savings."

She was right. I was scared, too, and tried to buffer the situation a little. "At least all of our meals and transportation are paid for. I know you want help to take care of the kids. I'll be on my feet by the time we get there and I'll get a job."

"What kind of job are you going to get? I'll get the job, and you take care of the kids." She stopped, hesitated a moment, then said, "I know what it is. I guess I'm just scared of the unknown."

"Let's see what's in the box," I said, wanting her mind off the subject.

She opened one end. "Looks like Mack sent along some baseball gear for the kids. Why would he do that? He didn't owe us anything."

"Large ball caps and XL shirts?"

"I know, right?"

"Hand me that," I said.

The box was plain brown cardboard with professional printing on the exterior: Sheriff's Benevolent Society, Widow's and Orphan's Fund, XL shirts, large baseball caps. I tore open the box and found wadded-up newspaper with a note on top.

Bruno,

   That night I wasn't far behind you but I was still behind you. You're a good cop. Don't ever forget that. Don't ever let anyone take that away from you. I found this at one of the places; I must've only missed you by seconds. From what you told me, I knew it was yours so I thought I would send it along.

Marie leaned over and pushed the wadded newspaper aside, awe in her tone. "Bruno, how much is there?"

"If I had to guess, I would say two hundred and fifty thousand." Money from Chantal's coffee table. The money from the train heists that I had buried in the backyard of the abandoned house on 117th and Alabama. Robby had found it, dug it up. Money he and Chantal were going to use to flee the country.

Marie covered her mouth and stared at me, her brown eyes filling with tears.